BLOOD ON THE IVORY TOWER

A scream, sharp and piercing, sent Will running toward Dr. Mellon's study.

Just inside the room, Mellon was crumpled against one of the bookcases, a stream of blood dripping from the side of his head, his eyes closed. In the middle of the carpeted floor, a pretty coed lay facedown in a pool of blood. A bronze Roman bust, its noble head wreathed in sharp and spiky laurel leaves, lay on its back beside her.

The old Latin professor was breathing, but the coed, her head severely battered, was like some buried Caesar, quite dead.

A
CAROL
IN THE
DARK

Cathleen
Jordan

A DELL BOOK

FOR

*Nick, who read and encouraged; Bob Stone, who dili-
gently pressed; Patricia Stone, Lois Adams, and Mary
Jane McKinney, who emboldened; John Jones, Hink
Johnson, and Steve Lynn, who generously assisted with
technical matters; and old friends, out there.*

Published by
Dell Publishing Co., Inc.
1 Dag Hammarskjold Plaza
New York, New York 10017

Dell ® TM 681510, Dell Publishing Co., Inc.

ISBN: 0-440-11184-6

Reprinted by arrangement with Walker and Company

Printed in the United States of America

December 1986

10 9 8 7 6 5 4 3 2 1

WFH

Calm on the listening ear of night
Come heaven's melodious strains,
Where wild Judea stretches far
Her silver-mantled plains.

Christmas carol
E. H. Sears, 1834

Contents

ONE
Gabriel's Ghost

Veiled by the falling snow, the buildings of Crosscreek University were ablaze with lights. Crossing the darkening campus among them, Dr. Will Gray felt a sudden surge of well-being in spite of the eternal cold, the snow down his neck, and the note in his pocket. Whatever old Mrs. Moffat wanted of him—the message was far from making that plain—it would probably lead to trouble, but at the moment, he didn't mind at all.

The campus walks were thronged with students and staff, moving less quickly than usual now that most classes were over for the day—not that many of the students would be around much longer. The Christmas break was almost upon them, and by the end of the week they would all have gone back to the little South Dakota towns where they'd grown up.

Since his arrival in South Dakota, and at the university, three years before, Will had crossed that particular section of ground nearly every day. His dark-haired, six-foot-tall figure, with its long navy-blue overcoat and hat, and his green eyes behind a pair of horn-rimmed glasses, was far more familiar to the thousands of people around him than they were to him. On that evening, as usual, his mind was mostly on fifteenth-century Florence, but at least half the students on the crowded walks tended to think of it as well when he passed, so firmly had his lectures in History 310—Western Civilization—impressed them.

Such information would have pleased Will, had he known it, but not much more. Since his and Dora's divorce the previous year, he had found new and preoccupying satisfactions in his own reading and, occasionally, even in the bleak world around him—these shafts of light rising out of the snow, for instance, and the old, familiar silhouettes of friends moving among them.

On the other side of the quadrangle in front of Marshall Hall, Will saw one student he did recognize, a shy but hardworking M.A. candidate named Barney Nealsson, who was just then tying a sign of some sort to a tree. Behind him, reading it over his shoulder by the light of a nearby lamppost, stood the English department chairman, Joey Livingston, swathed in masses of dove-gray tweed and topped with an umbrella. Those signs seemed to have sprung up everywhere since Will had crossed the campus several hours earlier. Bright green posters giving an unexpectedly springlike note to the December twilight. The nearest, however, was too far away to see, and his feet were already numb—it was something like ten below zero. He tucked his chin down into his collar, quickened his pace, and nearly collided with an elderly gentleman so clad in black from top to toe that he was nearly invisible in the gathering dusk.

"Sorry. . . ." Will regained his footing and turned to see if the other had fallen, but he was already disappearing down the path among the surging crowds of students, his shoulders stooped though his tread was firm. Under the wide brim of his hat, Will frowned briefly. That was old Mellon, he felt sure—long since retired from his post in the Latin department and getting a bit too frail to be out on such a night. Will shoved his hands back in his pockets, remembered the note again as he touched it, and headed up the sanded broad steps of Jaeckel Hall.

When Will emerged from the creaking elevator on Jaeckel Hall's fifth floor, he found Truitt Roberts, head of the history department, looking even more agonized than usual. He had planted himself in the middle of the dimly lit corridor opposite the office door and, with a wrath he attained only once or twice a year, was dressing down two moving men who had blocked the hall with their burden. "Enough!" he was saying furiously. "Just get these things out of here. Immediately!" His old suit (still his summer suit, Will noticed) hung limply on his frame, and his narrow, dark tie did nothing for a face pale with weariness. His graying brown hair stuck up wildly. "Wherever you got your orders, they were *not* from this office."

"That isn't what it says here. It's got your name right on the bottom. Right where it says 'Requested by.'" One of the workmen was trying to unfold a sheaf of papers in spite of his own gloved hands and a mass of paper clips and creases. "You can call—"

"Nonsense. *Nonsense*. I'm not calling anyone."

Will dodged around the three men and a pair of tall steel filing cabinets and came out before the open office door, guarded at present by the languid presence of Tom Donahue and Mary Savannah, the department secretary, who greeted him cheerfully.

"What on earth—" he began, but got no further; behind him, Truitt and the workmen had started shouting, and beyond him, in the history office, three phones had begun to ring. Donahue, who really belonged in the English department down the hall (he taught Elizabethan drama), had turned to reach for one of the phones, but Mary didn't move.

"Thank goodness you're here, Will." She was trying to keep from laughing. "Make those men go away before Tru has a stroke."

"What's going on?"

"They just appeared, bearing filing cabinets, and tried to get Truitt's other desk away from him. The old one he keeps in the corner. You should have seen his face."

Tom slammed down one phone, reached for another, and began scrabbling in drawers for a pencil. "Mary," he called, "get that other line."

"Phone's ringing," Will said.

"Oh, let it," she said comfortably. "It's after five."

"Who wants the desk?"

Tom was hunched over the second phone, writing quickly. "Stuck," they heard him say. And then, "Ghost here, too."

Mary gave Tom a surprised look, but he was still writing. She turned back to Will. "It's to be put in the new library wing when it opens," she said. "Part of the ground-floor display under that portrait Geoff Bordeaux is getting up. It once belonged to Gabriel McCrocken."

"Surely they don't need it right away?"

"Not if Tru can help it. It's still full of old department files. And I can't imagine who sent for . . ."

Truitt had evidently achieved at least a partial victory. The two workmen were stomping off downstairs, leaving the desk behind them. They had also, however, left the filing cabinets. Truitt hung over the railing and watched them all the way down. When they rounded the last landing, he straightened up with a triumphant grin. "Damned idiots."

"I *have* brought us all coffee," said Mary Savannah.

From the depths of her ancient, rattan-cushioned swivel chair, Will sighed and took the cup she handed him. "That's all right, Mary. Nobody really expected you to help."

"And ruin my best blue polyester blouse? Those cabinets are heavy."

"We know."

Tom Donahue was back on the phone, chatting up someone from the registrar's office named Mrs. Barclay. Will had to hand it to him. Despite their exertions, he was as good-natured and relaxed as ever; he must be having a particularly good day. Truitt, however, was certainly feeling his age. He was leaning back wearily in a straight chair, gazing out the window beside him at the lamplit quadrangle below. His face was a peculiar shade of gray, his hair no longer sticking up so much but flattened against his forehead with perspiration.

"What," he said, "are all those green signs out there?"

"Where?" Mary had turned to look when something in Tom's voice riveted her attention.

"Yes, Mrs. Barclay," he was saying lightly. His eyes were shining with mischief. "Yes indeed. Mrs. Savannah is out of the office at the moment, but she asked me to tell you that report will be on the registrar's desk at nine o'clock in the morning." Mary flinched, and even Truitt's head came around, but it was too late. "You have a nice evening, too." He hung up, but not before Mary had, without a word, moved his coffee cup well out of his reach.

"Before we all get to squabbling"—Will took the note from his overcoat pocket and pushed it across the desk toward Truitt—"I'd like to find out what this means. Evidently you sent it over."

Truitt put his head back again and closed his eyes. "I can't help. I swear it. I don't know any more about it than what it says. Mrs. Moffat called up about four-thirty, asking for you. I told her you were in class. She said she wanted to see you right away. She said the subject was Broadway."

"Broadway?" Will looked blank.

Truitt shrugged. "Beats me. Otherwise, she just wanted to know if Luke Vondervorste was still away at that conference." Vondervorste was the university's head librarian.

"We can be sure of that," Donahue told him. "You have received a cable."

"Why me?" Truitt asked tiredly.

"You'll see." Tom fished among the telephone messages and read the cable aloud: "STUCK IN PARIS CAN'T COME HOME DAMNED CHARTER WON'T FLY. GHOST HERE TOO, I GUESS. MAKE SURE DISPLAY OKAY, MAKE MAISIE PAY UP, MAKE JOEY MAKE TOM FINISH SPEECH HELP HIM. HOME SOON. LUKE."

The three men were silent. Truitt rubbed his eyes.

Across the office, however, at the student aide's desk, Mary Savannah leaned forward on her blue polyester elbows. "I beg your pardon," she said. "What was that about a ghost?"

* * *

"Well, I understood that." Will and Tom were standing on the side porch while Will buttoned his long overcoat and Donahue, his trench coat unbuttoned as usual, looked out at the falling snow. The parking lot beyond them was still so full of cars that Will concluded there must be something going on that night, and then remembered it was the last night of the fall concert series.

"Luke was carrying on about that damned ghost for a month before he left." He got the high button under his chin fastened, withdrew a yard of navy muffler from his pocket. "He seemed to think it was Mrs. Moffat's fault, with all the to-do she raised over the McCrocken Wing. He even said the early winter was the ghost's doing—I guess the winter McCrocken died was a bad one. Or so I've heard. But I confess I never quite saw the connection. Why would Gabriel McCrocken, or his spirit, want to cause trouble?"

"Because of the money, of course," Donahue answered easily. The steps from the porch to the sidewalk were deep in new snow, and both men had to hold on to the iron railing. "Car's that way," he nodded.

Donahue's antique Volkswagen resembled an igloo. "There's an ice scraper under you somewhere," said Tom as he started the engine while Will found it, then climbed out again to scratch little holes on the front and back windshields. Will fumbled in his pockets for a cigarette. He should have walked, instead of accepting a ride. He was going to be colder in that frozen little car than if he'd gone the dozen or so blocks to Maisie Moffat's on foot.

"That'll do it." Tom tossed the ice scraper into the backseat, on top of a striped Indian blanket folded there. In the faint light, his handsome features were profiled against the window. It occurred to Will that maybe Donahue's astonishing good looks really were enough for Dora. Will, though he liked Tom well enough, had not been able to understand the attraction Dora and he had shown for each other in the few months since Tom's arrival; it had seemed an unlikely match.

Tom had returned to the subject of Luke Vondervorste—now "stuck" in Paris. Paris at Christmas would be a web of lights and snow and river and cathedrals, a breathtaking business of bells and spires and rooftops. Will wanted to be there himself.

"The connection," Tom was saying, "is obvious—if you have Luke's kind of mind. Not that he really believes in that ghost, but he's impressionable, you know; all this unusually cold weather, so early, and all the talk about it, and all the troubles he's had with the new wing—all that made our Luke sit up and take notice."

"I'm still missing something," Will said from under his hat. "What was that about money?"

"Oh, you know." Tom stopped cautiously at the end of Indian Avenue before turning onto Victory. "Gabriel must have dropped around to inspect the new wing, found out the money was still missing, and is making his presence felt, in such ways as ghosts can manage. He wants it found."

"What money is this?"

"You really don't know?" Tom shrugged lightly. "There may not be any. Although Gabriel did make a lot more than he left. Or so it evidently seemed to anyone who was acquainted with him."

Lazily, Will searched his memory. Gabriel McCrocken, he knew, had once taught at the university, many years before. He had died in 1940. But he had been a man of many accomplishments; and as well as teaching at the university, he had taken part in the town's development over the years. Will's impression was that he had been both wealthy and unpretentious, a man to whom making money came easily but to whom scholarship was more important. He'd had several children; Maisie Moffat was the only one still living.

"That was his house, did you know that?" Tom gestured to his left. "Still is, in a way. That is, it belongs to Mrs. Moffat, though she's leased it to the university for decades. And, of course, is selling it to them now."

The house he indicated was familiar enough to both of them, inside and out; it was the only private residence remaining within the irregular perimeters of the university. At present, it occupied an L-shaped corner plot at Victory and Alcott Road, backed and sided by the Social Sciences Building, the library complex (including the law and medical libraries), and Faculty Hall, with its rooms upstairs for visiting professors.

In the midst of all this, the house stood peacefully on nearly an acre of land, amidst trees, grape arbors, flower and vegetable gardens. It was a gaunt, semi-Victorian structure standing three stories high, painted forest green with white trim, and embellished with a turret and three rows of curving verandas. Out back stood a shady summer house, a shed, and a lean-to. It was known locally as Corners, maybe because it had so many of them.

Will's green eyes flickered over the familiar iron fence, the tall, gingerbready structure, the glowing stained-glass fanlight. In an effort to keep the university appeased—and because Mr. Mellon, the present tenant, was an uncle to one of the deans—it was often used for receptions and dinner parties.

He would, in fact, be going there on Thursday. Mellon and his twenty-year-old great-niece were lending the place for the university's annual Christmas party. It would be the last one held there, for the house, long in need of repairs, had at last been judged to be beyond mending. The plumbing was cracked, and so were the foundation walls. The rooms were drafty, the furnace needed replacing, and the floors creaked noisily—the list of its faults went on and on. It was scheduled to be torn down soon. Mr. Mellon and his niece would be moving just after Christmas.

"Is there any real mystery about this money?" he asked.

"Sort of," said Tom. "At least, every other person I've met

since I came here has wanted to tell me about it. If you've missed it, you've been uncommonly lucky."

No, Will thought, people were just anxious to please Tom, and to entertain him. He had that humorous, inviting sort of manner.

When Tom turned again, they left the campus behind, entering the dark realm of houses on the west side of Main Street, a place of old, tree-lined streets and long-ago, small-town wealth. Will hadn't ventured there often; its hidden streets and squares were a world apart from the university. He knew only that everyone here was old and very much poorer than the houses and the shadowy old lawns bespoke. He had sometimes walked through the neighborhood on hot summer days, to enjoy the coolness of its trees and the melancholy of its dark-leafed ivy; then, the touches of shabbiness about the houses made them seem comfortable. In winter, however, they closed in upon themselves.

Mrs. Moffat lived there, on Elderberry Street.

"The mystery, if there is one," Tom said, "had to do with a letter Gabriel wrote to his children. He appended it to his will. In it he suggested, though not in so many words, that he'd hidden part of what he'd left. I'm told that during his last few years he had cancer and he knew it. By 1939 he didn't have much time left. So he did something odd; he began turning a big chunk of his fortune to cash. Rewrote his will for the last time, wrapped up his affairs, made a last business trip to New York in the spring of 1940. He resigned from the university that year, and died in the early part of September. By that time, most of the cash was gone. The small bequests were all for specific amounts, locked up in his safe. His children inherited equally whatever was left—Maisie, his daughter, and the two sons, Henry and Edward. Both the sons are dead now.

"When the will was first read, everything appeared to be very much in order. But the total assets of his estate didn't add up. By everybody's calculations, there was more than a quarter of a million dollars missing, or various holdings worth that amount. And that turned out to have been the cash, or the bulk of it. No one really knows what happened to it."

He turned onto Elderberry and eased the car up to the curb in front of Mrs. Moffat's. "Maybe it was just all gone, somehow, but Maisie and Henry and Edward certainly thought more should have been there. And there were, of course, records for sales of stock and property and so on, with no indication of subsequent purchases. So the three children turned the house inside out that winter, and pretty soon the whole town got into the act. Nobody ever found it, and there was, of course, talk of theft. Maisie always discounted that, and she still thinks the money exists. Principally because of that letter."

Will lit another cigarette. "Which said?"

"It was mostly a kind of farewell to the children, or so it seemed. But there were puzzling things in it. Ask Mrs. Moffat to let you read it someday. You'll see."

The porch light of Maisie Moffat's house came on. She evidently knew they were out there. Will reached for the door handle. "Thanks for the ride," he said. "It was out of your way."

"Not much. I have some errands in town."

Will got out. The tires spun momentarily in the snow; then the little car dragged itself out and chugged off down Elderberry toward the upper end of Main Street, and Will scrambled up Maisie's imperfectly shoveled walk to her front door.

TWO

Old Mrs. Moffat's Plan

Mrs. Moffat must have been waiting for him just inside. Will had no sooner found the bell, obscured by a mass of colored lights, than she opened the door with a rush and stood shimmering up at him.

"I don't know anything whatever about Broadway," he said gravely.

"That's two of us." She held the door open for him to enter. "Come in and I'll make you a big drink."

Will had never been there before. His previous encounters with Mrs. Moffat had in some way prepared him, however, for the dim and echoing entrance hall, its wooden floors, its paneled walls, and its dark oak staircase rising steeply to the shadowy upper floor. Despite her short, plump, comfortable presence, Maisie was as direct and unadorned as her foyer—and as likely to contain surprises as the hidden corners of the room.

He was distinctly unprepared, though, for the living room into which she ushered him. He didn't know what he had expected, but it wasn't this massive cream-colored interior, with its big black fireplace at one end, burning brightly, and its dark plank floors. The walls had wedding-cake picture molding some twelve feet up, but were otherwise bare. At the far end of the room was a collection of steel cabinetry crammed, above, with expensive stereo equipment and, below, with a bar. In front of the fireplace stood a glass table, surrounded by a circle of straight-backed, painstakingly carved walnut chairs that must have come from a monastery in Europe. To each of the chairs Maisie had tied cushions of Kelly-green corduroy. Over the fireplace hung an immense blue Matisse; in the bow window stood a gigantic blue spruce. The only other objects in the room were a long, darkly gleaming wooden worktable at the near end and, on it, a stained-glass lamp and a packet of yellowing papers.

"How about a bourbon and soda?"

Will nodded. "Please."

When they were settled before the fire, Will studied her wrinkled little face. She was docilely chatting about the weather and about her Christmas plans while she cracked peanuts from a big bowl on the glass table. He thought, watching her, that this rather odd and unexpected room, doubtless foisted off on her by some graduate student in the School of Design, lent her an unpredictable dignity, or brought it out. Her plump back was ramrod-straight, and the way she had her feet propped on the rungs of the medieval chair caused her long black skirt to fall in elegant lines. In the half light, the numerous rings on her fingers sparkled eerily.

She seemed content to go on making small talk, but at last he stopped her. "What was it about the theater?" he asked.

"On account of it, I'm broke."

He blinked. "What do you mean by that?"

"What you think I mean."

"Completely?"

She nodded. "I am, I'm afraid, a fallen angel, Dr. Gray. And since"—she grinned—"Mr. Vondervorste is so unfortunately away, I called on you to deal with this for me. You are in charge of the library committee this year. And you are much saner than Mr. Vondervorste."

"Just my luck. What happened?"

"Fear of God and a certain sympathy with the Enemy, oddly enough." She sighed. "That *always* leads to trouble. Once in a while, you see, I indulge in whims. That's rare, but the whims get expensive. Buying clothes for orphans. I've done that. Gilding the town lampposts. They wouldn't let me, but I tried; I did think they'd be pretty. Then there was this room. It cost a lot to do it. That Matisse alone . . ." She waved at it. "And all these rings. Most of the time, you see, it doesn't work."

She turned her hands over and studied them. "The rings never did look right. It could be my hands, of course—I've never had good hands, not even as a girl." She shot a sudden glance at Will's hands; he just barely kept from putting them behind him. "And this room is slick. I have three friends left alive, and every one of them hates it; so do I. Besides, I can't keep it the way it was meant to be." She reached across the glass table and took more peanuts from the bowl. "These are good, though." She dropped the peanuts in her lap and turned them over to select the best one. "Do you know the parable of the five talents?"

"I think so," Will answered. "One servant was criticized for hiding the money he was entrusted with. He was supposed to have invested it and increased it."

"Severely chastised. Not just criticized." She chewed the nuts thoughtfully. "Father Linnet preached a *stirring* sermon about it last New Year's Day. I heard it on the radio from my hospital bed. It was a galvanizing moment. He made me feel that I was very guilty."

"How do you mean?"

"This money that I gave the library building fund was left to me by Papa. Do you remember Papa? Of course you don't; don't answer that.

"For a long time I lived only off Toby's income—he was a wealthy man, too. Papa's money went for extras over the years. Trips, mostly. What was left a year ago had, of course, earned a good deal, but I certainly never tried to increase it as much as possible. And I had thought of another addition to the university that I could use extra money for."

She looked at him steadily. "However it would have seemed on the surface, it was a piece of self-indulgence that Father Linnet would have disapproved of."

"What was it?"

"I wanted to build a little campus museum, for the art students. That would be something to perk them up, I thought. And if we had a little house, behind the School of Education, I think . . . well, I paced it off one day last winter, the minute they let me out of bed. There's enough room."

"What about the parking lot?"

"Get rid of it. People around here don't walk enough anyway. It's bad for their hearts."

Will shook his head. "The trustees—"

"Bother the trustees. Stop." She held up her hand. "You've lost track of the point. The point is that the money I could spare had already been committed for the new library wing. I wanted more money." She opened another nut. "And Father Linnet had made me see that I had erred. So I decided to use what money I had before I had to give it up, and I stumbled upon a splendid scheme. I decided to back a play. Did you know Stuart Malone?"

"A little." Malone, from New York, had taught drama for a semester, as a visiting professor.

"A lovely man. I can't fault him. He did warn me. But the very idea of being an angel . . ." She smiled brightly. "I was introduced to him one afternoon last winter at a reception, you see. I don't often go to receptions, but I was so thrilled at having cheated Death that I was going everywhere. Besides, it was at our house, Papa's old house, and I went to see what had become of it. Let go to rack and ruin, of course. Mellon doesn't have good sense, though that niece of his is going to amount to something someday. Anyway, there, like it was fated, I met Malone. We fell to talking about the theater, of course, and one thing led to another. I think I got carried away. Anyway, to make a long story short, I put ever so much money into a new play, and now it's failed. It closed last night, actually." She shook her head. "Those poor actors, I'm so sorry for them. And it was such a nice story."

"How much had you invested in it?"

"Every cent of that hundred and fifty thousand."

"And you'll not be able to repay the university?"

"I am destitute. More or less."

In the hall, the telephone rang. Maisie brushed the crumbs from the peanut shells out of her skirt. "Excuse me, please. Fix yourself another drink. The good part comes next."

Will glanced at his watch. His cat was probably dismantling the icebox. He took his glass to the bar.

It seemed plain that Maisie had indeed let a small fortune get away from her. She had long ago promised the money for the improvement of the new library wing's design, on condition that it be used only for certain architectural luxuries and that the wing be called the Gabriel McCrocken Library.

As far as the actual construction of the building went, her contribution wouldn't have begun to cover the costs. But when the architect's plans had been published, she had appeared at a trustees' meeting in a flurry of irritation. Not exactly on a litter, he'd heard, but she'd given that impression, looking frail and tiny and delicate from one of her episodes with her own heart that had kept her in and out of the hospital for two years and that had nearly killed her. No wonder everyone had been afraid to upset her.

What was proposed, she had announced, was an ugly, uninteresting brick box, a boring, uninviting scar on the landscape. The campus of Crosscreek University deserved better. If she offered the trustees a little something extra—say, a hundred and fifty thousand—could they see to it that a less tiresome building were put up? She was even prepared with a few suggestions. . . .

It was a messy fight, but Maisie won in the end, as of course she had to. Everyone—except for the trustees and the bureaucrats and the architect, naturally—had been on her side, led by Jed McIngling at the *News*. Even then, Maisie didn't trust them to follow through. The entire library, she stipulated, must be finished as the new plans called for. When she saw it with her own eyes, she would produce the money. She was good for it. And then she went back to the hospital and nearly died again, and the trustees caved in.

Thereby, according to Luke, raising the ghost of Gabriel McCrocken to complicate things further. Luke would be near tears when he heard.

Nothing could be done now. The carved stone arcades were in place, and the pitched slate roof and the tile walks and the round windows. The building was complete.

It sounded to Will as if Maisie needed a lawyer. A very expensive one.

"That was the *News* again," Maisie said. She picked up the packet of papers from the worktable. Her slippers clapped against the floor as she came down the room. "I told Jed we're almost done. He'll be here in a few minutes."

"Why Jed? I thought you wanted to keep it quiet."

"He's helping me get up a flyer tonight, and his newsboys will distribute it tomorrow. I'm his godmother; he has to do something. Actually, he's enjoying himself." She laughed.

"And what will the flyer say?"

"Wonderful things. I can fix this up, you see, but not without help." She sat down carefully. "Maybe I was meant to lose that money."

Will lost his temper. Maisie had made a commitment that involved a substantial amount of money, and the university, whatever its sins, was always painfully poor. She seemed to be taking no more than a frivolous approach to the problem.

His green eyes snapped. "You're going to take up a collection? Start a fund drive? Have a garage sale? That won't do it, Maisie. This time the trustees are likely to commandeer this house, and every other asset you've got. Not much fun, the week before Christmas."

"They'll never have the chance. All we have to do is find Papa's money. It really was there, you know."

She opened the packet and spread its contents out before her. There were two large photographs, one of herself and one of old Gabriel; a sheaf of cracking clippings; a floor plan of the McCrocken—now the Mellon—home; a drawing of the layout of the town of Crosscreek in 1940; and a dog-eared letter.

"Gabriel's missing fortune." Will took his glasses off and polished them. Evidently Luke had been onto something.

"Lots more than what we need was unaccounted for, you know. If he invested it in something, it will be worth even more. I hope. Even if he didn't, the money's still there somewhere. My offer will be that the finder may keep the extra for himself, after the library is paid for."

"Do you seriously think it's there to be found?"

Maisie pursed her lips. "Do you have any better ideas? Besides buying me a tent?"

"Nothing comes to me."

"Well, then. Certainly it's there. Papa hid it, didn't he?"

"I thought there was some question about all that."

"Read the letter for yourself." She sighed. "Goodness knows there's no *other* way to explain it."

THREE
Signs and Portents

It was less than half a block from Maisie's house to the corner. Will walked along toward Main Street and the single faint streetlight there. Virtually no light at all came from any of the surrounding houses, and the yellowish glow of that one lamp, faded though it was, and partially obscured by the bare branches of the tree that overhung it, was all the lonelier for its isolation. But, isolated or not, it seemed that Nealsson had been here, too, for one of his green posters shone out like neon.

An unlikely place for it, Will thought. Almost no one went by here on foot, in any weather. He stopped to take a look.

On Friday, December 28th
at one-thirty
the contents of the house of Mr. S. F. Mellon,
64 Victory Street, will be sold at
AUCTION
Contents include certain remaining bric-a-brac and furnishings (some antiques), fixtures, draperies, carpets, and equipment. Complete list available in Carstairs Hall, Room 122, and at various Main Street locations. Viewing will be permitted on Thursday, December 27th, from 2–6 P.M.

So that was what was up. Will, wondering briefly if Mellon could be expected to leave anything worth buying—and deciding he probably wouldn't—was just turning away when the elm above him creaked in the rising wind and a load of snow slithered from one of its branches onto his shoulders.

He was still standing there, shivering and brushing himself off, when Dora shot down Main in her battered little car. She rocketed dangerously to a stop and rolled down the window to call to him. "Get in! I'll give you a ride."

Will sighed. The whole world seemed intent on keeping him off his feet this evening. It was easier to give in to Dora than to argue with her, though, so he climbed in beside her.

"I was just going to call you," she told him, with a glance behind her for oncoming traffic.

"I'm not home yet."

"No smart remarks, now. I have to ask a favor."

Will lighted a cigarette. "First, my dear, satisfy my burning curiosity. Where the hell have you been?" To have Dora come tearing down this end of Main Street from out of the emptiness to the north had taken him by surprise.

The expression under her furry hat had gone suddenly stern, and her usually rosy cheeks were pale.

"I've just been shopping," she told him. "That farm out yonder, you know. Where they sell things sometimes. The one where we went for the pumpkins."

"You need a pumpkin?"

"Of course not. I went for a Christmas tree."

"Did I miss it?"

"Don't be silly. They didn't have one I liked. I'll have to go back to Fewlinson's and get an already-cut one. Can I ask my favor now? I can't take you all the way home—I'm going to the store. So you'll have to get out in a minute."

"Ask away."

"This is serious, Will. You just can't say no. I need you to pick up Mother for me."

"Your mother?" Will frowned. "I didn't know she was here. You should have told me."

"She isn't here yet, that's just it. She's coming in the morning, on that nine o'clock plane. I can't possibly get her—

I've got a class at nine. But your first one isn't till two. You wouldn't mind, would you?"

"Mind driving ninety miles and back in subzero weather at six in the morning because you didn't think this out in advance? Why on earth would I mind?"

"Now, be sweet. You and Mother always got along." She stopped at the first light. "I just forgot about that class. It's easy to get days mixed up."

"Sure. There is, of course, Tom," Will said. "He might mind even less than I do."

"Why Tom? Besides, we're not speaking. I don't know why you think we're special friends, we're not at all."

Will sighed. "Forget I mentioned him then." Not a good solution anyway, he thought. For one thing, he did like Dora's mother. And Donahue, so far as he knew, hadn't met her.

"Will you get her?"

"Yes, I'll get her."

"You're a dear. I just knew it would be all right." She turned into the town square, maneuvered the car halfway around it, and shoehorned it into the tiny parking lot behind the grocery store. A station wagon began to pull out of its parking space ahead of her, and she stopped to wait for it.

"Come to think of it," she said, "you didn't tell me what *you* were doing out that way, at the end of Main."

Will opened the door and got out. "Well, I might one day," he said, "but not till you 'fess up."

"What do you mean?"

"That farm isn't doing business today, sugar. It belongs to Jones and his wife; Jones's kid is in my class. This afternoon Jones's kid made a complete mess of a presentation on Charlemagne he'd worked on for months. After class he apologized. His father's in surgery, in a bad way. Kidneys or something. Shop's closed, Christmas sale going down the drain, his mother's in a state. Stuff like that."

"Will—"

Behind them a car honked impatiently.

"Better get parked." Will stepped back from the window. "See you tomorrow." He gave the other driver an apologetic wave and walked along the line of cars to the curb. Across the street, on the corner of Main and the square, the lights of the bookshop made a bright spot next to the bank. There was something very soothing, Will thought, about the thought of being in the presence of its proprietor, Miss Louise Tree—small, unsure, auburn-haired, thoroughly independent Louise Tree—so he tightened his long navy muffler about his collar, pulled his hat down, and headed across the street.

Will stood helplessly before her under the ceiling light of the bare hall adjoining the shop. To his left a flight of stairs led up to her apartment; to his right a door led out to the sidewalk. Poised between the two stood Louise, her small face hurt and angry, her eyes swimming in tears. Under the ceiling light her silky hair, a little mussed, was bright with an admixture of coppery gold.

"You'll have Christmas dinner with me, then," Will said.

"Don't be silly, Will. I'd feel like such an idiot. I do now. You caught me at the wrong moment, I'm afraid. It's just—" She clamped her lips together and blinked the tears away. "Who in the world cares," she said firmly. "Right now I can't imagine why I thought I did."

"Well, I could kill Tom for you," he said. "Or I could at least rough him up pretty good. I could sabotage his car or tear up his plane ticket or bribe a New York cabdriver. I've got connections."

"Actually," she said, "Tom's fine and he can have his Christmas dinner wherever it suits him. I'm sorry I cried."

"That's all right. Your hair needs brushing," Will told her. "Just a little bit."

She turned to the mirror on the wall behind her. "You can't brush hair like this." It fell in a short braid down the back of her gray shirt.

"Well, whatever you do with it. Are you all right, really?"

"Yes." For a moment she reminded him of Dora, of any woman he'd ever known, standing preoccupied before a mirror, and then she didn't at all. Her shoulders sagged a little, and her hands dropped away from her hair. "Yes." She turned back to him, but her eyes, though dry, were blank.

"You look just great. Let's go back and sell books," he said. "I'll fix Tom first thing tomorrow."

Will lingered for a time inside the shop as Louise headed intently for the counter. Around him, browsing, were many strangers and a few acquaintances. Joey Livingston, head of the English department, was among them, and Truitt Roberts was hovering over the table of used books.

But Will scarcely noticed any of them. It was nearly eight-thirty—closing time—and he had a fleeting thought of his cat, Amigo, who was doubtless waiting impatiently by now on the dining-room windowsill that overlooked the front walk, a snug place in the shadow of the plum-colored velveteen curtains Dora had sent over after the divorce. But Amigo's black fur was sleek and his sides a little too rounded, as round almost as his serious golden eyes, and he wasn't likely to starve in the next half hour.

Not that Will had a very clear idea of what he should be doing instead of going home. He supposed he was waiting to help Louise lock up, to give her one more metaphorical pat on the back, one more drying of her eyes if necessary.

A few people were gathering up their purchases and taking them to the counter. Will stood with his hands in his pockets, looking out the narrow side windows, scarcely pretending to be interested in the shelves of books around him.

The town that night looked like a fairground. A divided and sectioned fairground, anyway. The plows had given up keeping even the square cleared completely, and a wall of snow some four feet high ran down the middle of the street, dividing it into two narrow lanes. The sidewalks, equally walled in, were filled with booted and hooded pedestrians; children, excited by the Christmas atmosphere, romped wildly among them. Will saw Dora, across the street, sail along through the parking lot to her car, followed by a boy pushing a cart heaped with grocery bags. Dora's tiny mother, even if she was a bit plump, wasn't going to come anywhere near eating all that.

The lights of the parking lot made her red coat stand out and her furry hat gleam. Another set of hurt feelings in the making, he supposed, if Tom hadn't yet told Dora he would be away. Perhaps he had, though, and that was what had made her so mad.

Will wasn't particularly clear about what Tom was going to be doing. It seemed, however, that he was required to be in New York on the evening of Christmas Day for a dinner party. The people giving the dinner weren't friends, he'd told Louise, not at all. He couldn't really explain. Nor were they academics. What had they in common, then? Well, nothing, really. No, they had no ties to anything in particular, or at least nothing he could think of. He couldn't even say who they were because he didn't know. They sounded like a bunch of hit men, Louise had said bitterly. At which Tom had laughed. No, not that. That wasn't it.

But he had Christmas dinner with these people every year. He had been doing so for a long time. He was expected.

He had seemed very cheerful, very delighted with himself.

For Louise, the disappointment was especially painful. Besides Tom, she had no other family. She had scarcely known her cousin before he came to Crosscreek the previous July, but she had quickly grown fond of him and had found a new and sudden happiness in the idea of being part of a family again. The past year or so, Will knew, since Tom's father had died, had been a strain for her, and her loneliness had sometimes shown in her small face.

Well, Tom had a right to spend Christmas with whatever old friends—or acquaintances—he chose to, of course. He had, after all, spent years living in New York, and he must miss it. Perfectly natural of him to want to go back. But it was too bad that his doing so hurt his cousin. Particularly since he was on a one-year leave of absence—there wouldn't be any Christmases together except this one.

Almost everyone else had left, and Louise was turning off the lights. Will found himself plunged into gloom as the window lights went out, followed by those on the whole lefthand side of the shop. Only Truitt Roberts remained.

"It got torn up," he was telling Louise with some embarrassment. "My dog, you know. . . ." His voice trailed off.

Will stood in the shadows, willing Truitt away. Whatever had been torn up, though, Truitt's aged collie was an unlikely culprit. More likely, his harum-scarum daughter, Angela. Though, he remembered, she must be about seventeen by now. And maybe outgrowing her foolish ways.

"Let me write it down." Louise's voice was kind. "Brewster, you said. *The Men Who Made the Midwest?*"

"That's right. I'm afraid Mrs. Moffat would have my hide if she knew." Truitt turned his coat collar up. "You've never even heard of it, have you?"

"Nope. But we get surprising things sometimes. It might turn up."

"If it does . . ." He made a vague gesture with his hands. "But don't go to a lot of trouble, or bother anyone else, Louise. I wouldn't want—"

Louise resumed her clearing up. "I understand, Truitt. I promise not to bother anybody." He flushed. "And don't worry. If I ever run across it, I'll call you."

He sighed. "Thank you."

When he was gone, Louise looked over at Will. "You should go home, too," she said. "If you don't, you'll just make me feel more embarrassed than I already do."

"I'll be off then," he said slowly. "One question. This bunch of cohorts Tom's so attached to—do they have a name?"

"Not one I could make any sense of. I thought maybe it was some fraternity or something, but Tom said not. He said they were called the Close Company of Perfect Strangers."

* * *

All the way down Main Street, where other lights were going out and shop doors were being locked for the night, Will thought about that, but his reflections did him no good at all.

The campus was deserted and suddenly desolate-looking, most of the buildings dark by now, and a film of snow blowing across the white lawns stretching out around them. At least the wind, which was picking up steadily, was at his back, coming out of the north.

He glanced up at Jaeckel Hall's fifth-floor windows as he passed. The history department had apparently shut down for the night, but at the other end of the building, one lighted square winked on as he watched, and he caught a glimpse of Tom's auburn head coming through his office door. He must have finished his errands, had his supper, and be planning to work all evening.

"Show-off," Will mumbled.

Ten minutes later, he let himself into his own front door and, in the dark foyer, braced himself for what always happened before he could reach for the light. Out of the darkness Amigo hurled himself at Will, the bundle of warm, furry cat hitting him squarely in the chest. Will caught him and carried him into the kitchen, switching on lamps as he went. "Let's eat," he said.

FOUR
The Deadly Fields

The airport was in Sioux Falls, ninety miles to the southwest. Will, alone on the streets of Crosscreek that morning, made his way along Parson Road through the dark neighborhoods behind the campus and silently blessed the snowplow drivers when he got to the edge of town and saw that even State Highway 1016, an old and now little-used farm-to-market road, had been cleared. It cut across the countryside to the south and joined the interstate some forty miles farther on, saving him some time. He turned onto it, reached down to assure himself that the heater really was working, and settled down for the drive, his foot as heavy on the accelerator as he dared. Not that he was all that short on time, but he found this road depressing.

It was a stretch almost completely without human life in its vicinity. Part of it was pasturage, the back side of a big spread that fronted on the interstate. Part was land belonging to two or three abandoned farms that were now in the possession of banks; another part was government-owned but unused land. All the way from Crosscreek to the interstate, and beyond as far as Marsdale, the road was empty and silent.

As he drove, the wind moaned around his car, and from the fields on either side, a thin dusting of snow blew and eddied over the highway. It was still pitch-dark—it would be half an hour yet before the east began to gray—and his headlights made long, bright paths down the straight road before him.

Will yawned. Dora certainly asked a lot, he thought, legal disassociations notwithstanding. Probably he ought to warn

Tom about that. She was the sort of person who never let go, who gathered people around her as she went along and ever thereafter regarded them as firmly fixed in place within her orbit, ready to be called on for parties or errands or to have their shoulders cried on. With Dora, relationships never changed; they always remained whatever they had been at the beginning. She had a kind of tunnel vision that was hard on her friends—on those, at least, who couldn't get away. Still, he reflected, it worked. However reluctantly, her friends did gather around her when required. They did pat her into shape and present themselves at the summer barbecues she threw in the park across Pebble River, where it flowed between narrow banks behind her apartment house, to be greeted warmly and sent for more hamburger buns and introduced to people they didn't really want to meet. They solved her tax problems and helped her hang curtains and fetched her mother from airports. They even, God help them, married her.

So preoccupied was Will with his thoughts, and with the discomfiting bleakness and menace of the windswept plains stretching out to the horizon, that he had had the other car in view long before it registered fully on his consciousness. It was apparently abandoned, hunched on the shoulder of the road and facing south, the direction he himself was headed. He glanced at his watch—it was about six-twenty—and reached in his pocket for his cigarettes at the moment he whipped past the car, automatically giving it something of a wide berth. And then, his hands trembling, scarcely knowing what he was doing, he was applying the brakes, stopping, shifting into reverse, backing unsteadily till he got near enough to get out and walk, on legs reluctant to take him to what he had seen in that split second of passing—something that looked uncommonly like a blanket tumbled carelessly across the back of the driver's seat, an Indian blanket bright in his headlights with colorful stripes.

* * *

The next few hours of that cold morning passed in a chaos of telephone calls and police cars, ambulances, and general confusion. The worst part had been the search, alone at first, finding the traces of tracks nearly obliterated by wind and snow, one near the car, another near a fence post, giving some suggestion of a direction. They had appeared to head west; Will had followed as best he could, striking out across a field, and then had known he couldn't do it. He'd fought his way back to the car, against the wind, and thrown himself into it at last, gasping and shuddering with a cold he thought would never leave him. He'd started the motor, pulled out blindly onto that empty road, too stiff and numb of mind to think of turning around—and found, a mile ahead, a turnoff to the right.

He didn't know why he took it. There was a bridge here, a wooden one over what must have been a stream, now snow-covered. He drove as far as he could, and then got out and walked some more. To his left, just where a rise in the ground made a blur against the somewhat less dark sky, he'd seen something that might have been a suggestion of buildings far below.

Will had given it up, cursed himself for wasting time, and gone back to his car. That was where they had found Tom, though, after he'd summoned help. Halfway between the bridge and the buildings—deserted anyway—some three miles from where he'd left the highway. Just a crumpled, figure in a trench coat, more than half-buried in snow and long since dead.

Will never did get to the airport. At some point he put in a call there, to leave a message for little Mrs. Chandler when her plane landed; later he was speaking to her faint and staticky voice, asking her to wait for him, have breakfast, read a paperback; he'd collect her as soon as he could. She was fine, she told him, whatever the problem was there, he should stay and deal with it. She'd been offered a ride in with someone, she'd manage. A nice woman from New York and another couple, some people from a nearby farm. Just tell Dora to leave the key under the mat.

But the problem that had kept Will from the airport wasn't one he could do much about. Much except be there. The three of them—Will; Dr. Lollo McIngling, father of Jed McIngling at the *News*; and Sheriff Mack Winterlin—were standing in an office outside the hospital's emergency room after everything had been done that could be done. "Happens every year," McIngling was saying, "and it's so damned unnecessary. Taking a car on a deserted road like that, in the middle of the night, when the wind is coming down like bloody murder. The chill factor must have been at least seventy-five below. He'd have been all right, of course, if he hadn't gotten out. These macho types never think. And him in a trench coat, for God's sake, with no lining. What was he trying to prove?" He started opening desk drawers, pulling out forms. "The hell of it is, what it's going to do to Louise Tree." He glanced at Sheriff Winterlin. "Has anyone told her yet? Or do you want me to?"

Winterlin had a snub nose, large ears that stuck out from his head, a mass of brown hair, and shiny brown eyes. "It hadn't occurred to us," he said. "What does Miss Tree have to do with it?"

"She's his cousin. Only living relative." Dr. McIngling looked unhappy. "Damn it to hell, she's going to take this badly. But I've known her for years, what with one thing and another. You'd better let me take care of it."

"Still, I'd like to go with you." Winterlin spoke with a determination in his voice that evidently struck McIngling as odd.

"No question of its being police business?"

"I'd rather think of it as routine."

"Because I haven't done the autopsy yet?"

"That, for one thing," Winterlin admitted, and then he raised the question that had been driving Will slowly mad since six-twenty that morning. "I'd also like to get a line on where the hell Donahue thought he was going."

There didn't seem to be a ready answer to that question. "Louise will ask the same thing," Will said.

"Same reason you were there?" McIngling suggested.

"That seems unlikely. But maybe. It depends on when he stalled."

McIngling frowned. "That's nearly impossible to say. He had been dead a couple of hours when he was found. How long he stayed in the car, how long it took him to get those three miles or so from it—who knows? Maybe he left the car at midnight? But I can't tell you when he got there, or how long he waited inside before he got out."

"Probably not all that long," Winterlin suggested. "I mean, it seems to me he wouldn't have stuck around much, given that he got out at all. He'd be sure to see that no one much went along there at that time of night, and he couldn't have been too comfortable. That Volkswagen wouldn't have got its heat going yet."

"Say he stalled at midnight then, for starters," McIngling shrugged. "See if it works out when you put it all together. But I'd think you'd need to work that out from this end."

"Well," said Will, "if he stalled at midnight or anywhere near it, he wasn't headed for the airport. The place closes down before that."

Nor could he have been on his way out of town for Christmas, of course. He had classes to teach still, he had other plans anyway, he had no luggage with him. To Marsdale, or Sioux Falls, or any other nearby town? But why at that hour? Dr. McIngling looked cautiously at Will. "Maybe he was calling on a lady? Some girls are just naturally up all night."

Will almost didn't bother to answer. That wouldn't have been Tom's style. And besides, he thought, another bed was doubtless kept warm for him.

"Is there anything at all along ten-sixteen that could interest him?" he asked. "I take it it's as deserted as it looks."

"Just about. Another mile on, as you found out, and you get to Wilde Road. Down that side road are a couple of farms. He appeared to be headed on foot for the nearer of them, the one Mrs. Ring owns. Beyond that is the Nealssons'."

"No Wildes?"

"That's the Rings. Mrs. Ring was a Wilde girl." Briefly, McIngling's eyes twinkled. "Bought out her father years ago so she could—"

Will stopped him. "Would Tom have had any business there?"

"Can't imagine what. Mrs. Ring has been away the past month. The Nealssons' hired man comes over every day to look after her livestock, but the house is all shut up. She's off visiting her grown kids."

"Still, it seems as if he knew—or thought—he could get help there."

"Thought. There wasn't any help for him to know about."

"The Nealsson farm was too far away," Winterlin said, "but is it possible that was his original destination? I understand that a Nealsson son is in school here."

"That's true, but I wouldn't think so," Will replied. "It's not customary for a professor to be calling on a student at midnight at his parents' house. And anyway, Barney Nealsson isn't studying English."

A nurse appeared in the doorway, carrying a manila envelope. She handed it to Dr. McIngling. "The contents of Tom's pockets," he said, and dumped it out on his desk. "Maybe something here will help us."

There was little besides the usual collection of wallet, comb, handkerchief, and so forth. One item, however, was an envelope. On the front was the return address of a publishing company and Donahue's name and university address. The back was a hodgepodge of notes, scribbled in pencil and crowded together.

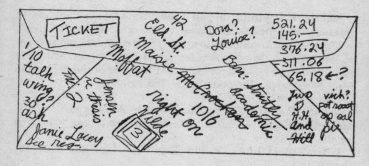

The three men studied it.

"Directions," Dr. McIngling said, pointing to *1016* and the words below it. "He wasn't out there for a pleasure drive, or going someplace he'd been before. Three miles past the turnoff is nothing at all. The Ring farm is six or seven miles from the junction; the Nealssons are a mile or so beyond that."

Winterlin turned the envelope about in his hands. "What's this other stuff?" He handed it to Will. "Make any sense to you? Why is 'McCrocken' crossed out, for instance?"

"He was going to give a talk for the opening of the new library wing," Will explained. "My guess is that his note had to do with that—maybe he'd looked up something he wanted to know. Or"—he peered more closely at the way Maisie Moffat's name and address were juxtaposed with the word *McCrocken*—"or he wrote down 'Maisie McCrocken' without thinking and changed it to 'Moffat.'"

"All right. Go on."

"He was planning a dinner party. There's the guest list and the menu."

"You got marked off," Winterlin observed. "Who is 'And'?"

"Andrea Mateas, I imagine." Will started up the other column of notes. "Jensen and Janie Lacey are English students." He elaborated on both till Winterlin was satisfied.

"Dora and Louise are almost the only two people to whom he'd be giving Christmas gifts, here in town anyway. That probably explains the question marks. Several people have been reading this Stringfellow Barr book lately, since Joey Livingston discovered it in the library and said it was good. 'Ticket' could refer to anything—maybe a plane ticket. He was going to New York for Christmas. These figures could correspond in some way. You could compare this with his checkbook."

Winterlin was making notes. "So it all seems to make sense," he said, "except for these directions. 'Wilde, three.'" He looked around at the others.

"I've told you," McIngling repeated. "That's empty fields. Check for yourself if you can't remember. *If* that's what the three means."

"I remember," Winterlin said shortly. "That doesn't mean I understand."

"Then you've got some questions to ask. Of course, it might have to do with something else altogether."

"Like what, though?" Will wondered.

Winterlin began returning things to the manila envelope. "I don't know. But he's right. It could be anything at all."

It was about nine-thirty. Will put on his coat and looked around for his hat. "Tell Louise I'll notify the college, and Dora. I've got to go by both places anyway."

The university first, he was thinking as he let himself out of the hospital. He left his car in the lot; the university was practically across the street. Joey Livingston should know as soon as possible. Tom might very well have had morning classes. And if he didn't show up, and couldn't be reached at home, word would get around the campus—to Dora before long, even if someone didn't think of asking her directly if she knew where Tom might be. And he wanted Dora not to know about it just that way.

To prevent it, he needed to make certain arrangements, and quick ones.

He had scarcely left the hospital grounds, though, when he changed his mind and made a short detour. A block or so away, on the corner of Main and Brown, stood Bo Jenkins's service station. Any car requiring official investigation was put in Bo's hands, and it was there Will headed. He found Tom's green Volkswagen parked beside the station.

Will crossed the cement apron and went in. The glass walls of the station were fogged over almost completely; inside, a space heater glowed fiercely, a coffee urn bubbled and perked on a table in the corner, and Bo himself, a towheaded, chunky man in his early fifties, was hidden behind the counter making a racket with an unruly dust cloth and a collection of apparent discards. He emerged at the sound of the door opening, his face lighting up when he saw it was Will.

"I didn't hear your car. Did the goddamn cold freeze the bell?"

"Nope. I came on foot."

"It's that bad, huh?"

Will shook his head. "Tom Donahue's car," he said. "Have you found out what was wrong with it?"

"It was easy." Bo sighed and looked at Will with clear yet troubled eyes. "He ran out of gas."

"No more than that?"

"It'll sure stop a car. Not that it makes sense. Unless he did a hell of a lot of driving around last night."

"Why do you say that?"

Bo shrugged. "I filled that tank about dinnertime."

"*Last* night? You couldn't be thinking of the night before?"

"It was last night, I know. But even if I didn't . . . well, maybe you don't know about those real old Volkswagens. That damn thing's a 1960 model."

Will looked blank. He knew all about that, of course—Tom had been half in love with his aged little car. He'd picked it up somewhere in his youth and had kept it ever since, tending it in the memory of his wilder, poorer days, turning it—with fresh paint and soft seat covers and shiny new parts—into a dowager with spirit. Everyone had laughed at Tom about that car, but he'd petted it nonetheless. "She's getting to be worth something," he'd said. "I wouldn't dream of deserting her anyway."

But Will still didn't understand. Gas was gas. You had it or you didn't. He looked at Bo inquiringly.

Bo spread his hands. "An old Volkswagen like that, there's no gas gauge on them, but there's a reserve tank. Activated by a lever. If you run out, you throw it and you've got about a gallon left. Which is generally enough to get you to a gas station." He folded his cloth and put it away. "You want some coffee?"

"No, thanks. What about the reserve tank?"

"He was running on it. The lever was turned, anyway."

"He did it himself, then?"

"Not unless he drove away a tankful."

"And if he didn't?"

"Someone stole it and threw the lever for him. They left him just enough to get out of town good." Bo stared at him. "Now why would anyone want to play a trick like that?"

All the way back to the campus, Will weighed the question of whether, somehow, Tom could have driven away some ten gallons of gas the night before. It scarcely seemed possible, but just maybe, from eight-forty-five on, when Will had seen him in his office, some inexplicable sequence of events had led to a crazy kind of marathon that might, just barely, account for it. But only if he'd set right out and had gone like the wind.

Will thought he could find out something about that without much trouble. A question or two put to Jessie Petrie, for instance, might be in order. Jessie dwelt just beyond the quadrangle in the precincts of the music department, and he didn't miss much about campus life.

Furthermore, it was Jessie who locked up after concerts. He didn't mind staying late to do that and to sweep up, since it got him into the concerts free, in a back-row seat. Will had often seen him there, transfixed, his old face dreaming of worlds of his own devising.

On the mornings after concerts, Jessie didn't have to come to work till ten.

From Jaeckel Hall, therefore, at about five minutes till the hour, Will headed across the quadrangle, through Marshall Hall, and stationed himself at the side door of the Music Building. He left behind him a stunned and grieving Joey Livingston. An earnest and reassuring Ellen Powell from the history department, one of Dora's friends, had been sent to intercept Dora after her class and to keep an eye on her for a couple of hours.

When Jessie Petrie came up the path between the quadrangle and the Music Building, Will was just coming out the door.

"How was it last night, Jessie?" he smiled.

"You really missed it, Dr. Gray." The old man stopped. "Mozart it was, a real happy piece, and then some Berlioz. You'd have liked that."

"How about your seat? Did you get a better one this time?" Jessie looked puzzled. "Same as always, Dr. Gray."

"I guess Dr. Donahue was there, then. He said he had a ticket but didn't think he could go. I told him he ought to pass his ticket along to you if he couldn't." That wasn't true, and Will disliked deceiving the old man, but he also didn't want to start talk about Tom's death.

"No, sir, he wasn't there, I'm sure of that. He must've forgot. He was up there last night when I went home." Jessie gestured in the direction of Jaeckel Hall. "In his office."

"That's too late for working," Will said. "You couldn't have locked up till ten-thirty or so."

"Closer to eleven. May not have been working, though. There was a girl with him."

"A girl?" Will was startled.

"Yes, sir. Not," he added quickly, "that there's anything

wrong with that. I just thought it was kind of late for office hours."

"Probably some female faculty member. Someone on the same floor."

The old man shook his head. "No, sir. Not that it matters, or is any business of yours or mine, but I think it was a student. I can't say how I know that—in the first place, I couldn't see more than the back of her head, just for a moment—but it was something about her hair. Kind of long brown hair, worn loose." He looked slightly embarrassed. "I didn't stop to watch or anything, I just kept on walking home."

"Jessie, I don't give a damn about Tom's morals, but this girl changes something. I'm afraid you're going to have to tell all this to the sheriff. Don't look so upset—I'll explain why. In fact, I think you'd better go on over there right now. But, for God's sake, don't tell anyone else about her. It might be a good way to get her killed."

If she hadn't been already, Will thought. Was it possible there'd been another body in the snow this morning—or, worse, someone not yet dead but who'd been overlooked in the confusion and the dim light and in their concentration on finding Tom?

Sheriff Winterlin didn't think so—"We don't have any reports of missing persons," he said, "and God knows we were all over the lot out there before Donahue turned up"—but on the off chance, they went back and looked again.

"You'd better come with us," Winterlin said to Will. "I'll get some men from the highway patrol, and I can send a few from here, but that's all I've got. We'll still be shorthanded."

For nearly two hours, they tramped and scrambled about once more, starting from the place Tom's body had been and fanning out beyond that on the assumption that once he'd fallen, his companion—if he'd had one—would have tried to go on in the same direction for help. The day was clear and sparkling and the wind had disappeared; the sun glared off the snow and showed clearly their tracks from the dawn hour, and the scuffed and rumpled place where they'd dug Tom out and brought in the ambulance.

Being there again so soon, and in such a different light, made Will feel slightly unnerved. He found himself walking over his own footprints more than once, and had to reassess landmarks—a line of fence, the creek, the road—in the new aspect of daylight. He was glad when Winterlin called a halt.

"We may have to wait for spring to be absolutely certain," he said, "but I'll be damned if I think so. I don't think she's here."

Will didn't either, and he was relieved. Winterlin's relief, however, was tempered with irritation. "Now I've got to find her among the living." He glanced at Will wryly as they tramped along to the car that was being brought up for them. "Any quick way you know of to sort out the coeds with long brown hair?"

It was nearly one o'clock when Will reached Dora's house. He greeted her mother with a kiss and thanked her for coping with the situation that morning, bowed Ellen out, with promises to explain her unusually interfering and kaffee-klatsching behavior to Dora, and then stilled Dora's angry outburst about where on earth had he been and why hadn't he *called* her to get her mother, she could have gotten the class covered if she'd had to. With further apologies to Mrs. Chandler, Will steered Dora into her little den and closed the door. There he told her about Tom.

When her shock and sobs had subsided, he asked her when she'd last talked to him and what his plans for the evening had been. But she hadn't known. She hadn't even seen him that day, though she'd tried. She had gone by his office for a few minutes between classes but had missed him so she'd left a note on his desk and . . . and, well, never mind. He evidently hadn't been in at all, not until his four o'clock class, anyway, she assumed. Yes, she'd been angry with him, but it was something silly, not anything that mattered. And when he hadn't called her last night—well, he didn't always. And he knew she had to clean house all evening to get ready for her mother.

Will took her back to the kitchen, made a fresh pot of coffee, explained things briefly to Mrs. Chandler, and left.

Louise's face was pale, but she seemed composed, and managed to make them some grilled cheese sandwiches. "You might as well let me," she told Will. "We've both had an awful morning, and we've got to eat. And this may be my last quiet moment for several days. I'd rather spend it with you than with anyone else."

Will saw that one or two offerings of flowers had already arrived, and he supposed he should send some, too. Mostly he watched Louise, listened to the tone of her voice more than her words. "I wish I understood it," she said, "this business about the car and everything. Whether it was all a terrible coincidence or whether it was planned. But that seems so unimaginable. Who could want to kill Tom?" Her voice broke a little, and Will wanted to reach out for her, but he didn't. Sheriff Winterlin had been back a second time, she told him, with some careful questions (after, Will supposed, he had found out himself about the gas tank). But even he didn't seem to be sure. "If it was boys playing a prank," Louise said, "maybe they'll be sorry." She was dropping things a lot this morning—a knife, a saucer, a loaf of bread. She picked them up without comment and brushed away the pieces of pottery, sliced pickles and buttered bread deftly in between. Will poured milk for them to drink.

"The funeral will be on Friday," she said, and then they ate their sandwiches quietly and sat over boxed cookies and the last of the milk while Will had a cigarette and they both looked down through the window beside them at the little backyard, marked only by an empty birdhouse on a post and by the heaped-up snow.

At two o'clock he went back to the university for his class.

At four, his last class for the day was over. In the near dark, Will headed for his car directly afterward, without going by the office. He was exhausted, not up to talking or any more of the dismay and emotion he would find in Jaeckel Hall.

When he got to the car, an inky-looking sheet of paper was fluttering from under the windshield wiper. Will unfolded it and grinned. It was covered, front and back, with a photostatted letter, a floor plan of a house, a map of the town in 1940, a pair of photographs. Jed had gotten out the flyer, and old Mrs. Moffat's treasure hunt was underway.

And at last he had a chance to read that mysterious letter.

FIVE
Will Gray's Visitor

There were, however, footprints on his front walk. Foot-prints that went up to the door and didn't come back again. Inside, the lights were on. And—sitting in the car in his driveway, Will peered up through the top of his windshield—there was smoke coming from his chimney. Feeling a little like one of the Three Bears, he collected his books and papers and got out of the car.

In the foyer, he found Amigo waiting for him in the middle of the rug, paws folded in at the wrist. Except for the small snapping sound of the fire from the living room, the house was quiet. Will took off his coat and hat, inspecting as he did so the tan suede coat hanging from one of the hooks on the foyer wall. It was a woman's coat and an expensive one, with a mink collar and cuffs. It looked, however, just a touch worn, as if its last good season had been the one before, or even the one before that.

A pair of damp beige suede boots, also expensive, stood under it, tilted against the low hall chest.

His Goldilocks was asleep all right, in an armchair beside the fire, but her hair was black and streaked in a fashionable way with gray. Will judged her to be in her midforties. Her skin was tanned, her thin necklaces and wide bracelets real gold, her dress well cut but unadorned, in a gray-and-tan plaid wool. Her legs were stretched out, her stockinged feet resting on an ottoman.

He had never seen her before in his life.

Amigo had come to stand beside him, purring a little and

just touching his leg. Will picked him up and carried him through the living room into the kitchen. When the cat food had been opened, he made a pitcher of martinis, put it on a tray with two glasses, and took it out to a table beside another chair. He set it down with a thump and clattered a spoon noisily about in the pitcher.

She came awake with a start, simultaneously reaching for the hem of her skirt with one hand and her bag on the floor with the other.

"You're among friends," he said. "At least I guess so. Want a drink?"

"Thank you." She struggled up straighter in her chair and withdrew her feet from the ottoman to the floor. Will grinned. A lady confronted by a stranger in his own house must feel that being barefoot was an unforeseen disadvantage. For the first time, he thought he had gained the upper hand.

"Shall we introduce ourselves?" he said, handing her one glass and taking the other to the opposite armchair.

"I know who you are," she snapped, "and if I feel like an idiot, I suppose it's my own fault." She put her glass down and began searching in her bag for a compact.

"Yes." He watched her briefly scrutinize her face, make a perfunctory pass at her perfectly arranged hair. She then exchanged the compact for a cigarette case, its lid enameled with a scene of herons against a pink-and-blue sky.

When she had the cigarette going, she looked directly at him. "The front door was unlocked," she said.

"That explains everything."

"Well, it doesn't, of course, but it was a long way back to the motel. On foot, that is. I didn't think you'd mind."

He didn't reply. He didn't know whether he minded or not.

"They told me you'd be out of class at three."

"They got it wrong. Are we talking about the history department office, by the way?"

"No, some scatterbrained child in the English department,

though it took her a while to find out. They did seem rather disorganized there."

"They would, today. May I ask why you tried to find me through the wrong department?" He hesitated. "That is, you really do have the right person? I'm Will Gray."

"I know. And I'm Poppy Ruth."

Will smiled, in spite of himself. "And your last name is—?"

"Ruth."

"Dear me." His wits seemed to have deserted him. "Your name is Poppy Ruth Ruth?" He reddened. "No. It couldn't be. It's just Poppy Ruth. Have I got it right now?"

"You do."

"And you're looking for me? *Were* looking for me?"

"That's right."

Will sighed. "All right, then. What for?"

"I need your help. You see, I'm really a friend of Tom Donahue's."

"Wonderful," he said, and she frowned.

She had arrived that morning, she told him, on the early plane from New York, stopping first in Chicago, where she had picked up the local flight to Sioux Falls—the plane Dora's mother had taken. Will had a sudden, though fuzzy, recollection of Mrs. Chandler's saying something about a New York woman she was coming in with from the airport. That seemed a very long time ago.

"I expected Tom to meet me," she said.

"You've heard what happened?"

She had. "But not until late this morning, when I gave up calling his house and started trying to find him. When I called the college. And then . . ." she shrugged ". . . I was given your name when I asked to be put in touch with one of his friends. I wasn't asking for you specifically, of course. Though I was rather surprised. Mrs. Chandler had already mentioned you so often, the whole time that farm couple were giving us a lift. In their *dreadful* old car. She kept saying that whatever kept you must have been serious. I didn't know, of course, that she was Dora's mother. Or that your problem was going to be my problem, too."

"Small world," Will murmured, and got up to freshen her drink. "So what did you want with Tom?"

She surveyed him thoughtfully. "It may be a smaller world, or at least a smaller town, than I'm used to. And what seemed so . . . so unproblematic a few hours ago strikes me now as questionable taste."

"But here we are."

"Yes." Slowly, she lighted another cigarette. "You see, Tom and I were very good friends. In New York."

"How good?"

"Oh . . . *very* good."

"I see."

"And now he has—had—a new friend."

"My former wife."

"Yes."

"And so?"

"Well, the old friendship hadn't quite died, you know. Might not, in fact, have come to that in the end at all."

"Not, I gather, if Tom was expecting you here."

"I did, I confess, invite myself. But I don't invite myself where I'm not wanted."

Will stirred impatiently. "All right. So you and Tom still had something going. Aside from Dora. I understood, by the way, that Tom was going to New York for Christmas. Couldn't you wait?"

A small flush stained her cheeks. "That wasn't the issue," she said. "I was expecting to spend Christmas elsewhere. In California, with friends."

"Ah. So on the way you stopped off to see him."

"That's right."

"Then why, finding him dead, didn't you just keep going?"

A brutal question; for a moment, the color drained from her face. Watching her, Will felt inclined to believe her. To believe, at least, that somewhere along the way, she and Tom *had* felt something for each other, however fleeting. Though he supposed Tom had been at least five or six years younger.

"Your wife," she said slowly, "might be, well, hurt. I'm afraid Tom may have kept me a little too much to himself. Since I don't want Dora to be hurt, and I assume you don't, I thought I'd tell you about myself and you'd help me get into Tom's house and just retrieve some letters and things I sent him and then there wouldn't be any risk that Dora would find them."

"I'm sorry, but I can't do that."

"I feel sure you could, really."

"No. And even if I could, I wouldn't."

"It *is* important."

Will shrugged.

"And if you're wrong?"

"If I'm wrong, Dora can look out for herself."

"That's a big chance to take."

"I don't think so," said Will.

"You won't reconsider?"

"I can't. It's not my choice."

"I see." She sat for a while, thinking and watching the fire. When she spoke again, it was to change the subject.

"Tom had family here, I believe?"

"A cousin. Her name is Louise Tree. She owns and runs the local bookstore."

"Miss Tree grew up here? I expect Tom's family in Iceberg Fields often came to visit?"

He wondered how much she knew about Tom's background and why she was interested. "No. Both wrong," he said. He reflected on the implications of her questions. Would it do any harm to Louise Tree to answer them? But he couldn't know yet what sort of answer, if any, might be damaging.

"Louise grew up in Arizona. She hardly knew Tom. She came back to South Dakota long after Tom had grown up and gone away, to be with his mother during her last illness. Her own parents, who were older than most when she was born, had died some years before."

"And she came on to Crosscreek because Dr. Donahue was here?"

"He was still teaching in New York. She came to Crosscreek three or four years ago because a college town is better for a bookstore than Iceberg Fields would have been."

"Why did she stay in this part of the country at all? Is it so interesting?"

"She liked it. It was the ancestral home, so to speak. And there was Tom's father nearby. So she had some family in the vicinity."

"What happened to him?"

"Killed in a car wreck last year." On his way back to Iceberg Fields from having Sunday dinner with Louise, Will had heard. He'd piled up against a guardrail—probably he'd been dozing at the wheel.

"I see." Poppy Ruth stared at the fire, as if she were thinking that over. Will hoped she'd run out of questions. He didn't much like talking to her about Louise Tree.

He remembered Louise's telling him most of this in August, one evening soon after Tom had arrived. He had been the only person in the bookstore at closing time. It was a hot night, very still, and he had lost track of the time. Louise had let him linger. It was almost nine when she'd said, a little shyly, "Can I persuade you to come out if I offer you something cold to drink?"

The two of them had sat in her backyard over an icy pitcher of white wine, listening to the locusts in the trees behind the shop. Louise's amazement had been matched only by her excitement that night at the recent appearance in town of her tall, debonair cousin, and she had poured it all out to Will. "You can feel so alone without any relatives," she'd said. "When I was a child, I used to think about Tom a lot. We were the only two children in the family anywhere. It was like having a make-believe friend. I saw him occasionally, you know. So he wasn't quite make-believe because he was real, and very dashing, I thought, and someday I'd know him, when we both grew up and found our way into the wider world. Well, I didn't find my way anywhere, but still, here he is."

A breeze had come up during the evening, ruffling the short sleeves of her white dress. Will had felt completely contented that night.

Poppy Ruth reached down for her purse. "I should like to call on her," she said. "Can you give me directions?"

He told her the way, then said, "However, I wouldn't do that tonight if I were you."

"Why not?"

"It's not exactly the appropriate moment, do you think? Louise's friends will be dropping in."

"I'll be brief." Poppy Ruth rose. "Perhaps I'll see you again before I leave?"

"No." Will stayed where he was.

"No, what?"

"No, I really don't want you going to Miss Tree's."

"I'm so sorry." She dropped the case with the herons on the lid into her bag. "Are you very fond of her?"

"That's immaterial."

"You seem quite protective."

"Probably I am. But you still can't go to see her."

"How do you think you can stop me?"

"I could have you arrested. For trespassing, entering, and theft. Theft of . . . of firewood. And for questioning in the possible murder of Tom Donahue."

"Murder?"

"Uh-huh."

Poppy Ruth sat down. "Murder?" Then she said slowly, "You're making too much of this, you know. There's nothing to be so suspicious about. I am just a friend of Tom's who arrived for a visit at an unfortunate time. I wanted to offer my sympathy to his cousin. If you think it's unwise, of course I won't go."

"It's entirely possible I'm making too much of it."

"Can I go, then?"

"No."

"What are we going to do, in that case?"

"We'll think of something."

It was almost one o'clock when Will got home. He threw his coat over the back of a chair and made some coffee. For a long time he sat at the kitchen table, the glow from the blue-shaded lamp making a warm circle of light on the oak. Gradually, his evening with Poppy Ruth (Mrs. Ruth, he'd discovered, but widowed) arranged itself in his memory, taking its place alongside the other sections of his disturbing day.

He had taken her to dinner at River Inn, on the edge of town, and then off to see a movie over her objections that she'd seen it already, years before. He was sorry about that, Will told her, but there was only one movie theater and there wasn't another thing in town to do but talk and he'd had enough of that. Unless she wanted to go bowling? She had shuddered faintly. Afterward they had gone to Green Tavern for drinks, and at last he'd let her off at the Drowsy Cowboy Motel, where she was staying. At the end of it, all he had done was to keep her from bothering Louise.

He had asked her about the Strangers, but she had had no knowledge of them. So she said, at least. He had asked her if any New Yorker of her acquaintance, including herself, might have wished Tom's death. She had said, very firmly, that that was impossible. Tom had been a joy and a delight to everyone who knew him. Handsome, entertaining, kind when he thought of it—everyone was crazy about him there. Did she know Will's own friends in New York—Roy and Junie Hill? Roy had been at Crosscreek a couple of years ago, was now something important at NYU. No, of course not, she told him.

She didn't fraternize with academics, except for Tom. They didn't come into her world. What *was* her world? Well, she lived on Central Park West. Beyond that . . . it was hard to explain, exactly. Well, did she work? Her blue eyes had gone dark. No, of course she didn't work. She had money, thanks to her lately departed husband. She . . . went to luncheons. Shopped. Had friends. Things like that.

Will said he got the general idea.

At the end of the kitchen, against the wall, he had put up a long writing table. He found himself standing before it, riffling through a pile of papers. He hesitated, suddenly at a loss, wondering what he was looking for, and then he found old Mrs. Moffat's flyer—he'd put it down there when he'd made the martinis earlier—and remembered the impulse that had driven him from his chair. He had had enough of Tom Donahue tonight. He needed something to work on that was entirely unrelated to Tom and his doings. Or undoings.

It took him three-quarters of an hour to transcribe the blurry photostat. At last he scribbled out the last line, put his feet up, and took up his tablet to read it through.

15 August
190

My dear Maisie and Henry and Edward:

It grows late—the crescent moon, though high, seems thin and pale and far away in a summer sky so thickly crossed with stars. Today, my today, will not be your today when you read this (one small but ironbound truth transcending so many brittle, painted imitations, though, of course, in itself of little account). Still, I hope you will return to my today in good earnest, for I am joyous in contemplation of my gifts to you. Surely you will; the bow, so thin it is only a token moon, bears down upon so high and bright a field of flowers that I think you must be able, as you read, weeks hence, to see it too, upon its plain. Look closely; they are dead and lost, you will tell me, but I say enduring in their march out of the past. It is well worth whatever trouble it may cost you.

Whatever passes for friendship among us can, I know, be wiped out by a too-precious impulse on my part, that may come to seem petty pridefulness, or a somewhat elephantine infidelity to your peerless integrity as individuals. I incline to think such will indeed be the result, and it has given me much cause to hesitate, not in my loyalty to you but in the course through which that loyalty should proclaim itself. I am far in the vanguard, however, and cannot distinctly hear your voices, through the train of years. If my support comes too late to do you service, or does not come at all, I beg you to pardon me. A father should dispense to his children all he knows and possesses of greatness; I fear that instead I shall but seem to you an old fool, caroling in the darkness of an old age.

But hardest won, highest prized, some say. You will know, and will often tell each other, that more from me than lies safe is yours by right. I agree. But, "right"?—kings and counselors have stumbled there. I have always believed, despite your courageous disbelief, that all my wealth is yours by right. And yet to give it is hard, in this case impossible, out of hand. Some I can bestow, some you must search for. My consolation, if you should, in the end, think the reward not worth the search, is that to receive a gift is often harder than to give one. This way may alleviate that.

One thing more remains to say: Once even unbelievers had magic guides, taken from the earth, to brighten the night and carry them in to shore. I could not fill the darkness with such light for you; I have tried to brighten it a bit, symbolically. The glow is false. May you, in your recovery of this final portion, release as well that more enduring flame.

> *Lovingly,*
> *Your father,*
> *Gabriel McCrocken*

He knew, or almost knew, what it was saying. Will took off his glasses and rubbed his eyes, his elbows on the table. A word, an image, had fled by him while he was reading it.

Much of it sounded simply like a letter written by an eccentric and somewhat romantic old gentleman given to a certain formality of phrasing and willing to be unusually open with his children. A farewell letter—affectionate, kind, confusing here and there, but that was all. And yet it wasn't what he would have expected, either as a farewell letter or as a directive to a hidden fortune. For, he supposed, it clearly was the latter as well, and the two were mixed together.

He went over it again: *More from me than lies safe is yours by right. . . . To give it is . . . impossible, out of hand. Some I can bestow, some you must search for. . . . This final portion. . . .*

Something of value, then, remained to be recovered, but exactly what—and where—was obscure, at best. The "what" had been calculated by others to be a sum of at least a quarter million dollars. The "where," however, was a total mystery. And what on earth was that "190" at the top of the paper supposed to indicate? Had Gabriel simply miswritten the date? He had died in 1940. Will stared at it doubtfully.

What, he wondered, had McCrocken intended? Why go to all this trouble, and why set his children such an odd, if kindly, puzzle? The letter contained no hint of asperity or hostility on Gabriel's part, and he had, in fact, left them very well off. Will wondered if the old man had been quite sane.

He fished the flyer from under the chair where it had fallen and spread it open. The photograph of Gabriel McCrocken, the same one that hung high up the wall outside the administrative offices, looked up at him from the page. Dark eyebrows that needed brushing sprang out at the foot of a low forehead topped with longish strands of gray hair, parted on the side. Below the eyebrows, the deep-set eyes were scarcely visible, only dark blurs with a gleam in them. There were high cheekbones, an unremarkable chin, and a gray mustache turning down a little over the corners of his mouth. The lips were tightly closed but protruded somewhat, and there was a small, horizontal crease between lower lip and chin.

He was not smiling, but the gleam in his eyes looked as if they might have been twinkling.

Will wanted to know a lot more about Gabriel McCrocken. Tomorrow, maybe, he could find time to drop in on Maisie. He was, after all, an interested party in this endeavor, such as it was.

A small, steady chipping against the window roused him. Through the blackness beyond the glass he could see a whirl of white, tossed by the wind. More snow.

It was late. In his corner, Amigo slept heavily, his head twisted so that the white of his throat showed. A gust of wind caught at the back door and rattled the windows in their frames. Will turned out the lamp and went upstairs to bed.

SIX

The Blind Jeweler's Companions

A tall black coupe hit the brakes in front of Will's house, and someone inside leaned on the horn. "Will! Will Gray!"

Through the slightly opened Venetian blinds that Thursday morning filtered another cloudless day, scattering ladders of light around the room. It was well past eleven o'clock when the commotion set up out front, but Will still slept under the twisted covers.

"Will Gray!" The shouting awakened him at last.

Will hauled up the blinds, looked out, and then raised the window in spite of the cold. In the car below, waving and calling from the passenger's side, was Maisie Moffat, in her good black coat.

"Come out!" she ordered.

He shook his head. "You come in. I'll be right down."

He shut the window, pausing only to see who was driving. Bo Jenkins climbed out and went around to help Maisie descend. Together they made their way up the walk.

"We did call," Maisie told him fifteen minutes later. He was brewing coffee; she and Bo were sitting at his kitchen table. "We called from the gas station and let it ring and ring."

"A late night," Will told her, setting cups before the two of them. "A late night and a long day before it."

"Yes. You poor thing, finding the body and all. But that's why we're here."

Will brought a cup for himself and sat down across from her. "What's up?" he asked.

"Well, maybe not so much, really." Maisie stirred her coffee critically, then added more cream. At the end of the table, Bo was sitting sideways in his chair, clearly indicating this was Maisie's show. "But," she went on, "we think you should pay a call on Miss Tree."

"I probably would have anyway." Will remembered Poppy Ruth and frowned. "Has someone been bothering her?"

"No, nothing like that. But there's something odd going on over there. Something that's making her unhappy."

"What kind of thing?"

"Flowers. *Lots* of flowers. From the most peculiar people."

"I don't think I understand."

"You will when you get there. Like we did. We went to pay our respects just now—that's how we found out. I don't drive any longer, you know, and on Thursdays Bo takes me to do my errands. So we seized the opportunity. And found Louise . . . well, if not upset exactly, at least out of patience." Maisie looked at Will over the rim of her cup. "I think," she said, setting it down, "it might have a bearing on the murder."

Will looked back at her curiously. "No one knows for sure that it was a murder. Has the sheriff's office said so?"

"Not yet. Not that I know of, anyway. But anybody with any sense can put two and two together. Me, for instance. Who in his right mind would leave town at that hour, for that place? Someone who was invited there, that's who." Maisie got up to refill her cup and to give Amigo a scratch on the head. "But what made the murderer think he'd get out of the car?"

"No one really knows about that, either," Will answered.

"Well, he must have planted something—the murderer, I mean. A light, some kind of signal. Only then—" She put her chin on her fist and thought. "The point, I'd think, would be the alibi. He wouldn't want to ruin it."

"What?" Bo asked, clearly confused.

"If this was murder, it was murder by long distance," Maisie said. "A message, a phone call, something like that. So

Tom Donahue goes off to die while the murderer, who summoned him, is really miles away."

"All right," Bo said cautiously, "I get that. He takes the gas, first. Then sometime later—or even before, I guess—he gets up some reason why Dr. Donahue should drive himself out there, beyond help. But I still don't see how he knows it will work. It wouldn't have, if he'd stayed in the car."

"So," Maisie said patiently, "he had to contrive it that way, but *without* putting himself on the scene. The scheme would be wasted if he had to do that."

"Then how was it managed?"

"Well, if he knew there were a light already—from a house that seemed occupied—"

"How about a set of false directions?" Will said.

"That would do it, yes." Maisie's eyes shone. "What were they?"

"Three miles along Wilde Road. *Maybe.* No one is sure of that bit because of the way Tom wrote those two things."

Maisie sat back, satisfied. "If that's what happened, though, it would do it. It's twice that to anywhere. Is there any way to prove it?"

"No way yet," he told her.

In the pause that followed, the next question—still unasked—hovered almost palpably between Will and Maisie, who looked suddenly ill at ease. Bo, however, came out with it. "Anybody know *why* Donahue'd be murdered?"

"Oh, who knows, Bo," Maisie said with irritation. "There could be all kinds of reasons we don't have any idea of. For one thing," she added brightly, "Dr. Donahue only just came here a few months ago. He probably had a *past.*"

"And someone came all the way out here to kill him for it? That doesn't sound very likely to me."

"I don't know why not. It's certainly not something to discount. After all, we didn't really know anything about him."

No, Will was thinking. Tom's past had actually turned up pretty quickly.

But Bo wasn't to be distracted from his original question. "Revenge or jealousy are good reasons," he said thoughtfully. "Or maybe he had some money put away."

"I don't know of any money he had," Will said. "He could have had some, for all I know, but he lived like all the rest of us, or seemed to. College teachers don't make that much, you know."

"Unless there was family money. What about that, Maisie?"

"That family never had ten cents," she said. "Maybe he knew too much."

Bo smiled at her. "Small-town secrets he stumbled on? You'd better watch out, then. If there's anything that bad to know, you know it, too."

"It's time to go," Maisie told him. "This wasn't supposed to be a social call." Bo blinked, but she just patted him on the shoulder and stood still for Will to help her into her coat. "You will call on Miss Tree, won't you?" she asked him. "A lot of people have been in and out since yesterday, but she is basically so alone. She's had to bury everybody close to her, and now this. And I just don't know what on earth she's going to *do* with all those flowers."

"I'll go see her," Will said, "if I can make a date with you tonight. I want to know more about your father."

"Done," Maisie told him. "Shall we say about eight-thirty? I'm busy till then."

Will smiled. "Does that mean we're going to the same party?"

"I guess so." Her cheeks went a little pink, but she stuck her chin up. "I guess we're *both* busy."

"Good God, Louise." Will stopped in the doorway. The yellow burlap curtains had been pulled back as far as they would go and the four windows opened a few inches, but the air in the apartment was still heavy with sweetness.

The room was banked with them. Pots and bowls of them covered every shelf and table and quite a bit of the floor. Colored tinfoil and ribbon gleamed in the sun.

He had not realized Tom had so many friends.

"Isn't it awful?" Louise agreed grimly. "Between calls, I've been hiding in the kitchen all morning, with the door closed. It's like living in *The Secret Garden*."

"Who are they from?"

"Look." She led him around the room, her slender fingers touching the cards attached to the ribbons. "This was the first. Yesterday."

It was a large gardenia plant, thick with blossoms. "'The Blind Jeweler,'" Will read.

"And then this." A vase of roses, tall red ones, had been sent by "The Renaissance Man."

"Prideful sort." Will turned to the next. The red petals and dark green leaves of a poinsettia drooped over the card of "The Chestnut Man." In front of it, an African violet, splendid in green foil and a purple ribbon, was signed by "Bess and Brandy."

"That could be legitimate," Louise said, "but somehow I don't think so."

"The Irishman at the Neighborhood Bar" had sent a pot of greenery. More poinsettias had come from "The Fat Twins." A small bunch of bronze chrysanthemums was apparently all "The Student in the Park" could afford.

It was bewildering, Will thought, and somehow macabre.

"Have you ever heard of any of them before?"

"Only one."

On one of the bookshelves stood an earthenware pot of dried flowers in bright colors. The card read, "The Etruscan."

"Tom once mentioned that he knew a man who looked just like an ancient Etruscan," Louise said. "Someone with crinkly long hair and an angular sort of body and a little *V* for a mouth, and who smiled a lot. He said he was also the timidest man in the world. Otherwise, they're strangers."

"'Perfect Strangers.'"

"I think so, too. But isn't it *funny* that they've found out about Tom so fast?"

"Maybe not. Any return addresses?"

"No. I asked Mr. Wicket. He could only tell me that they were all sent by wire from New York."

"A windfall for Wicket, isn't it?"

Will ambled about the room, reading the rest of the cards. "The African" had presented a big bunch of white gladiolas. "The Chinese Lamplighter" had sent a mixture of yellow daisies and yellow rosebuds. A blue hydrangea, potted, from "The Four Officers." An azalea from "The GI." A white poinsettia, done up in silver paper, from "The Cellist Across the Air Shaft."

He stopped in front of the windows and put his hands in his pockets. Louise had taken her own houseplants away; the windowsills were filled with more flowers. A red geranium from "Poppy and the Others" caught the brilliant light from the snowy street below.

That one didn't surprise him.

Poppy Ruth was certainly involved in it somehow, and apparently with these Strangers after all, if that was who the flowers were from. He couldn't keep her from calling on Louise forever, and possibly gaining access to Tom's house, if she spun a good enough story.

And just possibly for quite innocent reasons. Will couldn't see himself sicking Mack Winterlin onto her—not yet, anyway. Still, he wanted to know what she could actually want there—he couldn't bring himself to believe that trumped-up tale about letters, nor could he comfortably pick up with his own affairs where he'd left off while Winterlin and his colleagues sorted out questions like the ones Bo Jenkins had raised, or had been about to. Questions involving Louise's inheritance from Tom, if any. Or Dora's jealousy of someone or another.

He found himself wanting to have a look around Tom's

house, too—to know the worst, if there was a worst to be known. Or, as he firmly believed, to know there wasn't.

He was probably, of course, too late. Mack Winterlin had not only had a day's head start on him, he had almost certainly locked the house and taken possession of all the keys. Not that that would necessarily stop Poppy Ruth. Or stop Louise from helping her if Louise's sympathies were aroused. He turned abruptly and indicated the red geraniums. "Has she been here yet?" he asked.

Louise looked startled. "No. Of course not. She's one of the New Yorkers, isn't she?"

"As a matter of fact, she's in town. She wants to make your acquaintance."

"Well, she hasn't yet. Who is she, by the way?"

"Later. Louise—" Will surveyed her. Brilliant sunshine glistened in her auburn hair. Her small, stubborn face was anxious.

"When Sheriff Winterlin came yesterday," he said, "did he say anything about Tom's house?"

"Yes, he did. He said he meant to stop by. And he said I shouldn't go there without permission. Why?"

"I want to stop by Tom's house, too. This Poppy Ruth is up to something."

She looked at him quizzically. "All right, Will," she said at last. "I do have a key—Sheriff Winterlin didn't think to ask me if I did, so he didn't take it away." And then, with determination, "While you're there, if you don't mind too much, you can do me a favor. I had to go there yesterday myself, for his address book. There were people I knew I should notify. But I didn't think of getting a suit . . . for him to be buried in. So you can do that, if you wouldn't mind. And a fresh shirt and—well, you'll know."

"Of course. I'm an ass for not thinking of offering. I'd be glad to."

"Thank you. Let me get the key, and then there's something

I want to show you." She disappeared into the dining room. "Now, where did I put it?"

Will turned back to the window. Below him, about a block away, he saw a figure, in a tan suede coat and boots, marching along the snowy sidewalk. A dark-haired lady of his recent acquaintance.

"Louise!"

She came back into the living room, holding a blue square of paper. "Here it is, and here's the key." She handed it to him. "Look at this. Dora brought it over last night."

Will unfolded it hastily and saw it was a message for Tom, written on the university's telephone memo paper in the precise handwriting of Mrs. Hatch, the English department's secretary: *Ms. Ruth wishes to tell you she's coming Wednesday, 9:01 North Central. She's deliriously happy, darling, but you're insane. She wants to talk. She sends love.*

It was dated on Tuesday, at two.

"Where did Dora get this?" Will asked, feeling his heart sink.

"She found it on Tom's desk when she was looking for him. She was leaving a note for him herself, and she read it and kept it, in a fit of pique. Last night her conscience got the better of her."

Will read it twice, folded it carefully, and tucked it back into Louise's hand. "No wonder she was mad at him," he said, more casually than he felt. "Now listen. When Poppy Ruth shows up—" He glanced over his shoulder. She was on her way across the street. "Jesus. When Poppy Ruth shows up, do *not* take her to Tom's or promise to do so or send her there for me to let her in. She'll have a good tale. But don't even let her in here."

"Will—"

"One other thing. Make me a list of all these people who sent flowers. Not townspeople, just the odd ones. Is there a back door?"

"In the kitchen—"

He got his hat and steered her toward the back of the apartment. The kitchen door opened onto a flight of wooden steps leading to the backyard.

"And don't tell her anything we've talked about."

They heard footsteps on the front stairs.

"Got to go. Will you do those things?"

"Of course, Will. But—"

"Good." He hugged her briefly and was gone.

SEVEN

What Will Found, and
What Was Missing

Winterlin and his pals had been in Tom's office, and up and down the fifth-floor corridor of Jaeckel Hall, for what seemed like hours. Will, looking up occasionally from his work as they passed his open door, had wished repeatedly that they would go away. Their presence was distracting.

One of Winterlin's companions, a young, round-faced fellow, seemed to be less secretive than the rest. He was the photographer, and Will had watched him carry a tripod and a large camera into Tom's office, knocking the legs of the tripod against the walls everywhere he went. He whistled the school football chant or chewed gum as he went about his elaborate picture-taking, and sometimes he would whistle a line and then pound the gum loudly for several beats before the next line. "Cross 'em up, Crosscreek, X 'em out, mark 'em off," chew, chew, chew. He was called Ed.

After Ed had finished photographing Tom's office from every angle, he unwrapped a Hershey bar and leaned against the wall, eating it and watching the other men spreading fingerprint dust about the room and over the papers and books. Will didn't see what he did with the gum.

At one point Winterlin paused in Will's doorway to say hello. Will gave up on his work and kicked a chair around for him to sit in. Winterlin dropped into it gratefully.

"Have you found the girl yet?"

"No. We've asked around, yesterday and today, but no one seems to know who she might have been." He sighed. "We've been doing our damnedest to be discreet, but she's turning out to be pretty elusive."

"'Asked around'?" Will repeated. "Of anybody in particular?"

Winterlin shrugged. "We've gone up and down this building with routine stuff—who was here, who might have been seen going in or out at that hour." His bright brown eyes were thoughtful. "We've all assumed, of course, that the young woman might need protecting if she knows where Donahue was off to. But how about if she's the one responsible?"

"She'd have to have come up with a hell of a story. And siphoning off gas sounds more like a man than a woman, I'd think."

"Not these days. I'd as soon suspect our young lady as anybody else. You know some woman who couldn't do it if she wanted to? Starting, let's say, with Louise Tree? Or Mrs. Gray? Or old Mrs. Moffat, for that matter?" He smiled darkly as he got up to leave.

It was nearly four when Will entered the last grade in his grade book, glanced over the roll to see who would have to make up the test, and leaned back in his chair to stretch. The men in Tom's office had finished their work. The photographer had gone home. One of Winterlin's henchmen, standing in the hall looking through a bunch of keys, held a sheaf of papers rolled up in a rubber band. The door was still open. Will saw that Tom's desk was bare now, except for his typewriter and a neat stack of books. Another officer, inside, had begun to draw the curtains against the last rays of the sun, low and red in a pale purple sky. Will wondered what if anything, they'd found. Something more, he hoped, than the scraps of information he had brought away from Tom's house earlier.

The house, when he got there, had been warm and silent and locked. The curtains had been closed, and the remains of Tuesday night's dinner were still in the kitchen. Tom had evidently been burning papers in the fire in his den. Their scorched remnants had fluttered up from beneath the and-irons when Will opened the door from the front hall—remnants clearly raked through by Winterlin and company, leaving only wordless corners and edges of what might have been white notepaper.

He didn't have the house to himself for long, however. It was about that time that he'd surprised Dora on the back porch, trying to break in. In fact, he'd given her a considerable scare when, attracted to the kitchen by the scratching sounds he heard coming from that direction, he'd opened the door in her face. Literally. She'd been poking at the lock with a safety pin.

Her face had been tear-streaked and red, though part of the redness was from bending over. She couldn't stand it, she'd said—trying to show her mother a good time and listen to her chatter. She'd needed to get away and to do something, something for Tom, something to be close to him. She'd come to clean up. She hadn't thought anyone would mind.

"I was here Saturday night," Dora said after they'd both gone back to the den. "We sat in here."

The cotton throw on the daybed was rumpled, and the little fringed rug was skewed around. On a table, in front of the portable TV, the Sunday paper was heaped. It looked read.

Will had been in most of the rooms before. He roamed about downstairs while Dora went up to get a set of clothes together.

In the living room he found a cable. Will had taken it out of its envelope and read:

SNOW HERE HOW ABOUT THERE? BORDEAUX'S PORTRAIT IS THE KEY TO A CEREMONY WE CAN ALL BE PROUD OF. SPEAK TO HIM ABOUT IT, DON'T MIND IF HE'S CROSS. GABRIEL WAS GENTLEMAN FIRST, SCHOLAR SECOND, MAGNATE THIRD. THIS INFORMATION IS FOR YOUR TALK. FOLLOW THAT LINE. TIME IS SHORT BUT I'LL BE THERE. BE READY. THIS IS URGENT. LUKE.

Will smiled and put it back.

He continued to open drawers and closets but found nothing of interest. He went upstairs. Dora was trying to arrange all the clothes on one hanger.

"Why not use two?" he asked.

"I don't want to. Will, I can't find any socks. What were you looking for down there?"

He went into the next room and sat down at Tom's desk. Three of the drawers were empty. Tom did most of his work at school. One held only supplies—typing paper, pencils, and so forth. The fifth was a jumble: letters, book catalogs, old teaching contracts, snapshots, warrantees, outdated pocket calendars, and the like. At the bottom of the drawer were two flat folders and a manila envelope. Pictures of Tom's parents, side by side, were in one folder; in the other was a family tree written out neatly by hand—not Tom's—on stiff paper. A spreading, leafy tree painted in the center over *Arthur Drake Donahue, 1761–1838.* At the very bottom was Tom's name and date of birth. Will was tempted to add the date of death and close the parentheses. *That* would get Winterlin interested, he thought with a smile.

He shook the contents out of the manila envelope. More large photographs, taken years ago, Tom's high-school diploma, his college degrees, his birth certificate, a copy of his father's army commission, his parents' wedding invitation. Will put them all back. The remaining letters and snapshots were no more helpful.

It had grown quiet in the bedroom.

"Dora!" Will said, but there was no answer. From downstairs came the clatter of dishes and the sound of water running. She was straightening up the kitchen; he knew he shouldn't have let her do that. Then he heard a bit of music and a man's voice. Will remembered the radio on the windowsill over the sink. The murmur rising up the stairwell sounded like the news. They might at last, he thought, be stressing the possibilities of murder in Tom's death. Their original report, after all, was twenty-four hours old. There wasn't much left to say about it as it stood, and by now, given the chance to think it all over, the rest of Crosscreek had surely become as inquisitive about the murder angle as Maisie Moffat had been.

All of Crosscreek, that is, except for Dora, who had probably been too grief-stricken and too preoccupied with her mother to be thinking much at all.

Will put everything back where he had found it and opened the last drawer. Downstairs, the splashing had stopped.

Financial records. Bills, paid and unpaid, receipts, canceled checks, all tumbled together. He sighed and lifted out a double handful.

"Will!"

Footsteps dashed across the dining room below and up the stairs.

"Oh, Will!" Dora crossed the bedroom and stopped in the library door. "You knew," she said.

He was making notes and turning over a stack of small, squarish papers that rustled in his hand. Gasoline credit-card receipts. He was frowning. "There isn't anything to know yet. Not really."

"You might have said something. How long have you known?"

He didn't answer. When he looked up again, she had gone. He listened and heard, faintly, the back door open and shut. When Dora was upset, she always wanted to go outdoors. If there were back steps, she invariably wanted to go sit on them. Even if they were covered with snow. He returned to work.

"Will." He had not heard her approach. She was back in the doorway. "I'm ready to go, please."

"Okay." He shut the drawers, collected his notes, and stood up. On the way downstairs he asked her, "Was Tom fond of taking drives? To the towns around here, or to Sioux Falls? On weekday afternoons?"

"Sometimes," Dora answered. She was ahead of him, pulling on her gloves. "He went to newspaper offices—why, I don't know. I never went in with him except once. But he never said what he was looking up. And then we sometimes went to Sioux Falls for dinner on Saturday nights. Mostly we ate here, at home, though. We were rather on a cheese soufflé kick lately." She was keeping her voice very steady. "Poor Tom," she said in a nearly inaudible, squeaky voice, with tears in it.

He had found nothing out of order about Tom's papers, unless one counted a small curiosity: that during the fall, Tom had signed credit-card slips for gasoline in Iceberg Fields, Little Grove, Fitch, Eading, and Blue Hills. What had he found to interest him in those places?

"One more question." They were walking around the corner where Dora had parked her car. Will had put the clothes over his shoulder.

"Yes?" She was fumbling in her bag for her keys.

"It's time for you to tell me what you were doing Tuesday night, when you picked me up. The night you gave me that story about Christmas trees."

"Oh, Will, don't ask." He went around to the other side, put Tom's suit on the backseat, and got in.

"It can't be that bad."

"Well, it is. Not *bad*, it just hurts. I don't want to talk about it."

"Why not?"

She put her face on the steering wheel and cried.

"He was so cute," she said at last. "And so nice."

"Yes." Though Will wouldn't have thought of Tom as cute. "What were you up to, Dora?"

"Just getting him a Christmas present. A picture. Just a silly old picture." She sat up and sniffled mightily. "One he missed. That one time I went with him to the newspaper office. It was in Iceberg Fields, where his folks had lived, you know. He spoke to the editor and then went hunting up something in the morgue, and I was bored. So I looked in some of the files, too. And I found a picture from a long time ago. From the late thirties. It was a society item, about a picnic there. It was so pretty—a group shot of girls in summer dresses and young men in white shirts with their sleeves rolled up and those baggy pants. And big trees over them, and grass, and a creek in the background. One of the young men was Tom's father. He didn't look much like Tom. He was smaller and plainer, but he had nice blond hair and the sweetest face."

"So you had a print made."

"Yes. And I got it framed. That's where I was that day, picking it up. I'll show it to you tomorrow so you'll believe me."

"I believe you. Why didn't you tell me?"

"Oh, well, you know. I thought it might make you feel bad, my getting a present for Tom and all."

Will glanced at his watch. The faculty Christmas party at Mellon's began at five o'clock. He pushed the blue books aside, found a Renaissance text he meant to take home with him, and put on his coat. After buttoning it up, he reached well down into the righthand pocket and withdrew a slip of paper.

For there had been one other thing Winterlin had passed up in Tom's house, probably because it was of no interest to anyone. It interested Will only because it was a sort of coincidence, however unlikely.

He thumbed the paper open and looked at it again. He had found it being used as a bookmark in a copy of Ben Jonson's plays lying on Tom's desk. One of the books he used in class, Will knew. On it were only a few words: *The Men Who Made the Midwest*, by J. R. Brewster.

The same book Truitt's Angela had perhaps put a Coke

down on, or torn while flipping through it. Unless Wag the collie had forgotten that he'd entered his golden years. Or unless it had been Tom who had damaged it—thereby making things awkward for the university. Will remembered that Truitt had said something about Maisie that night to Louise Tree. The book must be hers. But if Tom had been at fault, why didn't Truitt make Tom go to the trouble of unearthing a replacement? What was he protecting Tom from?

Will thought about that as he descended the stairs and let himself out. If the book had had anything to do with McCrocken—as it was likely to if Maisie were involved—if it were one of those books Luke had foisted off on Tom, by way of Truitt, for the preparation of his speech, but one Tom couldn't use because it was torn up, Luke would certainly ask about it when he came back. And if Angela or Wag had been the sinner, Truitt would probably rather do anything than get himself in Dutch with Luke. He would know, with deadly certainty, that Luke would go on and on about it to him.

So a call on the public library, after a quick trip home to change clothes and get his car, was probably a waste of time. The book probably had nothing to do with anything except that speech. Except—Will brightened—then it would at least tell him something about McCrocken, if not about Tom, and maybe help with that confounded letter.

Forty-five minutes later, in his best dark suit and striped tie, Will found himself standing before a shelf in the little public library on Victory and Main Street. The book was there. It was a large one, brown with an ornate, embossed cover and faded gilt letters. He lifted it off the shelf and carried it over to a reading table.

The Men Who Made the Midwest. By J. R. Brewster. There, facing the title page, was a large studio portrait of Brewster himself, in a stiff collar and rimless eyeglasses. The pages smelled acrid and musty. Yellowish-brown spots had formed along the outer margin. First edition, 1934. Will turned it over and lifted the back cover. In a manila pocket glued to the endpaper was the checkout card. He slid it out of the pocket.

Thomas J. Aldrich   11-12-34
Cissie Warburton   4-17-41
Bobbie Bowers   5-20-41
Harley F. Carterman   9-3-47
Lydia Malone McKeown   12-23-48

Five names, all in faded, immature hands. High-school students, Will would have bet money on it. Three in almost indecipherable pencil, two in black ink gone brown with age.

No one had checked it out since.

He turned back to the contents page. Twenty-four lengthy chapters, all similarly titled: "The Men of the Soil," "The Men of the Mills," "The Men Who Broke the Iron Horse," "The Men Who Manned the Ship of State," and so on. At the end of each chapter, small-print biographies of the persons concerned were appended. In the index he found Gabriel McCrocken's name. He was in the chapter called "The Men Who Made the Little Towns."

McCrocken, Gabriel. 496–9, passim. Biog. 517.

But except for *passim*, he was out of luck. The whole chapter was gone, ripped out with rough hands. There was no way to tell how recently it had been done.

Will skimmed through the rest of the book but did not linger over the details he found here and there of McCrocken's real-estate acumen, or the references to his foresight in keeping the townspeople building within Pebble River's curves instead of away from them, or an approving note about his insistence, in town council, on footbridges over the river. Those scraps of information weren't going to tell him anything at all.

He returned the book to the shelf. The university library might have a copy. And that was across the street from the Mellon house, so he still had time to stop by there.

The library windows were warm and welcoming in the

dark. The McCrocken Wing, looking raw with newness and smelling sharply of cold stone, stood out in silhouette against their yellow light, attached to the main library by a short arcade of wide arches. At the card catalog on the ground floor of the main building, Will found that the Brewster book was indeed there, and that it was kept in the rare-books collection on six. He headed for the elevator.

The rare-books collection was housed in an unexpectedly breezy room at the top of the building. So many windows probably weren't good for old books, Will thought as he strode down the hall. But then it seemed to be the only space available, and it did have a pleasant, aerielike quality.

At the door, he paused. The room was almost crowded, as it had been all week. End-of-semester papers were due, either the next day or right after the Christmas recess. Most of the reading tables were occupied, and the open stacks rustled with shuffling feet and turning pages.

He nodded at the student guard—a sandy-haired, heavily muscled young man in blue jeans—and scribbled his name, as required, on the sign-in sheet. The Brewster book was in the stacks in an alcove to the right. He inspected it at length, without bothering this time to take it to a table. After a while he closed it and carefully put it away.

By now he was past due at the party. He didn't have time after all to go over the McCrocken chapter. But he had lost interest in it, though it was intact—almost. What wasn't there, what had been removed from this copy, too—though cleanly this time, as if with a razor blade—was a single page. Page 517, the one containing Gabriel's biography.

He was walking slowly, enveloped in thought, when he came out of the library, and it took him a moment to work up some interest in a university party. But the sky was Prussian blue with a few stars in it, and across the street the Mellon house was a blaze of lights behind its trim black iron fence. A good many latecomers, like himself, were approaching on the snowy walks. As far as he could see in every direction, cars lined the curbs.

The last party in the old house, Will thought as he started across the street. That was something; when it was all over, he wouldn't have wanted this business to have taken that away. He meant to enjoy himself, if he could.

And afterward, a hamburger in town, and then off to Mrs. Moffat's.

EIGHT

Mr. Mellon's Christmas Party

The tree was an ordinary-size tree, glittering in Mellon's front window—not an outsize spruce like Maisie Moffat's—but it partook of everything a Christmas tree should be. It bore white and yellow electric candles on its branches and was covered all over with toys and animals and dolls and the most wonderful balls of striped and dotted glass. On its top stood an angel in a pale blue gown with spreading, feathery wings. Will, with his Christmas punch and a plateful of food, captured a chair near the fire and watched the tree while he ate, half-expecting to see something magical in it if he watched long enough.

Around him, it was very noisy. The faculty and selected graduate students milled about in every room, with flushed faces, loud voices, and a lot of laughter.

The administration had thought of calling the whole thing off, on account of Tom. But it had seemed rather pointless, especially since the caterers and a team of cleaning women had been hired and a lot of money had been spent. Ten wives had been freezing milk cartons of ice for the punch for a week. And on top of that, Tom had been new. Not many people outside his own department had known him.

And so the party had taken place—and everyone, in the end, had turned out for it. Those members of the committee who had agonized about it at a special, closed meeting on Wednesday afternoon were relieved. Maisie Moffat was there, too, delivered in style by Bo. Everyone seemed to be having an unusually good time.

Will ate four cheese puffs and three stuffed olives and a cracker with pepperoni on it. His chair was pushed back somewhat, near the wall, and he could avoid having to talk while he was eating because he wasn't very easy to get to. He had spoken to Mrs. Moffat some time earlier, to see if she was still up to a visit later. "Of course," she'd told him. "I've been looking forward to it. I told Bo not to come back, that you'd be giving me a ride home."

So they were there for the duration. Will got as much food as he dared to replace his lost hamburger.

At the moment, Maisie was standing in the front hall, at the foot of the stairs, surrounded by a clutch of professors. Will smiled. They all seemed tense about each other, but they were questioning her closely—and listening soberly to her answers. They were trying to find out where the treasure was.

He glanced around. The graduate students in the crowd hadn't shown the least interest in Maisie's presence. They were probably all too tired to give any thought to missing treasure. Except for Barney Nealsson, who was leaning against a wall by himself, sneezing vigorously into a handkerchief. His cheeks were flushed and his eyes too bright. Too much tramping about putting up signs had given him a cold, Will supposed.

And except for Lucy Mellon, though Lucy, at twenty, wasn't a graduate student yet. She was everywhere in the crowd, refreshing drinks, putting bowls of nuts around, keeping the rooms tidy and pretty as people surged about. She was a tall, rangy young woman with long hair, a sunburned complexion, and a friendly grin. She never spent much time on her appearance, but she always seemed so healthy and good-humored that most people thought she was pretty. Especially so tonight, in her dress of dark blue cotton sprigged with white flowers.

Will found himself regretting the house's imminent destruction. He didn't know how it had been before, but it seemed to him that between them Lucy and Mellon had made it a charming and comfortable place. Though it was probably mostly Lucy. Mellon was a fusty old man with thinning gray hair, spectacles, and a sausage-shaped person. He was creaking of joint and high of voice and hadn't been seen in years when he wasn't wearing a black suit and a gray waistcoat. Except in the summer, of course; Will had often noticed him pottering in his garden in a striped shirt with the cuffs buttoned.

Since his retirement years before from the Latin department, Mellon had occupied himself with other interests— reading, gardening, and writing, mostly. It was only when he'd been persuaded to give an occasional lecture or two to one of the Latin classes that he ventured across the street to the main part of the campus. Otherwise, he kept to himself, in this house crammed with books.

Will didn't suppose he did more to the house than keep the books in order and pay the bills and hide in his den when Lucy wanted to repaint. But in spite of its structural problems, it had a snug and glistening air. The brass and wood and white paint gleamed, the floors were waxed and shining (except for the living room and Mellon's study, which had been richly carpeted); cranberry glass and pewter and bits of needlepoint in soft colors glowed throughout the many rooms. Over the front door the old stained-glass fanlight— with the porch light on behind it—scattered its colors across the marble floor of the little foyer, when it was empty, and just at present dappled the shoulders of Claire Bordeaux's white dress.

Claire, who could be a little dazzling, was holding a court of her own. Will saw Truitt Roberts hovering on the edge of a circle around her that included Zerner and Lowe from chemistry, Howard from math, and Barman from psychology. No one from the art department, though. Will supposed they had all been scared off long ago by knowing too well Geoff Bordeaux's infamous temper.

And Geoff himself? Will looked around for him while he

polished off his chicken salad and ate the stuffed mushroom he'd saved for last. In one corner he saw Dora—she was wearing her old navy suit and was listening politely to some counsel evidently being given her by gentle Joey Livingston. She made far less prepossessing an appearance than her smartly dressed mother, who was being entertained by a high-spirited group of older ladies on the living-room sofas. Will downed the rest of his punch and stood up with the intention of getting more, and it was then that he saw Geoff—loose-limbed, gangly, and coatless as usual—talking eagerly to Ellen Powell in the doorway to the back hall. A night when probably both Geoff and his wife would have been better off at home, Will thought, noting Ellen's shining eyes. Especially if Geoff still had the McCrocken portrait to finish.

The food and drink were spread out in the dining room on the other side of the jam-packed foyer. Will took a roundabout route through the kitchen. The catering staff had nearly all gone away, leaving boxes of things ready to be put out, or cheese puffs to be baked as needed, and the one remaining server was apparently out front somewhere, doing some serving. As was Lucy herself, he supposed, wondering how she managed so much on her own. He pushed open the swinging door and entered the shadowy, chandelier-lit dining room, emerging in the midst of a thicker mass of people than the living room had held.

He found Mellon standing alone at the end of the room, munching on a cupcake. Will paid his respects and stood with him for a while, talking with him about his work. At length, however, when Mellon removed his handkerchief to wipe his hands, Will noticed a cream-colored corner of paper protruding from his breast pocket.

"Not you, too," he said.

Mellon glanced down at it and immediately grew depressed. "It's from Luke Vondervorste," he said. "It came while I was dressing for the party." He fished it out with stiff old fingers. "I feel terribly boxed in."

DREADFUL NEWS ABOUT TOM. I'M HERE THROUGH CHRISTMAS I THINK EVERYTHING BOOKED FOR WEEKS MY HANDS ARE TIED. YOU'LL HAVE TO GIVE MCCROCKEN SPEECH, CAN'T SAY NO, IT'S YOUR DUTY. DON'T FORGET YOU LIVE IN HIS HOUSE. JOYEUX NOEL. LUKE.

Will laughed in spite of himself. "What can you do?" he asked.

"I don't know. I'm really at a loss. The house doesn't have anything to do with it, you know, and I certainly never knew McCrocken. I came here long after his time, in 1964."

"Perhaps it wouldn't be too bad," Will said. "You might be able to use Tom's notes. I guess Winterlin has them—they've been going through his papers and taking them away—but they might be done with them by now."

"I have a better idea," Mellon said. "I could cable back and tell him no—Lucy, my dear. How can we help you?"

Will turned. Lucy Mellon had come to stand beside him, holding an empty tray and looking slightly moist with the heat of the room. She smiled at her uncle. "I've been trying to find time all evening to say hello to Dr. Gray, that's all. And *guess what?* The cheese puffs are all gone." She laughed. "I've just put out every last snack and it's nearly eight o'clock."

Mellon's face went a little pink. "My dear, don't sound quite so pleased. Will is going to think you're telling him to go home."

"I would tell me that if I were you," Will said. "I'd be up on a chair banging a gong and saying, 'Okay, everybody. One more cheese puff each and then I want you all out of here. Pronto.'" He gave Lucy a grin. "What major is it this week?"

For months Lucy had been wavering between psychology and anthropology while she finished up her required courses.

"Psychology, I think. Or maybe pre-med. I like people. Live ones. But I've *got* to settle down. Everything new seems wonderful, and I keep going off in odd directions. I got so charmed with Dr. Donahue's class last month that I was even thinking of literature."

Mellon pursed his lips. "I think I'd ask first how much of

that was due to the literature in question and how much was due to Dr. Donahue."

"You needn't look quite so disapproving. He pretty much asked me the same thing Tuesday night. Not that he put it that way, of course, but—" She stopped. Will had laid a hand on her arm.

"Tuesday night? You'd gone up to see him?"

"The night she came home so late," Mellon said pointedly. "Handsome professors who find it necessary to have heart-to-heart talks with young women students at eleven o'clock at night, and no one else about—"

"But *I* was the one who went to see *him*. After the concert. It wasn't at all the way you think it was. I didn't even really get to talk to him because of that phone call."

Mellon's face, his rounded shoulders, his whole bearing went slowly still and cold, in just the way Will himself had been feeling.

Lucy was looking from one to the other of them.

"What *is* the matter?" she said, bewildered. "You both look—" She sighed and brushed her brown hair away from her face. "Oh, for goodness' sakes. It was just exactly like the sheriff has already guessed."

"That's only one guess," Mellon said, "and only very lately made public, by the way. My dear, where have you been all this time?" He looked miserable. "For that matter, why wasn't *I* thinking?"

"Because you were busy with your own work and because you just don't think those kinds of thoughts anyway," Lucy said comfortingly. "As for me, I didn't even know Dr. Donahue was dead till today. I don't listen to the radio, and we were so busy getting ready for the party. I only saw you once or twice all day, you remember"—she patted her uncle on the arm— "sort of hovering around looking anxious about the punch or the napkins or something. You didn't *tell* me—no one did. And then this morning I stayed shut up in my room till late, so I could get some studying done. By this afternoon, when I did find out, there wasn't anything for me to say."

"Well, what did happen?" Will asked.

"Just what they said on the radio," she repeated firmly. "Someone called—I don't know who—and arranged to meet him, or maybe to be picked up somewhere. Dr. Donahue just said things like 'Of course,' and 'No, it's no trouble,' and then he asked where the person was and he repeated the directions as he wrote them down on the back of an old envelope. He said he'd be there as soon as he could and put the envelope in his pocket and hung up. 'I guess you heard that,' he told me, and he said he'd give me a lift home. Which was silly, since it was a matter of a two-block walk, so I declined. After that, while he was putting on his coat and we were going downstairs, he was talking about my own plans and what I should watch out for."

She paused. "This afternoon, when I heard he was dead— had been killed—and realized he might have been talking to a murderer, I felt very . . . chilled. But when I thought about it, I knew I couldn't help. He certainly said no one's name; I can't imagine who it was."

Will brought up the question of the mysterious number three, and a little frown appeared between her eyes. "No, I don't remember that. If that was part of it, he may not have said it aloud, but I can't be sure."

Was that good enough? Will shoved his hands in his pockets and studied her face. Not in one sense. She would have to talk to Winterlin, who would make her go over it again and again, for some detail or inflection that would tell him something. But good enough to soothe any interested ears that might be listening? He was inclined to think so and began to relax. But Mellon had been too badly frightened.

"You won't leave this house, Lucy," he said clearly, "till we get Sheriff Winterlin here to talk to you. This evening. Nor leave my presence in the interim. I want you to agree to that."

If Lucy thought him foolish, she was too nice to say so. Will, who had thought well of her ever since he'd first met her two years before, had occasion again to admire her grace and good manners toward her uncle.

"Then let's get some more punch, shall we?" she smiled, "before it's all gone. And when Sheriff Winterlin comes over, I'll be glad to talk to him, but you'll see that that's really all there is. There's just nothing more, I'm afraid, not even if I thought about it for weeks."

Will didn't want more punch nearly as much as he wanted to fix in his mind who had been standing within earshot. As Lucy and Mellon threaded their way through the crowd, he dropped back against the dining-room windows and looked around him. He quickly realized, however, that it was impossible, as he had feared. As with all parties, the room where the food was laid out was the most popular, and the crowd was enormous as well as constantly changing.

He gave it up and went to find Maisie Moffat. She was probably still talking up her treasure hunt somewhere, he thought.

It took him twenty minutes, though, of sorting through dining room, entrance hall, living room, back hall, and solarium—twenty minutes during which he was stopped and stopped again, by this friend and that one, before he discovered her primping before the mirror in the empty guest bedroom across from Mellon's study. Will leaned against the doorjamb and watched her. She was opening all the half dozen or so bottles of perfume on the dresser, sniffing their contents, putting a little dab on the back of her hand, and sniffing again. When she saw him in the mirror, she gave a little jump.

"Now, how long have *you* been there?" She waved at the perfume bottles. "This is all good stuff. I'll bet people give it to Lucy as gifts and she doesn't use it. She doesn't strike me as a perfume-wearing girl. Yet. She'll learn. Are you ready to go?"

But Will wasn't. Probably silly, he told himself, yet it was a big house and Mellon was an old man.

"Are you tired?" he asked.

"Yes, I am a bit," Maisie admitted.

"Then, could you give Bo a ring after all? I think I'd better wait here a while—for reasons I can't explain right now. I'll join you as soon as I can. It won't be more than an hour."

"I can try," Maisie said doubtfully. "Though I wish . . . I wish I'd known sooner. I hate to drag Bo out again when he doesn't expect it."

"If it's not convenient for him, we'll work something else out. But try him anyway. He probably won't mind."

Maisie looked around. On a bedside table was a telephone. She sat down on the bed and dialed. But Bo wasn't at home, nor was he at the station. One of the men there told her Bo had left early. "He had Christmas shopping to do," Maisie reported when she hung up.

"Then let's see if someone else can give you a ride."

Will went back to the front part of the house, looking around him as he went for someone he could ask. He found a good many people still chatting, but near the front door he also found a clutch of others in coats and hats, milling about uneasily. Dora and her mother were among them.

"We can't find Mellon," she told him. "Or Lucy, either. And everyone wants to say good-bye."

"What do you mean you can't find them? Where have you looked?"

"Oh . . . all around," Dora said vaguely. "I didn't mean really *looked*, just that they don't seem to be—"

A scream, sharp and piercing, cut into her words. Will pushed her aside, moving toward it without consciously knowing where it had come from. Another scream, and another. He plunged through the paralyzed groups around him, in the entrance hall and then the back hall, and found himself at last, after some confusion and backtracking, and more unnerving screams, standing in the doorway of the study, gripping a woman by the shoulders, shaking her and hushing her. Just inside the room, frozen, stood her husband, a physics professor, bundled up in coat and muffler and gloves.

Mellon was crumpled against one of the bookcases on the righthand wall, a stream of blood dripping from the side of his head, his eyes closed, his hands outspread and turned up in a futile way. In the middle of the carpeted floor, Lucy lay face down in a pool of blood that spread around her face and soaked the neck of her sprigged blue dress. A bronze bust of Caesar, its head wreathed in sharp and spiky laurel leaves, lay on its back beside her.

Mellon was breathing, but Lucy, her head severely battered, was quite dead.

"He could have come from anywhere—one of the other rooms, or from the backyard, through the kitchen door." Sheriff Mack Winterlin was speaking to the few who were left—Maisie and Will and Mellon, who leaned against a sofa cushion with a cold compress bound to his head. The fire had nearly died, and shot up sparks and spits of light.

In the intervening hours, he and his men had come and done their work. While Lollo McIngling and the paramedics with the ambulance crew had been in the study, bent over Mellon, reviving and monitoring him, taking Lucy's body away, Winterlin had been in the front rooms writing down names, listening to accounts of who had been where. He had begun with Will, and now he was ending with him.

Maisie perched on one end of a sofa, looking round-eyed and serious.

"The caterer's helper was about to leave," he went on, "and was in the back hall, putting on her coat, so the kitchen was deserted. As you know, Lucy—accompanied by her uncle here—had gone into Mr. Mellon's study where they kept a little cash, in a jar, to get the woman a tip. They were attacked there, from behind."

Will glanced at Mellon, but the old man remained unresponsive, his eyes closed. It worried them all that he had refused to go to the hospital.

"The point is," Winterlin continued, "a guest here could have done it, or someone from outside—either a guest who had ostensibly left or someone else entirely." He looked at Will. "You still can't remember any more than you've told me?"

Again and again Will had recounted his conversation with Mellon and Lucy. Innocuous as it sounded, they all knew there must have been something they couldn't see in it, something the murderer feared.

He shook his head. "Anyone there could have overheard it, in theory. I can't positively eliminate more than a very few people. Dora's mother, for instance, and the ladies around her. They seemed to have been sitting in exactly the same place the whole time. And aren't very likely suspects to begin with. But even that wouldn't really hold up. I couldn't, of course, see who was behind me. And there were just too many people moving about."

"Then let's get some sleep." Winterlin rose. "Mr. Mellon, one of my men will be staying the night with you. Here in the living room. You needn't make any special arrangements."

Mellon gestured vaguely, negatively, his eyes still closed, but Winterlin was unmoved. "It will be better for you. You'll sleep better for not being alone."

Mellon's eyes opened at last—hopeless, steel-colored eyes. "You do whatever you want to do," he said. "But it's for you and not for me. Lucy wasn't yours, she was mine. And I'll never really sleep again."

On the sidewalk outside, Maisie leaned heavily on Will's arm. "Please come home with me," she said, "as we'd planned. We're into something, and we need to work it out. Ask me all the questions you'd meant to before this dreadful thing, and let's go on from there. I think somehow, by acting normally, we'll come to the end of it."

Will helped her into his car. "Maybe *you* will," he said. "I only wanted to ask about the treasure. What a frivolous thing."

Maisie looked up at him. "I don't know what else to do."

"All right, then," Will said. "We'll go on with what we have to go on with. Or we'll try."

And then he had to smile. Maisie's eyes had turned to black, inscrutable pools. "I could eat a table leg," she said. "I don't want to be irreverent, but I practically didn't get anything to eat at all. Before we go home, could we go through town? All I can think of is how much I want a hamburger."

NINE
Maisie's Clue

"If it's Papa you want to know about, you've come to the wellspring, all right," Maisie said an hour later. She had surprised him by offering him sambuca complete with coffee beans. "The sibyl sits before you, Dr. Gray, but a sibyl with a difference; I can give you masses of information from which the answer can be plucked out, but I can't get it out myself. I've never heard of a sibyl with that problem. Though the poor creatures did seem to be blind or crazy or mute or all three, and troubled by the most—*derelict* of companions, and I'm not, so that's something.

"And I do know so much more about Papa now than I did when he was alive. Not that it's all fact that's in question. I've lately come to realize that *essences* may be bound up in it. If they are, I wonder if any of us can solve the problem."

Since his last visit, Maisie had magically acquired two armchairs—soft, cushiony ones in bluish green inserted among the stiff wooden ones. ("I brought them in from the back sitting room for your benefit," she had said. "Both of them?" "Well, one looked funny by itself.") Will stretched his long legs out over the rug and relaxed. "What do you mean by 'essences'?" he said.

"Crosscreek in the thirties. Papa and the three of us. The game part of it. The things I think about when I think of Papa—hot summer afternoons and Papa walking along the sidewalk under the trees, coming home from the university, the nights we spent talking or playing something or sitting outside. Papa used to shake his head over us; he spent several hours after supper working in his study. But it was all mild and peaceful. I can't say how things have changed, but they have. It's still quiet and peaceful here now, but it's different."

"It's possible that you changed it yourself."

"How do you mean?"

"Is there any replacement now for the McCrocken family?" Will smiled slightly. "My guess is that your father's house was the first of Crosscreek's homes, in a social sense. It was big; it had sons and a lovely daughter; he was unquestionably somebody in the town's eyes. Maybe there were a few lesser but similar families in town. And after he died—"

"I believe you're right. After he died, and after the war, we all lived more quietly, more alone. Henry had been lost at Salerno, in 1943. Edward moved to Minneapolis. Toby and I had no children. All Papa's interests were taken over by several people instead of one. The same thing happened to our friends. Now we're a town of ordinary families, with old women living in the big houses. It seemed so permanent. It's strange it was so easily lost."

"Not very strange. It's the story of everybody's life."

"Still, some do seem to keep what they have a little longer. I think, you know, that the treasure was responsible. But I don't mean it made us avaricious and mean, just that there were years there when we might all have acted differently. I can see just how it would have been—Edward and his wife, rather stodgy but solid; Henry to take Papa's place, and Toby and me, with a big family . . . big houses, big yards, voices. . . . When it got quiet, it got quiet with a bang. I always wondered why. But those first few years were something you can't have dreamed of. We put everything else aside and looked for the money. We talked about it, night after night. We read, we searched, we made excursions, followed wild ideas, regarded that house as nothing more than a bank vault and our own houses as places to eat and sleep while we looked. And then, all of a sudden, we tired of it all and quit. We tried to reestablish the old way of living, but although in a way we did, the times had changed, too, by then, and the war was going on and Edward and Henry and Toby all had to go."

"And the town? I hear the townspeople hunted, too."

"Yes. People went on searching off and on for years after we quit. We gave out that anyone who found it could keep ten percent for himself. So some people looked during the war, and then afterward a lot of the men who came home got involved in it and were excited about it, since they'd scarcely had time to think of it before. Often Toby and I would see searchers, or evidence that they'd been looking somewhere. In 1946 a farmer turned up an old rusty tin box with his plow. It was empty, but a party of men went out there the next evening after work to dig his field. It seemed a likely place—the box was found only a few steps from some landmark—a tree, I suppose. And it was a new field. Before, it had always been a truck garden. They grew tomatoes in that patch. The grocer remembered that Papa had been especially fond of tomatoes." She smiled. "It was in the paper.

"Another time, about a year later, a boy brought home a bit of very old, wrinkled dollar bill. He'd found it in a bird's nest still under construction in a tree down by Pebble River. He got the scrap out and came back for his family. They all went down to see which way the birds went for nest materials. Pretty soon the word got around, and a lot of other people went down. They had a terrible time trying to follow those birds. I remember that one man fell in the underbrush and sprained his ankle. When he yelled with pain, everyone went running to the place, thinking he'd found the money, and after that the birds went off and put up their nest somewhere else. A lot of people were mad at that man for a long time."

"When did it finally stop?"

"About 1950, I think. It petered out gradually, and then one day I realized it was all over. Possibly someone found it a long time ago and went off with it without saying anything. I don't think so. I think it's still here."

"There's an old rolltop desk in the history department office—" Will began.

"I'd forgotten that." Maisie chuckled. "There *was* some hunting in later years. About the time dear Tippy Roberts came back to be chairman. That was Papa's old office desk, you know, when *he* was chairman—"

"Wait. *Tippy* Roberts?"

She reached for the peanuts on the glass table. "Truitt, of course. But he was called Tippy when he was a little fellow. Anyway, sometime along in the early 1960s, old Dean Moffat—Toby's half brother; we go about together quite a lot still, now that we're the only two left—anyway, in the early sixties he finally got to wondering in a serious way about that money. He conceived the notion after a few months that Papa might have hidden it in his desk. Did he ask *me*? No sir. Did he ask any soul who had looked for it back then? No again. But he went about the campus *wondering* about it to all the professors, especially the young ones, for a good four months more. At last he got up one day and locked his office and went over to see Tippy about it. He had to sit in the secretary's office for a long time because there was a meeting going on, but sit there he did, with his hat on his knees, and watched her type till she nearly screamed. It was a good hour, I heard. When he finally got in, Tippy hit the ceiling. It was unlike him—he's never been really volatile. Even now Gus still thinks about it. He still can't understand why Tippy should have been so mad. But of course, after all that mumbling and muttering about hidden money that Gus had been doing for all those months, half the faculty had already 'dropped in,' one by one, to have a look at it. Tippy nearly went crazy. He never knew Gus had started it, and Gus never got to look at that desk. I heard it had already been searched sixteen times."

"Not counting the time Truitt went through it himself."

"No. Nor the times Edward and Henry and I took it apart in 1940. There wasn't anything there."

"The question is"—Will's green eyes were direct—"whether there's anyplace else to look. It sounds as if the possible locations were exhausted."

"But it wasn't found. So there's at least one place left. Start with the letter," Maisie said. "It's the only thing you can do."

"What did you and your brothers make of it?"

"Nothing, at first. It made not a particle of sense. So we put it aside and looked without it. But in the end Edward went back to it. He sat Henry and Toby and me and his wife Rhoda down one night, and he made us a speech. He pointed out several things. One, that we had all been looking in the places where *we* would hide the money, not in the places where *Papa* would have been likely to hide it. Two, that we couldn't very well do the latter because we didn't know him very well and we didn't know the sort of place that would have appealed to him. Three, that Papa meant for us to profit from the search itself, as well as from its results. He based this observation on his knowledge of Papa and on two statements in the letter: '*all* my wealth is yours by right' and 'to give it is impossible, out of hand.' We were frivolous young people, and certainly Papa was rich in other things besides money, which we weren't especially, except for youth and beauty. Four—this one is connected with the last two—that Papa sometimes said he must have adopted us and forgotten about it. We were so unlike him, caring only for our own amusements and regarding him as a nice old person who lived in our house, that he often called us his wards instead of his children. Not that there was any hostility—we had a pleasant life together—but I do think he was genuinely puzzled by us. Therefore, Edward concluded that Papa was a bit lonely and wanted us to know more about *him*—we never asked—as well as being anxious for our education.

"To all this, Henry added a fifth point: that Papa had a strong sense of humor. He knew what greedy children we were. He knew we were also exceptionally lazy and yet that we would do anything we had to for that much money. Henry thought Papa saw it as a kind of posthumous game, in which he would see just how far he could string us out before we brought the search to an end. I think he was right. Papa was like that. A game—and he's practically won. I'm sure he would be sorry if he knew."

"After that, what did you discover in the letter?"

"Nothing." In the half dark, Maisie's eyes gleamed. "We ignored it again—Edward's speech only led us off on another tack. The hardest thing for anyone to do who has ever searched for the money has been to stick to that letter. We took up the discovery of Papa's life instead. Edward examined Papa's real-estate and stock-market interests. He had the idea that Papa had invested the missing money in something that had come to his attention in a business way, with the title or securities left in a bank we knew nothing of, perhaps under an assumed name. He also wrote to all the banks in the area and made two trips to New York. Papa occasionally went to New York on business and had done so the year all that money disappeared. Alternatively, Edward thought he had made some improvement on one of the pieces of land he still held at his death, something that cost more than anyone would have supposed and would have resulted in eventual great value."

"I thought he had no property at the time of his death except cash."

"That's not quite true. He had three deeds. Their value was reckoned into the value of the estate, of course, and they hadn't changed much for years."

"What were they?"

"The house, a scrap of land on the south side of town, and what we used to call the Water Pastures—about fifty acres now bounded by Harvest Street, Farley Street, and the river. We sold it after a few years, of course, and no one ever discovered any such improvement."

"What did Henry do?"

"Henry set the town on its ear. He loved making a production of things. While Edward was poking about in title offices and banks, Henry was supervising a team of students dragging Pebble River, or showing off for the crowd while Toby led a group that scoured the park, or rounding up all the owners of all the keys to the music department's lockers one night that April and marching them by torchlight over to the old auditorium, along with the town's only locksmith, to break into the mysterious unowned locker he expected to find.

"But he wasn't just fooling around. He had recalled Papa's perpetual interest in community and university affairs, you see. Papa had been responsible for suggesting those lockers in a faculty meeting, and in town council for creating the park, and for having zoning laws passed to keep the river within the town by making the river property the only residential lots for miles around."

"And you? Where did you look?"

"In his books. *And* I began by reading page 190 of every book in his library, with no enlightenment whatever. Enlightenment about the money, that is. I did pick up all sorts of odds and ends of information."

"What was your father's field?"

"American history, especially regional and western history. He taught all those subjects; bits of them were always creeping into his conversation. I was a young wife in 1940, with other duties to attend to, but in the afternoons I read. I tried to find out about all those things for myself, including Scandinavian and Indian lore, because they were related to what Papa taught. After every book, I read the letter again to see if it would begin to make sense. It never did."

"Speaking of books, did you ever find one called *The Men Who Made the Midwest*?"

"Yes, of course." She looked surprised. "Mr. Vondervorste has been his usual talkative self, I see. Mr. Brewster's book was never all that well known, and it's almost entirely forgotten now. I hadn't thought of it myself for years, until around Thanksgiving, but it's full of all sorts of information about this area. And it has several nice pieces about Papa in it. Do you know that he never brought that book to our attention? I remember that it lay around the house for some time—he brought it home one day and left it on the table in the hall and then in his study. After a while it went onto his shelves and we never knew he was mentioned in it till after he died."

"Do you still have that copy?"

"I did until three or four weeks ago. I gave it to Mr. Vondervorste. Under Papa's portrait in the new library, on top of the desk, will be a shelf of Papa's publications. I thought Mr. Brewster's book should be there, too, so I took it over to Mr. Vondervorste one day." She laughed. "He couldn't wait to get his hands on it. He wanted to show it to that poor Dr. Donahue to help him with the speech he'd been conned into making—new men *are* asked to do a lot—and he thought it ought to be available to students as soon as possible. He put it in the rare-books room, he told me."

"Did you know that a page is missing? The one containing biographical information about your father?"

"So soon?" Maisie looked pleased. "It shows that students do still work on my father's life. They used to come to see me often, from the university and from the high school, but I haven't had one for years."

"Can you tell me what was on that page? Treasure hunters might find it as useful as students."

"Oh, I shouldn't think so. Whatever the answer is, I'm sure it's something simple and obvious—Papa would have made certain of that. But I hope it's not so obvious as all that. I've read it, of course—several times. It just told when he was born and what he did and what our names were and what clubs he belonged to."

"He didn't happen to be a member of something called the Close Company of Perfect Strangers?"

"What . . . an odd name." A peanut shell cracked noisily between her fingers, and she looked ruefully at the smashed nuts within. "Oh no. *That* wasn't mentioned. And you really would do better to stick with the letter, Dr. Gray. You don't want to grow old and treasureless like the rest of us." She rose. "Now, you go and look at my tree. I have some cake and coffee for us. I'll be right back."

When he had eaten two pieces and Maisie was pouring his second cup of coffee, he said, "Did you ever meet Tom Donahue?"

"No. We spoke on the telephone once."

"About Mr. McCrocken?"

"Yes. We arranged to meet. It was to have been Wednesday—yesterday."

"When did he call?"

"On Tuesday. About noon, I believe."

"But he was killed that night."

"Yes." Maisie's fingers played slowly with the embroidery of the napkin in her lap. "Several things regarding the motive have occurred to me," she said. "But I have a hard time getting any two ideas to connect. I will tell you one thing, though. You might look into it. After you left on Tuesday, I had my supper and tried to occupy my mind, but then I just couldn't stand it anymore, so I called Bo to come for me. I so much wanted to see how Jed was putting the flyer together and how it was going to look. As you know, Bo has to come get me, or bring me the car when I want it myself, but it saves him time when all is said and done. If I kept it here, I would think of reasons to drive it, and Bo would be over here several times a week getting it started. We're old friends but still . . . He was ten or twelve when Papa died, you know. He spent most of that first winter at the house. He was a thin little thing in those days, and he could crawl into places we couldn't and put his fingers into chinks and holes. Once he found a fountain pen Edward had lost and once a mousetrap bit him. His father was Papa's doctor."

"So Bo came for you," Will said patiently. "Then what?"

"Then we went to Jed's office, but first we digressed. I

hadn't been out for several days, and I was surprised to see all the Christmas lights up around all the houses. I made Bo drive us around first, to look. We went up and down a lot of streets, and especially over to the east side of town where those blocks and blocks of new houses are. And everything *was* pretty. I never thought much of the Marshalls, but they have the whole house outlined in blue. And the Linnets have put little white lights in their trees. We drove along very slowly and looked at them all.

"Dr. Donahue's house was dark, but there was a car out front. A young woman opened the door of the house as we approached and came out. She had something in her hand, a smallish parcel, a flat one. She came down the walk and got into her car. We were past by then. I saw the lights come on and heard the car start just before we turned."

"What kind of car was it?"

"A station wagon—I don't know what color. You know how hard colors are to identify at night. It was light—a white or gray or tan or light blue. Maybe yellow."

Almost everyone Will knew drove a station wagon. Most were light-colored. Everyone but Dora, who had a foreign compact, and Louise, who drove a beat-up old Ford.

"I take it that you didn't know the woman."

"I can't tell you whether I did or not. I scarcely looked at her. It wasn't important at the time."

"Can you describe her at all?"

"Only to say that she was slender and dark-haired, I think, though her head was covered. Somehow she seemed secretive."

"Anything else?"

"One thing. As she came down the walk to her car, our headlights picked out something that flashed on the shoulder or collar of her coat. It was too far over for a button. I'm sure it must have been a large silver pin of some sort."

"And you are sure that she had been inside the house, not just on the porch?"

"I'm positive. I distinctly saw the door open, wide, and she came out. That was why I noticed her in the first place. The house was absolutely dark. It was odd to see someone come out of a pitch-dark house where I knew she didn't live."

"Have you told Mack Winterlin?"

"No. And I won't, without reason to believe it's connected with the murder. It's probably none of his business. I'd rather you found out who it was and what she was up to."

Will shook his head. "Why me? Besides, Winterlin wouldn't mention it to anyone unless it was important."

"Well, I don't know Mack Winterlin well enough to be sure of that. And I won't go around raising questions about somebody without a better reason than I've got. A little common sense is all that's needed. You have at least as much of that as Winterlin does."

Will studied her. "I must go. If I look into it for you, will you stay away from Mrs. Ruth and her friends?"

Maisie blushed. "Why should I?"

"She really might be involved in this murder."

"How did you know I had met her?" She sounded irritated.

"The way you looked when I mentioned the Perfect Strangers."

"You're unnecessarily observant. You don't need to observe *me* as closely as all that."

Will was silent.

"I can't stay away from her now. I've invited her to tea tomorrow." Her face was charged with annoyance. "I don't know why I should stay away from her. She and her group need help. Not financial, nothing financial at all. They are interested in relocating poor people from the east in this area, where they'll have a chance. Decent, hardworking people, with children." She was speaking very quickly. "What they need most is information—about jobs and the kinds of services there is a need for, and the town and the people. It's a worthy cause and one I'd *love* to be involved in. Mrs. Ring needs help on her farm, for instance, and I would like to have a family here. It's something I want to do, and it won't cost a cent."

"How did she get to you?"

"She didn't 'get to me.' She walked over here, poor thing, all the way from her motel this afternoon. She was cold and shivering. I asked her in. Who wouldn't have asked her in?"

"She just happened to pull your name out of thin air?"

"Of course not. She came about the car. Bo sent her."

"What about the car?"

"To rent it. She needed a car and she spoke to Bo and he sent her to me. And I asked her in. And of course it *happened* to come out that I was born here and know all about everything and she told me about her project and I offered to help. She had never heard of me till Bo gave her my name as a person who had a car to spare for a few days." Maisie stopped suddenly. "How do you know about her?"

Suppose it were true, Will was thinking. It would explain several things. Tom's out-of-town trips last fall. Poppy Ruth's anxiety to get into the house—he might have had money for her, contributions or something, that if unidentified would have been put back into Tom's account. Her story would not appeal to the sheriff's office.

It did not, of course, fit with her telephone message to Tom, but then, he supposed, a pleasure trip could have come to have a business purpose. Or both stories could be false.

The redness was draining out of Maisie's cheeks. She looked ashamed of herself. "I'm sorry," she said. "Me and my projects. I was looking forward to it so much."

"Mrs. Ruth is a remarkable person," Will said. "This is the second evening in a row that she has made me mad." He stood up. "I would like to come back again sometime, if that's all right."

Maisie's chin shot up. "It certainly is. I would be delighted."

"Do you have any reason to suppose," he asked, while she was getting his things, "that Tom Donahue ever looked for your father's money?"

"None whatsoever. What makes you think so?"

"A little while ago we were looking for motives for murder."

"Well, I can't see the connection. If he'd found it before he was killed, why didn't he just say so? Besides, I haven't heard that anything resembling Papa's fortune was in his house or bank account. If it was, I'd like to have a look at it."

"Maybe it was where he couldn't get at it."

"If it was where *I* couldn't get at it, I'd send for help."

Will put his coat on. "You're the one with common sense," he said. "You should be looking for the woman with the silver pin."

"The casual approach is what's needed there. Do I strike you as a casual person?"

He looked down at her. "You still intend to have Poppy Ruth to tea?"

"I do. Unless you want to insist on that bargain."

"I won't. But don't be taken in."

She opened the door for him. "Do you know any more about where to look for the treasure than you did before you came here?"

"I think so."

"Where?"

"I liked Edward's speech. I think you and your brothers were on the right track there. But one omission stood out glaringly."

"What was it?"

"You started to learn more about your father, and about his previous interests. It was supposed to be a deliberate switch from your previous way of life, which was self-centered, as you said, and also a switch from your previous method of search, based on what you yourselves would have done. Right?"

"That's right."

"But you took up the study of your father at the point in his life when the three of you were born." So thorough was her astonishment and so clear was her admiration that Will could scarcely keep a straight face. "Did it never occur to any of you that he worked and read and traveled and lived for years before you were thought of, or wanted?"

"It never *crossed* our minds. If it had, we wouldn't have expected to find he had changed."

"He might have changed a great deal. He might even have been like you once."

"So he might," she said with enthusiasm—and then saw his joke. "I think my father was a smart man."

"I think there's not much doubt about it."

TEN
Social Circles

"**G**ood morning." It was Poppy Ruth on the telephone. Her voice sounded stiff.

"Oh, Christ. Not you."

"I love your personality."

"It's got several advantages. It stops con women cold."

"If I can be civil, you can. I've had a bad night."

"Good. So did I. I wished for you." Will reached for a cigarette. "You called to say good-bye, I hope."

"I wish I could. I am being detained by the sheriff's office."

He grinned into the phone. "What did you do?"

"I didn't do a thing. I was just walking around Tom's backyard when Sheriff Winterman dropped by."

"Winterlin. That would do it, all right. So, where are you now? In jail?" He glanced at the clock. Nine-forty-five. The funeral was at ten-thirty. He had to be at the church a bit early. He was one of the pallbearers.

"Certainly not. But I can't leave town."

"All of us here are thrilled."

"I hate this place."

"You brought it on yourself, I think."

"The sheriff here is a *suspicious* man. I couldn't say anything right."

"What did you tell him?"

"What I told you. Of course."

"You really tried that stuff about love letters? No wonder he had a lot of questions. I liked the one about relocating the poor people better."

He snared a box of cereal and shook some into a bowl. Then he started slicing a banana.

"You won't vouch for me, then?" she asked.

"*Vouch* for you? What good would that do? I don't know you, or didn't two days ago."

"They think I had something to do with Tom's getting killed. And this girl."

"So do I, maybe. Wait a minute." He went to the refrigerator for milk. Amigo shot past him to peer in.

"What are those funny noises?"

"I'm eating breakfast. The funeral starts soon. It's a good time for you to operate, by the way. A lot of people will be there."

"Anyone halfway human would have offered me a ride."

"You don't need one. You've got a car."

"You're not going to help me at all, then?"

"I'm on the other side."

She hung up. Will finished the cereal and put the bowl on the floor. He was waiting for Amigo to lap up what was left of the milk when the phone rang again. This time it was Dora.

"Can I go with you to the funeral?"

"There's bound to be some reason why we paid all those lawyers all that money."

"Please, Will."

"Go with your mother, how about that?"

"She didn't know Tom. She's staying here."

"I told you there was more to breaking up a marriage than signing a lot of papers."

"It doesn't have anything to do with marriage. Do you really want me to go alone? It would look very dramatic. Or should I be cozy and find a girl friend? Or some nice married couple? You used to want me to develop some sense of style. Besides, our going together shows—"

"Dora, I'll take you on one condition. That you will not ever again tell me or anybody else that we are still good friends."

"I don't see—"

"You've got five minutes," he said.

"I'm ready right now. If you don't hurry, we'll be late. You're supposed to be there early."

"I just remembered the reason about the lawyers."

"What do you mean?"

"Forget it."

He put the bowl in the sink. On the way out the door, he thought of the Brewster book. If it was ten o'clock here, it was eleven in New York. Even Junie Hill, the only person he knew who had never seen a sunrise, might be up by now and willing to spend part of her day at the public library. He had just time enough to make the call.

Main Street and the square were jammed with traffic. After the graveside ceremonies and a half hour's call at Louise's apartment, Will, with Dora beside him on the front seat, had to make his way among the slow-moving cars pouring into and out of the cross streets. Classes were over for the holidays; the exodus of students that had begun last night and had resumed as a slow trickle at dawn was building now to its peak.

In his pocket he had Louise's list of the people who had sent flowers. The apartment had been nearly free of them; she had sent most of them to the church.

"Lunch?" he asked Dora as they waited for a light to change.

"No thanks, Will."

He glanced at her. She was looking out the window at the students driving by. By midafternoon the town would seem deserted, the streets empty, the university still and dark.

He knew her feeling of depression. It had nothing to do with the events of the last few days; it was the approaching silence, the long empty days ahead, the being left behind in a drowsing town for a long midafternoon nap that happened at Christmas and in June to those faculty members who were not taking trips themselves.

Will felt dragged down by it himself, but in the last year or so he had been able to watch it coming with a shred of perverse anticipation. Middle age creeping up on him, probably, taking this roundabout way to make itself acceptable to him. But he went on choosing to recognize it instead as something more like a tradition—familiar, persisting, inevitably part of his way of life. Should it cease, he would soon look back on it with nostalgia, regretting the flood of leave-taking and of coming back and, in between, the endless dreaming days, the aloneness, the unhurried breakfasts in his bathrobe with time to work the morning paper's crossword puzzle at his kitchen table with egg congealing on his plate, the earth smell of the cold, empty garage when he stood in it considering whether to turn it out and straighten the cluttered shelves.

"I brought the photograph," Dora said.

"What photograph?" he asked.

She was rummaging in her big leather bag. Will turned right, toward her apartment house.

"The one I told you about," she said. "Of Tom's father."

"You didn't have to bring that."

"I wanted to." She withdrew it and held it in her lap. "*Somebody* ought to look at it."

He made a left and stopped in front of her door.

"You're right. I'd like to see it." He turned the motor off.

She'd had it nicely framed—matted and everything. He held it carefully and studied it.

The scene was as she'd described—a gathering of a dozen or so young people in clothes that now seemed too formal for a picnic. She leaned across the seat and pointed. "That one. That's Tom's dad."

A bemused young face, guileless yet sophisticated, looked back at him, a slicked-down youth with one foot up on a picnic basket. Beside him stood a girl with hair as golden as his own. Will glanced at her and then looked more closely.

She was small and slim and dark-eyed. She had a sharp little chin and laughter in her eyes.

Against all odds, he knew that girl. The night before, he'd spent the evening with her.

He handed the picture back to Dora and waited till she put it away.

"You see, I told you the truth," she said. "The second time." There was an air of composure about her. She closed the clasp on her bag and turned to face him, her hands folded in her lap.

Will reached out and put his arms around her and rested his cheek against hers. "So you did." He sat up straight again. "You can do it if you try."

"Oh hush," she said, and got out. "Thank you for—"

He stopped her with a shake of his head. "Thank *you* for going with me."

She looked at him, biting her lip. "I don't understand you, Will. Sometimes you can be so nice."

"Don't let it bother you. It's not often."

"That kind of thing makes Mother laugh. You ought to save it for her. She thinks—her words—you're a peach."

"Tell her I'll take her to dinner one night."

"I will. She'd like that."

Will didn't go straight home. He had another stop to make. At Dora's corner he turned back toward his left; this time his destination was a house in the center of the wooded area that lay within a bend of the river.

Pebble River crossed Main Street in three places, giving Crosscreek, landlocked as it so profoundly was in the middle of the Great Plains, the air of a waterfront town, especially in the sector Maisie had told him was once called the Water Pastures. Dora lived on its edge; Tom and the Livingstons and the Robertses—and, in fact, a great many of the faculty— dwelt within it. It was a wild and muddy sort of place in the spring, reachable only by footbridges in several directions and harboring one or two trailers as well as houses. Where it ended at Main Street on the south was the skating pond.

The house he was headed for had been remodeled to look modern. Its sagging porches had been removed, and gray barn siding, two stories tall, had been put up; its windows had become irregularly spaced; it bore a three-story addition out back, with a pitched glass roof and a glass north wall, suitable for a studio.

Will parked at the curb. A car was in the driveway—a gray station wagon. And at the funeral that morning, Claire Bordeaux's coat had been trimmed with a jade-and-silver pin.

He sat there for a few moments, musing on the best approach to take. Claire wouldn't put up with subterfuge, and Geoff, if it came to that, was incapable of responding to subtlety. On the other hand, if he were direct, they would both laugh at him and join forces against him.

In fact, he wasn't quite sure he wanted to go in at all. He didn't know what to make of Maisie at the moment. That photograph had disturbed him more than he'd let Dora know. Angered him, even. So Maisie had known Tom's father when they were young. Had gone out with him, it appeared. She'd been very silent about that the night before, when he'd asked her if she and Tom were acquainted.

He stared sightlessly down the curving street, smoking and turning the implications of that over in his mind. Perhaps there was nothing to it. In Crosscreek, the young people in Maisie's social class would have been few in those days. It was natural, he supposed, to get up picnics and dances and heaven knew what else with the young people like them in the little towns around. It was probably so casual a part of her life that she wouldn't have thought it would seem remarkable to him. So she'd known Tom's father nearly fifty years before. Of course she had. So his son had returned to the vicinity to teach. So what?

Still . . .

The front door slammed and Claire strolled down to his car. He opened the door and she slid onto the seat beside him.

"If you're sitting out here hinting for an invitation to come in, you've got it."

"You took longer than I thought you would. I bet you went upstairs for your earrings." He had always liked teasing Claire. "Where's Geoff?"

"In back. Painting."

"Working on the portrait, I hope. Luke's going to come home one of these days." He looked again at the house, rising oddly out of the jumbled neighborhood with its campground air. "You've made a lot of changes in this place."

She shrugged. "We like it. At least we think we do." She glanced over her shoulder at the house as if she rarely paid much attention to it. "Luke Vondervorste thinks we mucked it up. He came here to tell us so one day, after we started building the carport. What do you think?"

"I think it's not your style. Geoff's, maybe."

"Is it one o'clock?"

"A little past."

"Come in, then. He stops painting for lunch."

Geoff was on his way down the hall from his studio, but he led Will back when he heard what he wanted. The studio was enormous, thirty feet high, with a balcony around three sides. Cold blue light poured in from the north wall of glass. It stained the bare floor and the gray boards of the walls with reflections from the snow.

"Treasure hunting, huh? Well, I can't see how I can help. But if you think it's of any use . . ."

As they crossed the studio, their voices and footsteps echoed back at them, caused by the absence of rugs or draperies.

The nearly finished portrait stood on an easel in the middle of the great space. The figure itself was done; Geoff was working on the background.

And Will had to admit it was good. McCrocken's black eyes,

so much like Maisie's, seemed to fasten on his as he entered the room; his gray hair showed the marks of a hairbrush; his slight frame, given an easygoing stance on a sidewalk in front of the university, nevertheless seemed full of life and energy; his flannel suit almost smelled of wool.

"What did you work from?" Will asked. "Whatever it was, you've done a fine job."

Geoff waved at a collection of photographs spread untidily on a worktable. "Mrs. Moffat gave me all those," he said. "You might want to look at them."

Will did, more to maintain his cover than anything else. He quickly saw, though, that Geoff hadn't directly copied anything. He'd come up with his own image of McCrocken from them, an image that fitted them all but that was McCrocken in a somewhat different mood, at a somewhat different age.

"What do you get from all this?" Geoff asked curiously.

"Sanity, for one thing." Will smiled. "Though that crazy letter made me wonder. And—" He had also seen a touch of wistfulness, but he didn't voice that. "And intelligence, and good humor. Maisie thinks her father was playing a game with them, one with a certain point to it. That could be true."

He looked around him with interest. He'd never been in Geoff's studio before. Various canvases, apparently depicting scenes of Crosscreek, were propped against the walls, but almost none was wholly visible. The exception was a small painting less than a foot-and-a-half square that stood in a torn piece of brown wrapping paper pulled off it and left on the floor.

The house it showed was an old one, one much like others in the immediate area. It looked comfortable but seedy, with screened porches up and down and a vaguely prewar design. A small brown dog was just rounding a corner of the house; a gaunt old maple stood between the other side and the driveway; the grass out front was scanty. A hot summer sun lay over everything.

"That's this place," Geoff said, "before we had it done over."

He smiled oddly. "We almost sold that one the other day, but—" He shrugged.

"What happened?"

"The client died."

He was half-sitting on a kitchen stool near his table, one foot on the floor, the other on a rung. Claire was leaning against the wall by the door, in the far corner of the room.

Will crouched down to examine the painting more closely. "Who was the client?"

"Tom."

"Sorry to hear that." The painting was exceedingly well done, and evocative, but Will couldn't see anything special about it otherwise. "Why did he want it?" he asked.

Geoff looked hurt. "He liked it, I suppose."

From the door, Claire laughed. "What a thing to ask, Will."

"Sorry. I didn't mean it that way."

"We don't know why he wanted it especially. He was over here for lunch Tuesday, to look at the portrait. He said he probably ought to work it into his talk somewhere. Or at least make sure his presentation of the old man agreed with Geoff's." Claire shrugged lightly. "He looked at all the rest of Geoff's pictures after that, and Geoff was telling him about them. At the end he said he'd like to buy that one."

"So you took it over to him—" Will gestured at the brown paper.

"She took it over that night." Geoff spoke abruptly. "But he wasn't home. And then it was too late."

"You should be glad I brought it back. I almost left it in his front hall, but something stopped me. My untrusting nature, no doubt. No money, no picture. Otherwise, no telling when we could have recovered it."

"Did the house have any particular historical significance?"

"Not that I know of," Geoff answered. "McCrocken owned it once—built it, I guess—but never lived in it. It was just a rent house. He had three or four of them along the river here." He spread his thin hands. "What Tom *said* was that he liked the summertime look of it."

"He was right." And Will thought he was. The dried-up front yard and the hot blue sky in the background fairly baked in the heat. "It's something I'd like to have myself. What would it put me out?"

Geoff named a figure that make Will blink. "I guess I'd better come back after payday."

Claire was regarding him with amused eyes. "Prices have gone up this week, dear. Geoff's going to have a show."

"Really?" Will—a little put off by the amount Geoff was asking, and thinking privately that the reason Tom had tried to buy this particular canvas was that it was the only small one; God knew what Geoff thought the other ones were worth—looked up and found two different people before him. Two excited people, with starry eyes and all the hardness dropped away. He peered at them through his glasses. "Where?"

"In Chicago."

"A gallery?"

"A top one." Geoff's face was bright with pleasure. "We made the final arrangements yesterday."

"That's great, Geoff. Congratulations. You'll send me an invitation, I hope."

"Natch." They walked with him to the door. Claire had begun to recover some of her brittleness.

"Are you really looking for that treasure, Will? Or is it—I hope—just a short-lived whim? Mrs. Moffat is a bit much, don't you think?" She smiled knowingly at him. "A case of a person clearly wrapped up in herself."

Will, startled, looked down at her.

"If you *do* find it, though, we've got lots of paintings for sale."

"But you needn't come looking for it here," Geoff said genially. "That, at least, wasn't what Tom was after. As I told him, McCrocken only owned these houses for a few years in the 1920s, long before he died. And if anybody needs a clincher, I'm sure that any money found on the property after his death would have legally belonged to the owners."

The phone was ringing as he pushed open his back door. It was Poppy Ruth again.

"I apologize for this morning," she said stiffly. "It was a nice funeral, don't you think?"

"You didn't call me up to chat about that. What do you need this time?"

"Just feeling rather lonely. I thought I'd see if I could take you to dinner."

"I'll pick you up at seven, but it's on me." He looked at his watch. "Where are you calling from, by the way? I thought you would be at Mrs. Moffat's about now."

"I am. She's in the kitchen, getting the tea ready." Will thought he detected some strain.

"How many poor people has she volunteered to give jobs to?"

"A family of four." She was silent for a moment. "She's a nice person."

"I know."

He rang off and put in a call to Junie Hill in New York. Over the wire, behind her "Hello," came the unexpected noise of voices, lots of them, sounds of music, glasses rattling, laughter, and through them again, her faint "Hello."

"Junie!" he shouted.

"Will? Why are you yelling? Are you all right?"

"What's all that noise? Are you having a party?"

"You bet. We're pregnant. And celebrating."

"It's about time. I'm delighted, my dear. Is Roy pregnant, too? Or just you?"

"Both of us," she said firmly. "Hold on a minute."

Will waited. He knew she was going to close the door to the living room, a room he remembered distinctly from past trips to New York and one that Junie and Roy Hill loved because it had a working fireplace and a magnificent carved mantel and a bow window and a high stamped-tin ceiling.

The party sounds were abruptly cut off. "I'm back."

"Did you find the Brewster?"

"Yes. I had the page copied. I'll read it to you."

It took quite a while. When she had finished and Will had gotten it all down, he said, "I appreciate that. Can you do me a couple more favors? First, I'm going to need a hotel room for Christmas Eve and Christmas night."

"Will! You're coming! But you must stay with us."

"I can't. I might not even have time to see you."

They had an argument about that; he won.

"What hotel do you want?"

"The Chevensey, please." It was a small, old place on Central Park West, comfortable and sparkling clean and chintzy. He had always been fond of it. "I don't know where I want to be, but that's handy to both sides of town. And familiar."

They argued again, more briefly, and he was again told about the folding bed in Roy's study and again rejected it.

"Second," he said, "ask Roy to lay hands on a reverse directory for me. I may need it."

"What's going on there?" she asked.

"It will surprise you—not pleasantly." He hadn't gone into it that morning. "Murder and mystery and sinister flowers and a lost treasure. It's been pretty bad."

"Who got murdered?"

"It was Tom, Junie." And after more explanations, because she and Roy had also been acquainted with Tom while he was in New York, he said, "Did you ever hear of a woman named Poppy Ruth?"

"*That* woman! Did she *murder* Tom?"

"No. I don't know. But it looks like it was someone here, name and reasons unknown. What do you know about her?"

"Only that she's horribly rich and that Tom was batty about her for a while. She let him follow her about. But she got tired of being followed eventually and told him to buzz off."

"When was that?"

"Last spring. He was very bitter and hurt. Roy and I thought that was why he left."

"This sounds kind of Edwardian."

"So was Tom. Or tried to be."

"How do you know she was rich?"

"Good grief, Will. How do you know anybody's rich? Tom said she was and she looked like it and dressed like it and lived in a big apartment. Also, I know because of the callous way she let Tom spend money on her. She made him take her to expensive restaurants and to plays and concerts, more than he could afford. Do you know what the theater costs these days? And he was always buying her beautiful little gifts."

They talked awhile longer, about Tom and about themselves. When Will hung up, he found that he had been on the phone almost an hour. He made himself a stiff drink, carried it into the living room, kicked off his shoes, pulled on a sweater he found lying on the end of the couch, found his dog-eared copy of Machiavelli's history of Florence, settled down in the armchair against an ancient brown cushion Dora had picked up somewhere, and fell asleep.

ELEVEN
The Missing Page

He took her to dinner at Green Tavern, near campus. She wore the same gray velvet suit she'd had on at the funeral. He pointed that out to her.

"Even for me, you might have changed," he said. "I expect that a woman who was going away for Christmas would have a lot of clothes with her." But it was an elegant suit, with wide cuffs and a long jacket. It could, Will admitted to himself, be exciting to be taking her out to dinner under other circumstances.

"You'd better not stay much longer," he told her. "There's only one restaurant in town you haven't been to. Then we'll have to start over."

"We would soon be talked about. We probably are already. I feel like you must know everyone here."

"Not everyone. Enough, though."

Will could pick out two former students of his nearby, an education professor he knew, and a sociologist. He had had one of the waiters in class, and some of the foreign-language faculty were gathered at the bar.

"There's an odd-looking fellow," he said. "At least, I've never seen him before."

At a small table in an uncomfortable-looking alcove near the door sat a man remarkable for his height and thinness. He was shabbily dressed, had kept his overcoat on, and had hung his hat on the back of his chair where people coming in kept knocking it off, forcing him to keep looking for it under the table. His overlong yellow hair was crimped and hung almost to his shoulders. He had a small, V-shaped mouth and angular shoulders.

Seeing him, Mrs. Ruth paled. "He's not *that* scary," Will said.

"Yes, he is. Eerie." She really looked as if she were about to cry.

"Interesting, I'd say. Have you ever seen Etruscan statues anywhere? The Met, at least? He reminds me of them."

She closed her eyes.

The man showed no sign of having seen them; neither did he leave. Green Tavern was getting a good crowd that night, and he was soon hemmed in by a line of people waiting for tables. A waiter fought his way through to him now and then, and came back looking exasperated; the man seemed to have ordered nothing more than soup. Only the poor location of his table was keeping the waiter from objecting. For on top of that, he nursed the soup forever, his bony shoulders outlined against the colored lights of the jukebox.

Will ordered steaks for them both, but Poppy Ruth seemed to have lost her appetite, too. "That makes two of you in town," Will said when their waiter had gone away. "If we just wait long enough—"

"Two of whom?"

"Two members of the Close Company of Perfect Strangers. You and our friend over there."

"I've already told you. I belong to no such group."

"If I asked the gentleman to join us—"

She blanched again. "Oh, all right," she said. "It's a private club. And none of your business."

"Tell me about them."

"What do you want to know?"

"The purpose of the group."

"The one I'm here for."

"Ah. Right. Relocating the poor of New York. What about the real purpose?"

She didn't answer.

"How did Tom get mixed up with them, anyway? Your doing?"

"No. He got there the same way everyone else did."

"How was that?"

"Word of mouth. If you lived in New York, some December day you might get an invitation in the mail. At the bottom of the invitation, if you were a new member, would be written the name of the person who recommended you—some name by which you might know him, that is. 'The Redhaired Man on the IND,' for example. To get that invitation, you must have come to know—slightly—someone in the group who, through chance conversation, decides you are a likely addition. Someone you happen to sit beside at a concert, at the park, in a bar, on a train. It could be a neighborhood shopkeeper. It could be a business acquaintance. It could be someone who read about you in the newspaper, or who sees you often on the street, or someone your lawyer consulted about your affairs. The variations are endless."

"But that's all? There's no other way to get in?"

"None. Nor any way even to know that the Company exists. Tom should never have told anyone."

"A new height in exclusiveness. What are the requirements for membership?"

"Five. The means of entry, as I've explained. Patience with detail. Imagination. A certain freedom of movement. And, oh, a certain largeness of spirit."

"Must one be single?"

"No, but most of us are. For one thing, few persons with families can get away on Christmas night."

"Why is that dinner party so important?"

"It's the only time the Company meets."

"What's wrong with meeting more often?"

"We would cease to be strangers."

"And why is that important?"

"It would take all the fun out."

After that she wouldn't answer any more questions. And

when Will looked again, over coffee, the yellow-haired man was gone.

"It depends on the denominations," Will said in answer to Bo's question. "Did anyone look into that the first time around?"

"Look into it?" Bo looked surprised. "How could they? If they didn't know where it was—"

Will had found Louise's apartment dark when he glanced at it on his way home, but the closed and shuttered shop showed a chink of yellow light around the door. Not sleepy yet, he had stopped and been admitted to a small gathering around the coffeepot in back, where Louise, Bo, and Dora were deep in conversation about how big a stack the missing money would make.

"You're right, of course. But they could make a guess. The money had to have come from somewhere, presumably some bank. But which bank? That amount of cash—maybe they kept a record."

"Well, nobody told me about it. Of course, I was just a kid."

"You'd probably have heard. I understand from Mrs. Moffat that you did quite a bit of treasure hunting for them."

Bo grinned. "I certainly did. This time around, I think I'll pass. I don't have time like that anymore. Unless I can find it by just thinking about it." He jerked a thumb at Dora. "She's the one asking the questions."

"I'd like to be rich for a change," Dora said with determination. "Besides, Mother and I want to take a trip." Dora turned to Bo. "I didn't know you were involved back then."

"Lord. Was I ever. Mostly because my dad was the old man's doctor, so when they needed somebody little, they thought of me. And it was all pretty dramatic and secretive for a while. I had fun."

"How old were you?" Dora asked.

"About eleven. I remember the day Gabriel died. We were in the school yard—you know, up there on Indian Avenue?

Where the stationery store is now and those other shops along the drag?"

Dora nodded.

"Well, they weren't there then—that was all open ground. And on the other side of Indian Avenue was the school, the old elementary school. The playground beside it faced south, and the nearest building we could see from there was the old McCrocken home. We were all out at recess that day and we saw the blinds being drawn all over the house and Miss Maisie driving up in her little roadster and running in, and one of the servants going on horseback—they still kept a couple of horses then—to look for the second son, Henry. Edward, the oldest, was in the house already, and my dad's car was parked out front. So we knew what had happened."

"And you helped look for the money afterward?" Louise asked.

"Not right at the beginning—nobody did but the McCrockens at first, before they published the letter and asked everyone to help. But pretty soon Maisie came over to the house one day and asked if I'd like to help. They needed a boy to wiggle in places but someone strong enough to give Edward and Henry a hand with the lifting and all. I was young but kind of rough and tough. So I did treasure hunting sooner than most."

"I hope they paid you for it," Louise said. "It sounds like a lot of hard work."

"You don't need to pay a kid to hunt for treasure. But we had an arrangement. I got a quarter a day, and I could keep anything I found that they didn't want. I found a lot of stuff, too. I used to keep it in a cigar box at home. Some old playing cards and a yellow pig and some bits of broken glass and a seashell. Things like that."

"Have you kept them all these years?" From a cupboard in the shop storeroom Louise brought out a bottle of brandy and some plastic glasses.

"Nope," Bo answered. "At least, I did, but the last time I

looked, a long time ago, I couldn't find the box. My copy of the letter was in it. It's gone, too."

"That's no great loss," said Dora firmly. "I don't see how he expected anyone to make sense of it."

"It isn't that bad," Will said.

Bo sipped at the brandy Louise handed him. "I thought it was awful."

"Take a look at this, then." Will took a folded sheet of paper from his pocket. "It comes from a book by a man named Brewster," he told them. Out of the corner of his eye he saw Louise's puzzled glance. "Someone has defaced the only two publicly available copies in town, recently in the case of at least one of them. This is part of the missing material."

Instantly Dora wanted to know how he'd come by it, but he didn't answer. Instead he said to Bo: "Is there anything there that you didn't know about McCrocken? Or would it all have been old news to the town?" He pushed the paper around so they could all see it.

> *McCrocken, Gabriel Drummond.* (1/6/68–   ) *B.* Surrey Co., Va., to Sarah McLean and Donald Drummond McCrocken (estate agent and acct.), Sc. immigrants. Sixth child of ten. Moved to Memphis (1876), thence to St. Louis and to Kan. Cy., Mo., shortly thereafter. *Educ.* Miss Bright's School (Kan. Cy.), St. Roper's Acad. (Va.), Columbia (N.Y.C.). A.B. 1888; Ph.D. 1895. Instr. Columbia 1895–1896. Pub. monographs on Eur. warfare (1893), Fr. rom. (1894), theory on birth and devel. of towns, esp. comp. Med. and Am. towns (1895). Invited by Chilton Black & Co., N.Y.C. (now defunct), to expand latter; traveled west on tour of study (via Gr. Nor. R.R.). *Settled* Crosscreek, S.D. (1896). *Mar.* Cornelia Isabelle Nilsson (1905). *Children:* Edward McLean (1908), Henry Nilsson (1909), Maisie Ann (1910), Sarah Margaret (1911). *Rel.:* Epis. *Membs.:* Crosscreek City Council; His. Soc. Am.; Soc. Am.

West; Friends of Scand.; C.U. Loyal Order Yellow Panthers. *Professor,* Crosscreek Univ. (1896 to present); chaired Dept. Hist. (1923 to present). *Major pubs.: The Northmen in the North Plains; The Cycle from Settlement to Town; The Dakota Territory: Beginnings to Statehood; Travelling in the Rockies.* Also num. art.

"I don't know if I knew it or not," Bo said, halfway through. "I can barely read it." When he finished, he shook his head. "I knew most of that at the end. I didn't know any of the beginning."

"Four children?" Dora asked. "What happened to Sarah Margaret?"

"Died young," said Bo. "Or so I heard."

Dora was rereading it. *"Who* was St. Roper?" she asked. "And what is the Loyal Order of Yellow Panthers? Do they still exist on campus?"

"There's too much there," Bo said flatly.

Will was watching Louise. Her head was bent over the page. "What do you see?" he asked her.

She looked up with a smile. "New York? Such a different life. He might have been almost a different person."

"Possibly. But how do you mean?"

"I don't really know what I mean. I was only thinking that he didn't step off that train tailored to Crosscreek and that big house on Victory Street. He was a young man, a New Yorker—" She spread her hands. "I had an odd feeling after reading that. Of all the people I've heard talking about Gabriel McCrocken, no one quite gave me that impression of him."

"Maisie needed you," Will said.

Bo Jenkins pushed back his chair. "I'm tired."

"We should all go," Dora said. "Louise looks ready to drop." She began handing around the coats and scarves. "Come on, Will. It's not past *your* bedtime, I know, but you have to think of others."

But Will contrived to linger behind.

"I am so very sorry about Lucy Mellon," Louise told him, in the shadows of the front of the shop. "I guess you don't have any idea who did it?"

Will surveyed her soberly. "I've narrowed the list a little, that's all. But it's still longish. Or nonexistent, depending on how you look at it."

"Who's on it? Can you tell me? Oh, Will, what an awful business this is. That we're all making lists—in our minds, anyway. Lists of our friends. But who else might have wanted to kill Tom, and then Lucy, except someone we all know?"

"Yes. The first problem, of course, is the motive."

"I suppose I had one. To some people."

"For each other, you and I should head the list. You because of money." He shoved his glasses up on his nose. "I looked for insurance policies in Tom's house yesterday, Louise. If there were any, Winterlin must have them."

"I don't know about that. Tom never mentioned it."

"No. But at least his university group insurance would have been in force. Thirty thousand dollars or so to his beneficiary. Whoever that was. I'd guess his next of kin. And, God knows, you could use it."

His chest hurt from saying these things, but he went on. And the more he talked, the more the uncertainty dropped away from her. She wasn't angry, she was just reflective. He hoped she knew he was making a necessary confession.

"You have been surrounded by death," he told her, "and now you have at last profited from it. Winterlin will have thought of that, too."

"And so have I."

"Of course. And also wondered about me. I was angry at Tom that night and told you so. And after all, how well do you know me?"

She smiled. "You *can't* care about me that much. Not even if it had been a . . . a kind of hoax, with an unforeseen ending."

His reply died on his lips. That night he hadn't. Since then . . . but they weren't talking about since then.

"What do you think about me?" she asked. "And if you're sure of me, why?"

"You weren't there last night. You couldn't have heard what Lucy said."

"That's true. And wouldn't, couldn't ever, have killed him. What I wanted was to keep him. So who's left?"

"Oh, it's still a hell of a list. Dora, possibly, for jealousy of Poppy Ruth. Poppy Ruth wasn't at the party, either, but I still don't trust her. She's up to something. Geoff and Claire Bordeaux are mixed up in it somehow. Your Etruscan is in town. The people at the party, for reasons unknown. At the moment, though, I'm most interested in what these Strangers are doing."

"Me, too."

"Louise, I'm going to have to renege on that invitation to Christmas dinner."

"That's all right," she said.

"Is it?" He felt let down.

"I even have another invitation. Dora asked me tonight to join her and her mother."

"That's good. You'll like Mrs. Chandler. In the meantime—"

"Yes?"

"I don't know. Just be careful." He gestured impatiently. "I wish there was something I could to do to help solve this, but the best thing is certainly to stay out of Winterlin's way. I can't find out anything he's not better at except check up on those Strangers. But it's damned frustrating."

"Perhaps he should follow up on that, too?"

"Go to New York?" Will shook his head. "On what evidence? It's a long shot. An inquiry by the New York cops wouldn't help much, either. I'd be afraid the Strangers would just melt away before it. So I'll do that and you'll be careful and I'll also try to find McCrocken's money. Maisie needs it."

"Do you think Tom could have been looking for it?"

"It's possible. But there's no particular reason to think he had been. Now," he said, "you go to bed. Dora was right. You do look tired."

"Tonight is better than last night," she said. "Still, I'm glad today is over."

"Yes," he said. "A good day to be done with."

But his own day wasn't quite finished. As he stepped out onto the sidewalk, he saw that a light was burning in the *News* offices. Bo's mention of his missing letter had started a small train of thought in the back of Will's head.

The *News* occupied a narrow building on the opposite side of the square. The secretary–receptionist–advertising manager who helped Jed put out the paper was just letting herself out when he arrived; she told him to go on down to the basement reference room and help himself. Will thought he recognized one of last year's graduating journalism students under the immense blue plaid scarf that covered her head and face except for a pair of sharp blue eyes.

Under a glaring ceiling bulb, he discovered that the paper kept bound volumes of its back issues on bookshelves along the wall. In the center of the room were filing cabinets, and in them were manila envelopes of clippings.

Will opened the drawer where McCrocken's file should be. There was an envelope there all right, labeled *McCrocken Library*, and another marked *McCrocken, Maisie (Mrs. Toby Moffat)*. There was no envelope for Gabriel. He flipped rapidly through the rest of the M's, to see if it had been misplaced. As he had expected, it wasn't there.

Unless somone had taken it upstairs. He turned to the bound copies, kneeling and hunting along the shelves in the semidarkness. *1940.*

As he drew the volume out, leaning forward to blow dust from the top of the pages, he felt the back cover move under his fingers. About two-thirds of the way through, most of the pages were missing, leaving a fringe of edges. Will put the book on the floor and turned to September. From the middle of the month on, almost everything was gone.

He replaced the book and lifted out the volume for 1941. The first months were similarly riddled.

On the second floor, in what the small *News* staff called the city room, he found Jed McIngling. He sat at his desk, his feet up on an opened drawer, hunched over a paperback novel and smoking. A Styrofoam cup of black coffee was at his elbow. The other two desks in the room were bare, typewriters covered, phones quiet.

Jed looked up from his book as Will came up the stairs. "What's up?"

Will told him. "Somebody's got the Gabriel McCrocken file. Do you suppose it's up here?"

"You wanted that? Could've saved you the trouble. Should've asked. It's been gone for"—he squeezed his eyes shut and furrowed his brow—"eight years." He opened his eyes. "That we know of. Nothing since—about McCrocken, that is. Ergo, no new file."

"Who took it?"

"Who took it? Dastards and vandals. Rats. Same rats that ate up 'forty and 'forty-one, I imagine."

"Rats with pockets. And razor-blade teeth."

"The same. Was it important, what you wanted?"

"I found what I wanted, so I'll say good night. Merry Christmas, Jed."

"So glad we could oblige." Jed went back to his book.

TWELVE
The Letter Revealed

For others, the Saturday and Sunday before Christmas were busy; for Will they dragged endlessly on.

He was restless, but for all his moving about, up and down Crosscreek, he found no relief. The days were overcast and cold, the town without the students seemed too quiet, the house was utterly silent. He spent hours hunched over the kitchen table with Gabriel McCrocken's letter in front of him; he seemed to walk miles in the muffled streets thinking, letting his mind wander, sometimes dropping in to have a drink with someone.

Now and then a car would go by, or a bundled-up figure plodding along through the snow. Because it was cloudy, most of the houses stayed lighted up all day long; there was an atmosphere of privacy about each house—families inside getting ready for Christmas, bright kitchens, packages being wrapped, relatives in the living rooms.

Dora and her mother put up their tree. Joey Livingston, Will found, was spending most of his time on bird-watching hikes in the country. On Saturday afternoon, Lucy Mellon was buried. Will went; he was somewhat surprised to see that Maisie Moffat was there, too.

Poppy Ruth didn't call him that day.

Mack Winterlin, he discovered, had been from one end of town to the other. He showed around the envelope found in Tom's pocket. He asked questions about all sorts of things. He talked to all the people who could be regarded as Tom's friends. He talked to colleagues who were only acquaintances, who had done no more than serve on a committee with him, or cosponsor a student group. He interviewed the neighbors—such as they were, for Tom's house was nearly hidden by some woods and by a turning in the street—about Tom's habits and inquired of each, again, whom they had seen near Tom's house on Tuesday night. Again and again he went over who was where at Thursday night's party, who went home early, who was talking to whom.

He was doing his best to tread delicately, it appeared, to accuse no one, to alarm no one. Mrs. Bordeaux was amused at his cautious inquiries; Dr. Livingston was laconic. Geoff Bordeaux was impatient with him; he had the McCrocken portrait to finish and was too edgy to sit still and too preoccupied, when he did sit down, to listen. Dora and Mrs. Chandler were polite but, for their various reasons, not much help. Dora told Will that Winterlin seemed to be running out of questions.

Louise Tree had asked if Winterlin was finished in Tom's house. She needed to get it in order. It had only been rented, furnished, and she wanted to turn it back over to the rental agent. She told Will that Winterlin had asked her to wait for a few days.

Poppy Ruth respectfully requested permission to return to New York for Christmas. She called Will once on Sunday, in a fret over not having yet received an answer. She said she'd canceled her trip to California. He told her to drop that piece of track covering; she'd never been going there in the first place. She hissed at him and hung up.

Packages came in the mail for Will, from his family. He stacked the parcels in the living room without opening them, and went on prowling about the town, and thinking.

"Tell me about Maisie," Will said to Bo on Sunday about noon. He'd stopped by the station on one of his walks, and the two of them were sitting inside, their feet propped on the low sill of the big front window, listening to the coffeepot burble behind them and watching the cars go by on Main Street.

"What about her?"

"I hear she used to go out with Tom's father."

Bo shot him an odd look. "I wasn't born then, you know." He turned his coffee cup in his hands. "But as a matter of fact, that's true."

Will waited, and finally Bo went on.

"I know that because she mentioned it once when Tom's dad was coming here to see Louise before he was killed. We saw him once, coming out of the bookstore, when I was driving Maisie around one day. Maisie nearly fell out of the car. Said he hadn't changed at all, except for some creases. But she wouldn't let me take her back to say hello. She said she was just glad to see him looking so well and that if Louise Tree was any evidence, he'd married into a nice family. And a hardworking one."

The bell clanged as a car drove in. Bo got slowly to his feet. "Goodness knows that's the truth," he said. "The other night Maisie made me take her over to Jed's late, so she could hang around and bother him while he put that flyer together. I couldn't bear to be a party to it, so I went over to see Louise. Ten-thirty at night it was, and she was still there in the shop, doing accounts or something, and the place still a mess the way people had left it. I straightened up for her while she got the paperwork done. Good thing, too." His face was dark. "She'd never have gotten to bed. As it was, it was almost midnight before we knocked off. That was when Maisie showed up, and by then I could tell Louise was nearly dead. She says she can't afford a helper, but she sure needs one."

The car outside honked impatiently, and Bo went out to see to it. When he came back, Will said, "Seems to me like you've been putting in hours beyond the call of duty, too. Does Maisie require a lot of unscheduled driving around like that?"

"No, not so much. I don't mind."

"You must have gotten to be pretty good friends after all these years."

"I guess so. A shared past is what counts the most, though. In our way we've got that."

So they did, Will thought as he walked home. Two people, he'd bet, who would do a lot for each other, too, if they ever had to.

On Sunday afternoon, Will decided to call Mr. Mellon. Either way, he thought as he dialed the number, there might be some value here. Penance for his time-wasting foolishness, or repayment for information. It might help Mellon out, as well.

Mr. Mellon answered after many rings. His voice was dull.

"I'll take that talk, and Luke, off your hands if you want me to," Will said. "But I'd need Tom's notes; it would be easier if I didn't have to start from scratch. I wondered if you'd given it any further thought, or spoken to Winterlin about them."

Mellon, with difficulty, put together a few sentences from the other end of the line. Truitt Roberts was going to do the talk. Mellon greatly appreciated Will's offer, but it wasn't necessary. Anyway, there weren't any notes. Nothing at all. He'd spoken to Winterlin about it the night before, thinking it might take his mind off things. Oh yes, they were quite sure. Only a folder on his desk with one item in it: a photocopy of McCrocken's letter—with Bo Jenkins's name printed across the top in what looked like crayon, oddly enough.

Will hung up, whistling under his breath. It wasn't much, but it was the best news he'd had in days.

Dusk fell early, that day before Christmas Eve. It had been a dark, cold day, windless and damp, with the smell of snow in the air.

His empty coffee cup beside him, Will stretched out on the couch with a pillow under his head and his heels up on the couch arm. He'd started a small fire in the fireplace; the house was quiet and getting warmer at last. Amigo passed across his field of vision from time to time, on business of his own, his tail held in a question mark.

McCrocken, he reflected, had been a historian, a businessman, a builder of sorts. A specialist in western and American studies. Devoted to Crosscreek; closely involved with the town and the university. Humorous, kind, hardheaded, shrewd, capable of many things. A scholar and a wealthy man. And he had died over forty years ago.

The points of resemblance between McCrocken and himself—history, Crosscreek, the university—had never satisfied Will's feeling, as he'd read that letter, that in some way they had a common point of view. The town and campus that Will knew were greatly changed; their fields were worlds apart . . . What the hell was he overlooking?

With a thump, out of the near-dark, Amigo landed on his chest, purring throatily. He rubbed his cheeks against Will's, one side and then the other, and sat down on his chest and stared at him.

"Supper?" Will asked. "I bet it's time."

But he didn't move. The color had almost gone from the room; in the last light through the window beside the fireplace, the crimsons and dark browns of furniture and wallpaper had faded together into a background of dull shades whose outlines ran together and were lost. Amigo's black fur was edged in flame by the glow in the fireplace; he looked flat and two-dimensional, like a figure in a medieval tapestry, shabby with age.

The north windows rattled in their frames, and his cat made a mewling sound in his throat.

"Jack Frost on the prowl," he said. "Can you see him?" Then, "Let's go find out if there's any cat food in the kitchen." And halfway up, as Amigo bounded onto the floor, Will froze in place at last with understanding. That was it. That was the connection between them. Gabriel McCrocken had spent most of his academic life as an American West historian, but he had started it as a medievalist.

In the kitchen, as he opened a can of cat food and spooned it out into Amigo's bowl, he recalled the line from Brewster's biography as he had read it on Friday afternoon, as they had all interpreted it on Friday night at the bookstore: *Published monographs on European warfare (1893), the French romantics (1894), the theory on birth and development of towns, especially comparing Mediterranean and American towns (1895).*

With the bowl in his hand and Amigo trotting anxiously at his heels, he went to the worktable at the end of the room, moved papers and books about till he found it, and read the sentence again.

For it could be interpreted differently: *Published monographs on European warfare (1893), the French romances (1894), the theory on birth and development of towns, especially comparing medieval and American towns (1895).*

The abbreviation *rom.* could stand for romantics or romances, but seven hundred years' difference lay between them. Brewster should have had the wits to make it plain. And *Med.* with a capital *M*, especially up against another place name, *American*, suggested only Mediterranean. But it had to be *medieval*. It made far more sense for McCrocken, as a student of small towns, to take an interest in comparing the new settlements of the American continent to the villages of medieval Europe, with their similar climates, agricultural conditions, and isolation—and their subsequent cultural links—than it would to look instead at the very different Mediterranean world.

But could he be sure of that? Will stared down at the paper. There would have been the desolation of the plains to compare with Spain and Africa and the Middle East. The heat. The absence of timber. Sheep. And maybe he had been right in the first place; maybe *rom.* stood for romantics after all.

He set the bowl of cat food on the windowsill and dialed

Maisie Moffat's number. At his feet, Amigo wore a desperate face. The phone rang a long time.

At last she answered. She sounded out of breath.

"Mrs. Moffat?" Will told her about the three monographs. "Do you have copies of them?"

"Three monographs? I don't think so, dear. I have all of Papa's books, of course, but . . ." She hesitated. "Now wait. There's an old pamphlet, I remember. Would that be what you mean?"

"It could be. Do you know the name of it?"

Amigo leaped onto the worktable. Will lifted him down again.

"No, I don't. If you'd like to come by after dinner, I can get it for you."

"If I could just know the name . . ."

"Well, suppose I go look it up?"

"Would you?"

Will caught the bowl just as it began to slide off the sill from the force of Amigo's second leap. "What's wrong with you?" he whispered fiercely. And then realized what he was after. "Hell, Amigo, I'm sorry." He put cat food and cat on the floor.

Maisie was back.

"I've got it, Dr. Gray. It's just the one. I don't know what happened to the other two. I never saw them."

"That's all right. What's the one called?"

"It's . . . let me get it under the light. There. It's dated 1893. The title is 'Methods and Tools of Frankish and Teutonic Warfare from the Sixth to the Tenth Centuries.'"

Will sighed with relief.

"Good enough. Did you know your father was a medievalist?"

"I did not. How on earth—"

"What about his library? Did he have any books on medieval history or literature?"

"No. All he had was American history."

"What about Mediterranean cultures?" Will still wanted to be sure about that. "Or the French romantic poets?"

"Not a line."

"And nothing but this monograph about the medieval period. Did you ever hear him mention it?"

"All he ever talked about was Indians and pioneers and Scandinavians."

"Okay. Thanks a lot."

It was surprising but not too surprising, he thought as he watched Amigo eat. Gabriel had moved from an early interest in the medieval period to a particular interest in towns. He had been sent west to do a special study by a New York publisher and had gone not to live but for a short stay. He wouldn't have brought his books with him, or anything else but a suitcase of clothes.

But he had liked the plains, particularly the new little settlement of Crosscreek, building itself up, talking about a university, needing the twisting, tree-lined Pebble River but tending to edge away from it in its unplanned growth.

He could stay and watch the town grow. Maybe have a hand in shaping it. But he was a scholar first and a businessman second—then, in fact, the latter only embryonically. He had to earn his living. The brand-new Crosscreek University, still on paper that first year, did not yet need a medievalist, but it did need American historians. He could learn to do that, too.

There was a frozen pizza in the refrigerator. Will got it out, turned on the oven, and laid a place for himself at the kitchen table. From a cabinet he brought out a jug of red wine and put it on the table next to the blue-shaded lamp. It wasn't long before he could smell the sausage and cheese and tomato sauce beginning to heat up.

He had no idea where the treasure was. But it was closer now than it had ever been to Maisie and Henry and Edward. He *would* know, tonight, if it took all night to find out.

Had Tom known? Had Tom seen the significance of that

page, or had he come to the treasure from some other direction? But if so, how? Apparently Brewster had discovered and put down, although carelessly, the one major bit of information about Gabriel's past that had not been known in Crosscreek. And if Tom, reading up on McCrocken for his talk, had seen it, too . . . but Will thought something else had been going on regarding Tom and that book. He carried his plate to the sink. That came next. It wasn't something he could make sense of tonight.

The letter stared up at him from the kitchen table. The hands of the clock stood at ten. *It grows late—the crescent moon, though high, seems thin and pale and far away in a summer sky so thickly crossed with stars.*

Maisie had thought the number 190 referred to a page number in a book. It could, but in what book, for God's sake? The letter should be telling him that.

She had compared herself to a sibyl. "I can give you masses of information," she had told him, "from which the answer can be plucked out, but I can't get it out myself." He had never followed up on that remark.

He glanced at his watch. Not late, but would she be asleep? He brought the feet of his chair down to the floor with a bang that made Amigo open his eyes, and went to the phone. She answered almost immediately.

"I thought it would be you. I've been waiting up. Have you solved it?"

"Not yet. Tell me something. What struck you particularly when you first read your father's letter?"

"How ill he must have been. How pain and age had changed him in ways we had been blind to till then. And how—well, *stoic* and brave, to have fought it and managed to hide his real message in all that."

"In all what?"

"Oh . . . the adjectives. The funny, sentimental way of

putting things. The elaborateness. Papa's ordinary style was rather spare. I cried at the time."

Will smiled. "Go to bed," he said. "It may take me a long time yet. I'll call you in the morning."

"Have you had a chance to look for that woman I saw?"

"Yes. That's taken care of, sort of. I'll tell you about that tomorrow, too."

The adjectives, the words, the adorned style, working in lots of words that would not otherwise have fit. Words that were meant to suggest something. Not a hiding place but the source of the "190."

Will went back to work.

It did take him a long time. His sense of recognition had come, like Maisie's sense of unfamiliarity, from certain words that seemed to gather themselves into clusters he had seen somewhere before. He read and marked and made lists. He eliminated what seemed to be direct and untrimmed statements. He let associations gather in his mind.

Loyalty and its course, hidden wealth, something taken from earth, lost but enduring. The gold of the Nibelungs?

Elephantine infidelity, peerless integrity, the question of right, the mention of kings. Something from the Arthurian cycle?

An old fool, caroling in the darkness of an old age. Some song or ballad—Caedmon's hymn, perhaps, or "The Wanderer"?

The aged, uncertain friendship, loyalty, a hard battle. *Beowulf?*

Or would it be something French? Two of the three monographs were specifically studies of Frankish warfare and literature.

Amigo stretched and yawned and rolled over on his back, paws bent loosely over his chest. He flexed his toes, glinted at Will through sleepy eyes, and sighed.

With his pencil, Will carefully circled two words: *caroling* and *elephantine*. In the margin he wrote others: *carol, Carolus, Charles; elephant, olifant.*

So that was it. *The Song of Roland.*

He got up stiffly, searched among odds and ends over the stove, and brought out a teapot and a tea caddy. While he waited for the water to boil, he opened the back door and stepped out on the porch.

The cold was bitter. He stood on the porch and absorbed it as Amigo liked to absorb the sun's heat on his fur.

A simple and obvious solution after all.

But Maisie would want to have it spelled out, to show her friends. Will took a clean sheet of paper and went through the letter from beginning to end, putting down a number of references to the poem, with notes of explanation.

15 August	15 August 778; the Battle of Roncesvalles, of which the poem tells the story
crescent	the emblem of the Saracens, whom the French had gone to fight
cross[ed]	the emblem of the Christians (Charlemagne's men)
joyous	Joyeuse, the name of Charlemagne's sword
high and bright	Hauteclair, the sword of Oliver, Roland's friend
field of flowers	field of battle; flower of French knighthood, destroyed in the fight
enduring	Durendal, Roland's sword

their march	Charlemagne and his men were marching back to France from Spain when the rear guard was ambushed; also, Roland, Duke of the Marches of Brittany and leader of the guard
passes	the pass through the Pyrenees, where the ambush took place
friendship	the notable friendship between Roland and Oliver, celebrated in the poem
wiped out	the French troops, killed to a man in the battle
elephantine	*olifant*, Roland's horn
infidel	another reference to the Saracens
peer	the lost Twelve Peers of France, of whom Roland was one, who died in the battle
I am far in the vanguard	Charlemagne and the army
train	the baggage train that the rear guard was protecting
if my support comes too late	Charlemagne's did

caroling	Carolus, Charles, Charlemagne
unbelievers	Saracens again

None of them, Will felt sure, was meaningful in itself; the aggregate, though, gave him the source he had been looking for, in which *190* would be important. With a list like that, no one could doubt that *Roland* was the reference.

At the letter's last paragraph, Will paused. *One thing more remains to say: Once even unbelievers had magic guides, taken from the earth, to brighten the night and carry them in to shore.* There it was, he thought—the particular clue within *Roland* to which *190* pointed. Not that he remembered *Roland*, chapter and verse, that well, but he would have bet on it.

He kept most of his books at home, on shelves in the dining room. *Roland* should be among them.

He brought two editions back into the kitchen, one a copy in the original Old Norman, the other a prized and battered translation by Léonce Rabillon. The latter differed somewhat from the Oxford manuscript that the Old Norman edition reproduced, but it was probably close enough for Will's purpose and his Old Norman was rusty, at best. Unless, of course, his supposition about the magic guides were incorrect and McCrocken meant instead to point to page 190 of his own translation, whatever that might have been. Maisie had said he'd kept no such books, though, and Will was sure McCrocken had been too much of a scholar to have used anything less than an original source. He turned to stanza 190.

> *Granz sunt les oz de cele gent averse*
> *Siglent a fort e nagent e guvernent*
> *En sum cez maz e en cez haltes vernes*
> *Asez i ad carbuncles e lanternes*
> *La sus amunt pargetent tel luiserne*
> *Par la noit la mer en est plus bele*

E cum il vienent en Espaigne la tere
Tut li pais en reluist e esclairet
Jesqua Marsilie en parvunt les noveles

A quick reading filled him with elation. Rusty or not, no one could have missed the fourth line, and the reference to carbuncles and lanterns. Carbuncles, he knew, were red jewels valued for their lanternlike properties. Superstition had it that a carbuncle could light up the darkness with its own fire.

So, according to stanza 190, Gabriel had not hidden his quarter million in cash but had converted it instead to jewels. Perhaps to red ones—garnets, rubies. And where were the jewels? He had been led to *The Song of Roland* and within it to this reference to gems. It should also lead him to their location. He opened the Rabillon and found the same passage.

> Great are the forces of their hostile horde;
> They swiftly skim the waves, and steer, and sail;
> Their masts and yards so blazing with the light
> Of carbuncles and lanterns, night gives up
> Its darkness and still fairer shows the sea.
> As they approached the shores of Spain, the land
> Was all aglow, and tidings reached Marsile.

Well, they weren't, at least, on masts. Pebble River supported only the occasional rowboat. But they might be hung high, nevertheless.

Hung high, with lanterns? Did that make any sense? Not that he could tell, but it was the only starting place he had. He went back to the letter. Were there any other mentions of light and its location?

In the first paragraph he found what he was looking for. The reference to the high crescent moon, and then the strange line, *The bow, so thin it is only a token moon, bears down upon so high and bright a field of flowers that I think you must be able, as you read, weeks hence, to see it, too.* Assuming

McCrocken hadn't left the jewels on the moon . . . well, of course not—a "token moon," he'd said. A bow above and . . . yes, of course. For Will had seen, countless times, another high, thin crescent curving down over a bright field of flowers. Lit by a lantern, of sorts.

I could not fill the darkness with such [magic] light for you; I have tried to brighten it a bit, symbolically. The glow is false. False. Will smiled. That was so, but it was a clever and highly misleading way to put it.

It was almost three o'clock. A good four hours before daylight. He knew where the treasure was; the last check, to be absolutely sure, could wait till morning. But he wasn't sleepy, and in the morning there would be people about. He couldn't bring it home, but he could go look at it.

Most of the clouds were gone. No moon tonight, but a lot of stars. Between the starlight and the streetlights and the brightness of the snow, Will had no trouble seeing his way. He didn't have far to go.

In front of the Mellon house, Will stopped and leaned on the black iron fence. No one was out; not even a car passed within his hearing. Occasionally, an ice-covered bush rustled stiffly in the breeze. Will leaned on the fence and waited, watching the house and letting his eyes adjust to the light. The house was dark; Mr. Mellon was, he hoped, fast asleep.

Over the front door, the fanlight was shaded by the high porch ceiling. A semicircle of black wrought iron; beneath it, a stained-glass pattern of fruit and flowers and leaves. With no light behind it, and very little light on it, it should have been perfectly dark.

But as he watched, one gleam and then another winked out at him, above the tall, heavy door. A shot of red, of green, of white. There were purples and blues there, too, Will knew, but no color came from them.

Gabriel had mixed them, then—stained glass and precious stones set in the same pattern.

He stood there a long time. At last a car, going north on

Alcott Road from the university, turned onto Victory. Its headlights swung over the front of the McCrocken-Mellon house and glanced along the porch.

A burst of red cherries, a mass of green ivy, a field of white daisies rambled haphazardly above the lintel.

The car passed behind him, creaking in the snow, and turned up Indian Avenue. In a moment the night was still again. Will turned away from the fence and walked home to bed.

THIRTEEN

New York

It was Monday noon and Christmas Eve Day, and there was a lot to do. Will had put on a white shirt and suit and tie. In the kitchen, nothing remained of his night's work. All of it, including the two copies of *Roland*, was in an envelope on the car seat beside him.

In his pocket he had Louise's list of flower senders; on the backseat was a carry-on suitcase. Lined up on the kitchen floor, to Amigo's amazement, he had left four large bowls of dry food, interspersed with four bowls of water.

Clipped to Louise's list was the result of a conversation he'd had with Mr. Wicket, florist. Wicket, with a lot of coaxing and encouragement, had produced a little data—amounting to the information that six orders for flowers from people on Louise's list had come from the same establishment in New York: the Mary Gold Flower Shop on Columbus Avenue. "Good enough," Will had told him. "You're a champ."

He hadn't bothered to call Poppy Ruth. Mack Winterlin's orders notwithstanding, he knew they'd meet again in New York.

The big house on Elderberry Street was his first stop. Will took the manila envelope in with him.

Maisie was in her best dress. It differed from the black dresses she often wore only in its scoop neck bordered with flat black cotton lace roses over pink silk. She was even wearing a hat, a twenty-five-year-old black felt hat that made a half moon on the top of her head. Appropriate, Will noticed, with a smile.

"I'm going to lunch at River Inn," she announced as she opened the door. "I'm taking Mellon. I just called him up and said so. He needs to get out more." She led him into the living room and sat down on the edge of a chair. "Are we rich or poor this morning?"

"Rich." Will handed her the envelope.

"Should I open it?"

"Not yet. Let me tell you about it first."

His second stop was a brief one at the bookstore, where he collected the key to Tom's house from Louise. "If you're caught, you stole it," she told him. "He still won't let even me in."

"He'll never know," Will said.

The house had a deserted feeling that had grown in the last few days. Once the front door had closed behind him, the musty smell of the shaded and airless rooms made him want to tiptoe.

Finding the invitation took longer than he had expected. Tom had been careless with his mail. A few Christmas cards were strewn on the hall table along with Luke's cable, some in their envelopes, some out. He found a phone bill on top of the refrigerator and a couple of circulars on the dining-room table.

Upstairs, on the bedroom chest, lay a bank statement. Beside it, the invitation to the university's Christmas party. A thick envelope of Christmas seals was under the alarm clock. It had run down long ago.

Maybe there just wasn't one. It could have been understood. Will walked back to the head of the staircase.

The hall table. He had forgotten the drawer.

The drawer was empty except for a broken pencil and a candle end. He put his hands in his pockets and looked around. Stuck in some book, perhaps? Or fallen under the couch? Taken into the den, maybe.

Under the Sunday paper he'd seen there before was what

must have been that last Saturday's mail. He glanced rapidly at each item. Christmas cards, mostly, a bill, junk mail, two little envelopes that looked like invitations and that bore Crosscreek postmarks, and one large heavy one from New York.

Will opened it and pulled out a cream-colored card, engraved in small black capitals:

AS IN THE PAST
THE CHRISTMAS NIGHT FEAST
OF
THE CLOSE COMPANY OF PERFECT STRANGERS
WILL TAKE PLACE
AT 9 O'CLOCK
IN
THE ROOM BELOW
THE STREET

Nuts, he thought. At least this wasn't what Poppy Ruth had been after in Tom's house. She would have known it was too innocuous to matter. He put it in his pocket and locked the front door behind him.

Between Crosscreek and Sioux Falls, his mind was occupied with the questions of whether the "room below the street" was, in fact, a restaurant or referred to a private house, and how he was to go about finding it in time. Still, he had the invitation. If he could find the place, he could get in. Till Poppy Ruth saw him, at least. And when that happened— well, he thought he'd have the Etruscan's help.

From the air at night, the canyons of New York turned into depths of light, gold and pink and orange, with blue strings for the bridges, layered endlessly deep in the blackness and run through with the dark channels of the sea. Will peered down through the little window, as glad as ever to see them.

And then the plane stopped circling and dipped sharply, and there were ordinary houses and traffic signals and streets crowded together, more water, and the end of the runway.

La Guardia was showy with noise and people and decorations, the rumble of jets and the sweet-voiced flight announcers. Inside the terminal, Will bought the most detailed map of Manhattan he could find and three paperbound restaurant guides.

Outside, along the curb, little clusters of people lined up at the cab stand, waiting for the yellow taxis that wheeled down from the street above in an endless procession, their windshield wipers going.

Then someone was opening a yellow door and hoisting his bag up front beside the driver.

"Manhattan," he said.

Roy Hill turned up at the Chevensey only minutes after Will checked in, full of Christmas cheer and bearing the reverse directory Will had asked for under his arm, wrapped up in brown paper and spotted with rain.

"Junie says I can't come home unless I bring you back with me," he announced. "For at least an hour. She's sure you can spare an hour. Good grief, Will, what are you up to?" He looked around at the litter of papers and books and maps Will had already spread out. His long face was benevolent over the collar of his belted coat. The Manhattan yellow pages captured his attention. "Whom could you possibly be calling on Christmas Eve?"

"Anybody I can raise," Will grinned. "How've you been? I do seem to be considerably short on time. Got any to spare? I might need help. I don't know if I can accommodate Junie just yet."

"You've got any help I can give. Around here it's a holiday, so I'm all yours. But you've got to see Junie first. Then we'll come back here and tie into it."

On those grounds Will allowed himself to be taken away

and put into Roy's car. The traffic was nonexistent; within minutes Junie was hugging him and making a place on the sofa, among a dozen crewelwork cushions, and Roy was putting a drink in his hand, and the fragrant branches of the Christmas tree were thrusting out over the top of his head.

"I wish you hadn't asked Junie how she knew Mrs. Ruth was rich," Roy said, after they had exchanged news about mutual friends and made sure each other was contented with life and that the present was secure and the future bright. "She's been dreaming up schemes ever since to prove she was right."

"I suppose it's obvious." Will looked at her with affection. He could have predicted she would take his doubt as some kind of challenge. "But there's a hell of a lot of money floating around in the background of Tom's murder. At least, it seems a lot to me and would to you two. I guess that Mrs. Ruth wouldn't exactly be overcome with greed, though."

He found an ashtray on the end table beside him.

"Beyond that, I can't justify my asking. It was one of those indefinable impressions one sometimes gets of people. Maybe those who are worried about money develop a different set of wrinkles that we recognize but don't know why. Or think we recognize." He had to laugh at Junie's smug expression.

"Will, you're remarkable," she said. "Just remarkable."

They all sat and beamed at each other for a minute, pleased with each other and themselves.

"Well, it was embarrassing," Roy said. "She has untold amounts of gall. I had to leave the house sometimes. At any rate, you made a convert. The kind who thinks it was all her own idea in the first place. Aren't you going to tell him?" he asked his wife. "He's been here forty-five minutes now. You must be about to burst."

"It was low," Junie warned him. "Do you really want to know about her? If it's not important, I won't tell you."

"I want to know."

"She's in trouble. Don't ask me how I know, but I do. I've

been engaging in a lot of trickery. But she has enormous bills everywhere, I've heard."

"The rich are notorious for not paying bills," Will said. "What makes you so sure?"

"Trust me. She's got to be positively strapped."

"So . . ." said Will.

"You look absolutely doubled up with thought," Roy commented.

"I am." Will told them a little of the story. "Perhaps these Strangers are what Mrs. Ruth says they are, and they have nothing to do with Tom's death. Perhaps, if she was involved at all in his search for the McCrocken money, it was between the two of them only. But if the Strangers *are* part of it, how does Mrs. Ruth's personal financial situation fit in? And if they aren't, what was the Etruscan doing in Crosscreek?"

"Why don't you ask him?" Roy said. "Or would that be too easy?"

Will laughed. "I intend to. But I have to find him first."

The rain was turning to sleet by the time they got back to the hotel. Will and Roy sent for food and drink from room service; then Will showed him what he'd been doing with his batches of papers so far.

The Mary Gold he'd found, was on the corner of West Seventy-fourth Street and Columbus Avenue, not many blocks from the Chevensey. Will spread his map on a writing table and circled the spot. A few blocks away, on Central Park West, he made another mark for Mrs. Ruth's apartment. On West Seventy-seventh, between the park and Columbus, he circled a third spot, Tom Donahue's last New York address. Then he drew a triangle around the whole area, bounded by Broadway, Central Park West, and West Seventy-ninth Street, with the apex at Lincoln Center.

Roy was consulting Wicket's list of the six flower orders that had come from the Mary Gold. They had been sent by the Train Mender, Oscar, the Irishman at the Neighborhood Bar, the Blind Jeweler, Bess and Brandy, and the Four Officers. Two of them, they decided, might be findable: the Train Mender and the Irishman.

"Before long," Will said, "one of us should take a walk."

While they were waiting for their supper, they went through the reverse directory. Will read out names, addresses, and phone numbers; Roy copied them down.

Within their triangle they found nine Oscars, fourteen Besses, three Bessies, and untold other persons with an initial O., E., or B., or some name like Elizabeth or Betty.

"You want to start, or shall I?" Will asked.

"You," Roy said. "I wouldn't know how to handle it. Give me something else to do."

Will handed him the restaurant guides, the directory, and the map.

"Look for restaurants in this area or near it that say they're open on Christmas Day. There won't be many, I'd guess. Double stars if they seem to be below street level or mention private dining rooms. God knows it could be anywhere in town, but this is still our best bet."

Roy set to work at the writing table. Will propped himself up on one of the twin beds, surrounded by the telephone, the names, paper and pencils, and an ashtray.

Bess Mindelstein, on West Sixty-eighth Street, sounded small, sleepy, and suffering from a cold.

"Brandy?" The girl was struggling drowsily to understand. "I don't have any. I could bring some gin." She sniffed. "Is this Terry?"

"I don't mean a bottle, Bess. I mean Brandy."

She blew her nose. "I should bring it in a teacup? Is this Terry?"

"It's Tom Donahue, love. Calling for Mrs. Ruth."

"*Not* Terry. I see." She was awake now, and the little voice was cold. "I don't know you. Or Ruth. Or what you're talking about. Do you mean the Murphys' party?"

"The annual feast, Bess. For the Strangers."

"Oh dear Lord. Some charity deal. Count me out, huh? Good night." She sneezed and hung up.

Room service arrived, with an array of cold cuts and potables. Will worked bites in between calls; Roy's meal was taken more comfortably.

Bess Bellini was not at home. Bess Deeds's phone had been disconnected. Bess Umberman was an elderly invalid, according to the whispering nurse who answered the phone. Will started on the Bessies.

"Finding anything?" he asked Roy.

"Nope. Lots of restaurants, all right, but not one that fits. Not in these books, anyway."

An hour later, they were no further along. It was nearly eleven o'clock.

The streets, when he reached them, were nearly deserted. The fine sleet that was still falling slid under his collar and stung his face, in spite of his wide-brimmed hat. The wind was wet and piercing and miserable.

Will headed up Columbus at West Sixty-fifth Street. Most of the lights were out; the sleet obscured his vision; the number of shops was prodigious. The few bars were still open, but there were many fewer than there once had been. Columbus seemed to have changed since Will had visited it last, to be slicker and less comfortable, less old-fashioned.

Still, some of the neon signs he was looking for glimmered ahead of him, floating orange and pink and green here and there along the way.

Delicatessens, laundries, fruit stands, liquor stores, shoe-repair shops. Restaurants, flower shops, hardware, antiques. A carpenter's, a bookstore, a candle-seller's. Grocery stores, newsstands. Bar. BAR.

Will opened the door of O'Rourke's. There was a marble floor, a lot of dark woodwork, and practically no one there. It was warm and musty and smelled of beer. But the bartender was Italian. Will didn't stay.

Food that was French, Cuban, Turkish, Czechoslovakian, Szechuan, Indian, Mexican, continental, sea. A frame shop, several dry cleaners, bakeries, art supplies. Tobacco, boutiques. Bread, bread and cheese, bread and pasta. Leather goods, ice cream, ice cream again. He slogged on. The sleet was heavier. A car or two went by, and an occasional brightly lighted empty bus. Taxis now and then. A 20th Precinct police car. Antiques again, restaurants forever, travel agency, babythings. BAR. In big orange letters, Ballou's. Was Ballou an Irish name?

A soft whooo-o whisked through the patter of sleet. Will's head jerked from the bar sign to the shop he was approaching. The Train of Thought, the sign over it said. And in the window, a perfect little display of a lighted town at night, with hills around it and a lake in the middle, and clicking in and out through the tunnels and down through the station, an HO-gauge engine pulling a dozen cars, whistling into the distance beyond the town and the window and the dripping sleet.

A small card, stained with age, was stuck in the window's corner. Typed on it: *Trains—Mended—For Sale—Traded. Jonah Dale, Prop. Monday–Saturday 10–4.*

Will copied down the name and crossed the street to Ballou's. Through the inner door he saw that it was smaller, brighter, more crowded than O'Rourke's had been. Two men were drinking beer and playing chess at one of the two tables. At the other was a young couple. Two men and a girl at the bar. Farther down, behind two large women, were several men in a row, the last one wearing a hat. Christmas decorations were everywhere, including an Advent calendar atop a row of bottles, with all its paper doors wide. Ballou was opening the last one, the one for Christmas Day, as Will stepped in.

"There we are, everybody," he said cheerfully. "Merry Christmas, my friends!"

There was a friendly clatter of response.

Ballou—if it was Ballou—was a cartoon of an Irishman. Rosy cheeks, snowy sideburns, deep blue eyes under heavy gray brows. Will ordered a beer.

"Have one yourself," he said. "On me. Merry Christmas."

"Ay, Christmas. But what's the occasion, lad? That's good enough, but maybe it's something more?"

"To drink to Tom Donahue."

"Tom Donahue?" Ballou chuckled. "Well, he sounds Irish, but who is he? Should I know, and be solemn? Or be glad? Tell me about your Tom Donahue now."

Everyone else was talking loudly, not paying attention to anything else. Ballou, still standing in front of him, gave him a friendly but appraising look.

"Will you be at the feast tomorrow?" Will asked.

"There'll be a proper Irish dinner, and plenty of it. At home with the family. That's the only feast on my docket. You were thinking of another one?"

"I'm looking for the Irishman at the Neighborhood Bar. I think he's here, or not far away."

One of the men at the end, the one with the hat, rose. Will couldn't see his face, the way he was turned in the direction of the back wall. He had laid down a five-dollar bill and was buttoning his coat. Ballou started toward him.

"Well, I'm that, I guess. It's neighborly, it's a bar, and I'm Irish. Not another more Irish"—he took the bill and went to the cash register—"unless you count O'Rourke's." He laughed softly to himself.

"I've been to O'Rourke's," Will said. "O'Rourke wasn't there. An Italian."

"No, O'Rourke wasn't there. O'Rourke died six years ago." Ballou gave the man his change. "But it was the Italian I meant. Name of Otranto. O'Tranto, see? Calls himself an Irishman. He thinks it's a good joke."

The skirts of the other man's coat brushed against him. Will felt for change.

"He says it's good for business. O'Tranto at O'Rourke's."

"Do you know where he lives?"

"Which one? O'Tranto lives at O'Rourke's." He sketched the apostrophe in the air. "Otranto"—he shrugged—"who knows?"

Outside, Will stood on the curb waiting for a car to pass. His eyes searched down the street, on the other side, for O'Rourke's. A blue sign. Sleet and streetlights and faintly lighted shop windows. It was two blocks, or three. Three. No blue sign. O'Rourke's had closed.

He went back, to be sure, walking as fast as he could, cursing himself as a failure of a detective. O'Rourke's was dark, and empty. He pounded on the door, but no one came. At last he started back to the hotel.

Partway up Seventieth Street, between Columbus and Central Park West, a man was standing at the outer door of a brownstone, at the top of a flight of steps. He was fumbling for his keys. It was the impatient customer at Ballou's, and Will suddenly realized who he was.

He paused in a doorway. The man hadn't been in front of him on Columbus. He must have gone all the way up to the park and come back down Seventieth.

He waited, shivering, the sleet spattering on his shoulders. The key was found. The man pushed through the outer door, key in hand. Just as he stepped onto the threshold, he glanced sharply down the block, toward Columbus. The entry light fell on his face.

It was flat, with a red, triangular mouth and uptilted eyes. From under his hat, a thickness of crinkled blond hair protruded. From beneath his coat, bony shoulders stuck up.

The Etruscan now had an address.

FOURTEEN

At the Feast

Christmas morning. Will woke suddenly, about nine o'clock. The room was quiet with the special quietness of hotel rooms. Pink and yellow light wavered on the ceiling, in the patterns of the closed drapes. Beyond his door he heard, faintly, the hum of a vacuum cleaner down the carpeted hall.

Still, for no reason that he could identify, it felt like Christmas Day.

He dressed and went downstairs for a walk, alongside the park.

A Central Park West doorman, leaning against the wall and wearing a cap with earflaps, wished him Merry Christmas. He had gray wool gloves on his hands and was beating them softly together. A yellow taxi coming down the street veered at him hopefully; Will waved it on and it righted itself with a disappointed waggle.

It was one of those white, frosty days. Sky and sidewalks and trees and even the air were a solid white world, picked out with stop signs and parked cars and traffic signals, that made a high tunnel of Central Park West and turned the park on his right into a stage setting of something between stone and marble, with trees cut out in bas-relief from the formless backdrop of air and sky.

He walked as far as the Museum of Natural History. By then, he reflected, he would have walked straight out of Crosscreek. He could almost smell the eggs and sausages and black coffee he was aiming for all the way back to the hotel.

* * *

Soon after breakfast, Roy Hill came back, bringing Junie with him. They'd opened their presents, they said, and couldn't think of another thing to do. So the three of them spent the early afternoon submerged in maps, notes, telephone calls, and talk.

The restaurant they were looking for, they concluded at last, was probably the Silver Tankard on West Seventieth Street. It could, however, be Skip's Hat on West Sixty-fifth or the Old Dutch Brewer's on West Sixty-third, around the corner from Broadway, or even, though more dubious, the Tenor of Our Conversation, facing Lincoln Center. Or it could be none of those, if they were mistaken in assuming that they wanted a restaurant rather than someone's home, and one in the vicinity. "One of these people might even *own* a restaurant," Will said. "One we've discounted because it's closed to the public today."

Roy had been around to look at them all. It was impossible to tell from the outside, he said, whether they had downstairs dining rooms. All were closed till five o'clock.

But according to one of the restaurant guides, the Silver Tankard had such a room. The guide was ambivalent about it: It got high marks for having a working fireplace, good artichokes, and tender veal, but sharp and disapproving comments for allowing food to get cold on the way down from the kitchen.

"The thing to do," said Junie, "is to get a table near the fire. And a long fork."

Slowly Will gained confidence that he would, in fact, be having dinner with the Strangers that night. They had not been able to find Otranto. Either he didn't have a telephone or he lived with someone else or he didn't live in Manhattan. Bess and Oscar had both eluded them. Although Will was sure Poppy Ruth would be in town by nightfall—if she wasn't already—the doorman at her building had told Roy she had not come home. He didn't know when she was expected.

But a Mr. Jonah Dale lived on West Seventy-fourth Street, and they knew how to find the Etruscan.

Toward the middle of the afternoon, they agreed that it would be best to leave Junie at the hotel, beside the telephone, to act as liaison in the event that either Mr. Dale or the man Will thought was the Etruscan turned out to have nothing to do with the Strangers. "You follow the Etruscan tonight," Will told Roy. "Believe me, you can't miss him. He's seen me with Poppy Ruth and he probably can't be sure whose side I'm on. If he spotted me behind him, he'd run. I'll take Dale."

From the landing above the fourth floor, Will looked down through the banister rails to the closed door of Apartment 4A. His right shoe swung by his fingers from its laces. Now and then he flexed his toes in the thick red carpet.

Someone was having a party upstairs, in 5B. The uproar filled the stairwell, disco music thumped through the walls, shrieks of laughter rose above the hubbub, but no one in the building seemed to object. Maybe it was too early for complaints.

It was better than waiting outside in the cold, but he hoped that most of the guests had arrived. He had followed one couple in, with smiles and thank-you's because they were holding the door open for him, and had gone slowly up after them, turning off on the second floor and ostensibly searching for keys till they disappeared. Since then he had sat at the top of the landing in his overcoat, retying his shoelace twice, once for the benefit of another group of party-goers and again for a short, pale man who had come up carrying a newspaper under his arm and gone into 5A.

It was twenty minutes till nine. Will put his shoe on and tied it. About time to go, he should think. One would expect a trainman to be punctual.

Behind the door of 4A there were three sharp clacks, of

bolts being thrown and latches turned. Will stepped back onto the landing, out of sight, just as the door opened.

Mr. Jonah Dale had a mop of thick gray curls. He was wrapped in a long gabardine coat, with the collar turned up. His cheeks were pink, his eyes blue, and his teeth beaverish.

He locked the door, tested the knob twice, and went downstairs. A moment later Will also let himself out into the street. Mr. Dale was just ahead of him, hurrying toward the corner, his arm raised to hail a taxi.

Damn, Will thought. What did he need a taxi for, unless the restaurant was farther away than they had thought? If it was, there was no letting Mr. Dale get away from him at this point or they'd never find it.

He had visions of himself saying, "Follow that cab," but since there was only one in sight, stopped at a light a block uptown in a sea of empty street, his visions evaporated as instantly as they'd come. That left bluff.

"Mr. Dale?" He came up on the elderly train mender so swiftly that the other man jumped a little. "My name's Gray. I think you know—that is, are *acquainted* with—the Etruscan?"

The taxi wheeled up and Mr. Dale leaned forward automatically to open the door.

"Bless us all," he said. "This is truly astonishing. The Etruscan has never introduced a new member before. He is most respected, you understand, as our treasurer, but he is painfully shy. Painfully. This is *quite* an occasion!" He stuck out his hand. "Get in, Mr. Gray!" he said enthusiastically. "We'll go together, if you're willing. But we have a stop to make, and we'd better hurry. Mr. Collier will be wondering where I've gone to. We call him the Blind Jeweler, you know. I always pick him up for the feast."

"Sorry," Will said. "This place is taken." He half-rose, with an apologetic smile for the man who had paused behind the chair next to his own. The African had asked to have it saved while he spoke to someone across the room. "Perhaps at the next table?"

But the tables around them were full. "The Renaissance Man," murmured Mr. Jonah Dale at his elbow. The man stared at Will coolly. He had black hair and the shadow of a beard along his jaws.

"Over there, sir?" the Train Mender suggested. Near the fireplace the Student in the Park, the Chinese Lamplighter, and the Cellist had a place left. Will pointed it out, and the Renaissance Man bowed and turned away, moving stiffly in his evening clothes.

The room was filling up rapidly. It was pleasant down here, in the Silver Tankard's cellar. Under pink lights in low, beamed ceilings, a number of tables—some for four, some for eight—gleamed with silver and glassware and pink linen. One table, decorated with branching silver candelabra, was clearly the head table. It had been set apart, on a raised platform. Six high-backed chairs faced the room.

"That is our president, Mr. Lou Butterton," Mr. Dale told him. "Of course you already know our treasurer, Mr. Crowder." The president and the Etruscan had their heads together and were deep in conversation. They were flanked by four still-empty chairs.

Poppy Ruth had not yet turned up.

So far, though he had only just come in, Crowder had not seen him. But Will had been fortunate, he thought, in Mr. Dale's choice of a table. The three of them were tucked away at one end of a long one. Will edged a little more deeply into the shadow of the arch in which it stood.

It was getting late. Roy must have reported to Junie by now. Will spoke to Mr. Dale and Mr. Collier. "If you'll excuse me? I need to make a phone call."

The Blind Jeweler smiled and nodded, his dark glasses winking in the candlelight. Mr. Dale looked worried. "Tip your chair forward, then," he said. "It will help me save your place."

Will hurried up the stairs, praying that he wouldn't meet Poppy Ruth coming down. There was a pay phone in the foyer.

Roy, Junie told him when he reached her, had indeed called. He was on his way back to the hotel. He'd found and followed the Etruscan successfully, and they'd been right. His destination had been the Silver Tankard.

"I'm there already," Will said. "Thank you both for all you've done."

"We'll want to hear the end of the story."

"You will," he promised.

"Tell me who is here, Jonah," the Blind Jeweler was saying when Will resumed his seat. He was short and thin, with a downturned but smiling mouth. His gray hair was shaggy, and his long, delicate fingers rested lightly on the base of his cocktail glass. "It sounds like quite a crowd."

"It is." Mr. Dale looked around. "Nearly everyone is here tonight, I think. Except for our secretary-treasurer—or rather our secretary, now that Mr. Crowder has taken over the books. She is late."

Will supposed that the secretary was Poppy Ruth.

So she had previously been the treasurer as well? Will sat quietly for a moment, thinking over the implications of that.

It was an extraordinary group in the cellar room. The Strangers were much more numerous than he had expected. Most were men, and most of the men were formally dressed. The clothes of a few, however, stood out. The African was swathed in purple robes, and the Chinese Lamplighter wore a long, straight gown of flame-colored silk. The Four Officers, together at one table, were in dress uniform, with swords and boots. The Chestnut Man had on his old clothes and leather apron, the Student in the Park was in threadbare corduroy and a too-narrow tie. Otranto, the Italian Irishman, glittered in a tuxedo with a dark green brocade coat, and the Fat Twins wore puce ruffled shirts.

"Do you know them all?" Will asked Mr. Dale.

"Oh yes." The Train Mender gave him a small smile. "Mr. Collier and myself were among the earliest members. Since 1970, Mr. Collier?"

The dark glasses flashed. "Mr. Dale knows it's since 1970," he said in Will's direction, "but he always likes to confirm it. It's a little ritual that is part of tonight's larger ritual." His shaggy gray head swung toward Jonah Dale. "But it is wrong to suppose that you or I or anyone else *knows* the other members. We are a society of strangers, you know."

Mr. Dale's pink cheeks grew pinker. "I keep a shop in the neighborhood," he reminded Mr. Collier. "It's very hard to stay strangers with everyone."

"Do all these people live in this area, then?" Will asked.

"No." The Blind Jeweler shook his head. "A dozen or so. Most of them did at one time, but now they live all over the country." Mr. Dale pointed out one man who had moved to New Mexico and another from South America as examples.

"And they come back to New York for tonight only?"

"Of course," Mr. Dale said. "The two benefits of sustained membership are—"

"Compelling," finished Mr. Collier, with decision.

"And what *are* the benefits?" Will asked.

Mr. Collier was cocking his head this way and that, picking up scraps of conversation from nearby tables. Mr. Dale answered him.

"The chance of wealth, of course. It doesn't always happen, but about one out of three tries pays off—wouldn't you say, Mr. Collier?" His eyes gleamed with enthusiasm.

"Four successes out of ten tries," the Blind Jeweler said. "Mr. Dale! We can begin. I believe I hear Mrs. Ruth."

Will watched her descend the narrow stone staircase in a long black dinner dress, nod to the waiter at the foot, and thread her way through the crowded room. The men at her table rose as she approached, and a waiter hurried to hold her chair. Will saw, before he bent to tie his much-tied shoe again, that while he'd been talking to Mr. Dale and Mr. Collier, an elderly couple had taken two of the remaining places at the head table.

"Who is speaking tonight?" Mr. Collier was asking.

"The Renaissance Man, I think. You should have agreed to do so, too, I believe."

"No." Mr. Collier turned his dark glasses toward Will. "I was invited, but I declined. Mr. Butterton will handle it better."

"How do you mean?"

"The sixth place."

"I see it. Are we still waiting for someone?"

"No. It will remain empty. It is a tribute of sorts to a Dr. Tom Donahue. You will hear the story later in the evening. My name may be mentioned. We are very fortunate," he added. "Someday we will lose someone, but Dr. Donahue's tragedy had nothing to do with the Strangers."

Waiters were streaming down the stairs holding enormous trays of food on their shoulders. Poppy Ruth's entrance had been the signal to begin serving, it seemed, and there were to be no preliminary remarks.

"You were telling me about the benefits of membership," Will said, once they'd been served.

"So I was," Jonah Dale answered. "And the Company's chief virtue is that it relieves one of the problems of Christmas night."

"In what way?" Poppy Ruth had not so much as glanced in his direction, and for the moment, the waiters, looming up enormously tall in the candlelight, blocked out the head table.

"I expect that for you, as for most of us," Mr. Dale replied, "Christmas is a difficult day. If you are alone in the world, you are lonely. You feel that you ought to have something special to do, and you don't. Your friends all seem to have plans, or to go away. It seems artificial to go out for entertainment;

besides, everything is closed except the movies. I've been to the movies on Christmas Day; it makes you feel even lonelier.

"But if you *do* have a family, it can be almost worse. That, at least, has been my experience. You can't escape; you have to be with them. The rooms are hot and stuffy; the people sit for hours, telling old, dull stories; you have to seem to be enjoying yourself. Everyone is pretending that it is all a great deal of fun when they've been ready for hours for it to be over. And yet there you all must sit. Unless, of course, you are a member of the Close Company of Perfect Strangers. And then, just as the afternoon is getting intolerable, you can rise with a smile and say you must be off to dress for dinner. Their evening is tedious, but your Christmas night is a night of romance."

"Mr. Dale feels strongly on this subject," said Mr. Collier. He gave his friend a sweet smile, while his fingertips, at the edge of the table, found his knife and fork and rested lightly on them.

Behind him, a waiter, noting the dark glasses, looked inquiringly at Mr. Dale. Mr. Dale shook his head, the waiter moved on, and Mr. Collier, with as much precision as if he could see, cut into his roast beef.

"Your tie clasp is unusual," Will told him.

An emerald, shaped a little like a leaf, uncut and only slightly polished, burned in the silk of his tie, just above his stomach.

"It is not very valuable because badly flawed. But I thought it was beautiful, when I could see it." He found his Yorkshire pudding and speared a bite of it on his fork with a bite of beef. "Besides, it is a memento of my most peculiar order. I wore it tonight on purpose."

Mrs. Ruth, Will saw, was engaged in conversation with Mr. Butterton. Through the rose-colored bars of the candles rising from the elaborate candelabrum before her, he saw her shake her head repeatedly at something the old man was saying.

"Where does the money come in?" Will asked.

It was Mr. Collier who answered. "We find lost wealth."

"You are hired to do so, do you mean?"

"No. No one hires or commissions us."

"Then how do you know about it?"

"Legend. Local tales. Chance. Have you ever heard of any stories of hidden treasure, Dr. Gray?"

"Of course. Everyone has. Sunken ships. Oak Island. Lost gold and silver mines all over Mexico and the West. I once heard that a moving van had crashed on a highway near our house when I was a kid. It was carrying a millionaire's belongings. Everything was found except for a pair of ivory goblets. Curiosities—but old, and worth a fair amount. Somebody thought later that they saw one of them in a sharecropper's house on the other side of the county. I never learned what happened."

"You never looked for them?"

"No. But even if I had, the goblets belonged to the man who lost them—or his insurance company. What would have been the point?"

Mr. Collier spread his napkin on his lap. "As you said, everyone has heard such stories. Often there is no longer a legitimate owner, or a legal claim can be established. If nothing else, there might be a substantial reward, or a share worked out for one's efforts. The mines, for instance."

"That would be an enormous undertaking."

"Perhaps too enormous," Mr. Collier agreed. "But suppose that, among us, there were someone free to spend a year in their vicinity. And suppose there were a second man with some knowledge of geology or mining—or even just one with access to a computer, who could collate the information already available. And surely we could find someone here with the temperament to sort through old documents, and another who could speak Spanish." He broke open a roll and buttered it calmly. "You see? In no time at all, we could produce a respectable team. As a group, we are many-talented."

"How long do you go on investigating a particular story?"

"One year. That's all we ever allow."

The tumult of conversation around them was growing steadily louder. "For strangers," Will said, "everyone seems to have plenty to say."

"Anticipation," said the Blind Jeweler. "We all look forward to the stories after dinner."

"This isn't just anticipation." Will looked around at the noisy crowd.

"Oh no. Everyone," Mr. Dale said, "has a good time here. We all try hard to be entertaining tonight."

"Which means," said Mr. Collier, "that you can tell all the old stories that your family and friends are sick of."

"It's more than that." Mr. Dale spoke eagerly. "You feel good about yourself. You are probably the only one of your kind around, and every class, every profession, in that circumstance becomes romantic. There's something exotic, almost Eastern, about us—we are a bazaar. Merchants in jewels and . . . and model trains, and chestnuts and learning.

"The Close Company of Perfect Strangers," he went on, "could, you know, only have happened in New York. At least a thousand people live on my block, for example. Strangers don't bother us—in fact, after a while, one comes to enjoy them. One feels better around strangers, though out-of-towners find that hard to understand. So we're all quite comfortable here together."

"How did it get started?" Will asked.

Mr. Collier laughed. "Mr. Dale," he said, "point out Bess to our friend."

"She's at the head table," Mr. Dale told Will. "The woman with the hat."

"Good God." The night before, propped on the twin bed with the telephone in his lap, Will had pictured Bess as a girl in her early twenties. Round-faced, he had guessed, with long blond hair. The woman at the head table was blond, but a yellow, dyed blond with thick, frizzy hair. She was cushiony and sixtyish, in a flowered suit, a mass of red beads, and a trailing blue scarf. Her eyes were heavily made up, and her laugh was infectious. Sitting next to her was a small man with a bald head, a neat gray mustache, and a deep suntan. He was wearing a starched plaid shirt under his suit coat, and he looked at his wife with great pride.

"That's Brandy," Mr. Dale said. "Her husband. His real name is Bertram Randolph Allen."

"What do they do?" Will asked. Bess was clearly having a good time; Brandy didn't say much, but several people had gone up to the table to greet him, evidently with pleasure.

"Brandy was a lawyer, up in the West Eighties somewhere," Mr. Collier told him. "Someday that area's going to be fashionable, but it wasn't then; it was a pretty gone-downhill place. Parts of it were dangerous, and he kept trying to move away, but he felt responsible for the people. A widower he was, of long standing, with a daughter to raise. He knew it wasn't the best neighborhood for her, but it seems he couldn't help staying."

"And Bess?"

"Bess drove a gypsy cab of sorts. They're both retired now, by the way. They live in Florida.

"Bess was never a true gypsy. She operated by phone call only, and she took her calls only from within the neighborhood. Some years ago she got tired of driving a cab all day and called it quits. She was unmarried, reasonably well off, lived alone, and quickly found herself at loose ends. Christmas came; Bess decided she was lonely. She hadn't had time to make all the friends she wanted, and a lot of those had moved away or died or something. But she had certainly known hundreds of people. And she especially remembered one she'd helped out a good deal over the years, taking his daughter places and even helping to look for her one night when she appeared to be lost. That one, of course, was Brandy." The downturned lips smiled again. "She thought

Brandy was a dear, she tells us, and a rather special kind of fellow."

"So she asked him to dinner."

"That's right. But she was pretty sure it wouldn't be correct to ask just him. And so she went through her records of all her old clients. Most were strangers to her, but about many of them she knew a little. And in the end she selected four whose looks she'd liked, who were also alone, she thought, and whom she'd gotten on well with. And she sent them all little cards, inviting them to Christmas dinner.

"Well, it went on from there. Brandy liked her cooking and her company and stayed late. By the next winter they were engaged, and to celebrate, they repeated the Christmas dinner. Only, each guest had had such a good time at the first one that each asked if he could bring a friend. By the third year, the custom was established—except that Bess stipulated that only strangers be brought. An odd acquaintance struck up in a bar or on the subway. They had started out as strangers, she said, and that was what had made it fun."

"That was the year," Mr. Dale interrupted, "that the dinner was moved over here, and the year the fortune hunting started. Mr. Collier and I met that year. We all sat at one big table under the stairs. You can see how we've grown."

The candles were burning low; their wicks swam in melted tallow. Talk at the other tables was erratic, with expectant gaps.

Mr. Butterton had taken some papers from his pocket and was smoothing them out on the tablecloth. The Strangers were turning in their chairs to face him. Under the clattering and scraping of chairs on the stone floor, Will said quickly, his heart in his mouth, "Your emerald *is* remarkable, Mr. Collier. If Tom Donahue had seen that, why did he have such a hard time finding the rest of them?"

Mr. Collier's lips parted in surprise. "It is true, then?" he asked at last. "You seem to know; it must be true."

"How did *he* know?"

"An accident. We met by chance in the park one November day last year. It was gray and cold; no one was about; we sat on a bench in front of the band shell and talked about the upcoming feast. I told him I had a scrap of a story to tell, but only a scrap—I'd never mentioned it all these years because I really didn't think it was enough to present. When I'd given him an outline of it, he was very interested. It seemed that certain facts corresponded with a rumor he himself had heard."

"Mr. Gray, did you *know* Dr. Donahue?" Mr. Dale broke in.

"I am a friend of his from Crosscreek."

The shock on Mr. Dale's face was plain. "But then you don't really belong here?"

"No, I don't. I've crashed your party, but for a good reason. I came here to try to find out why Tom was murdered."

"We had not heard that he was murdered." Mr. Collier leaned across the table. "I should like to hear about him from you."

"And I would like to know what Tom communicated to this group, or at least to Mr. Butterton, before he died. And how Mrs. Ruth figures in."

The president had risen and was waiting for silence. The dim ceiling lights went out, leaving them all in the sputtering candlelight.

"Afterward?" Will asked. "I also want to talk to the Etruscan, if that can be arranged."

The Blind Jeweler nodded. "At my apartment. And we will certainly invite him." Then he turned, like the others, toward the head table.

"Merry Christmas, all. Welcome to the Christmas Night Feast of the Close Company of Perfect Strangers." Lou Butterton leaned on his knuckles and surveyed the room out of pale eyes. He was tall, gaunt, and big-boned. "If there are any strangers here, you have come to the right place."

A rustle of laughter stirred through the crowd.

"The thirteenth annual feast," Lou Butterton added. "We

are Perfect Strangers in two senses," he went on. His bass voice rolled out, slow and speculative, reaching the far corners of the room without effort. "One, acquaintanceship among us, to even the slightest degree, is extraordinary. Two, the hope of perfection in another is eroded by acquaintance. We might all be perfect, for we are not friends. It is a heady illusion, and if the noun is accurate, so also is the adjective, and the sensation is rare. There is no acquaintance without watchfulness, no friendship without 'in spite of.' Camaraderie assumes faults forgiven and obstacles overcome.

"To some, we sound like a contradiction. We are not. We can be a close company only because we are, and to the extent that we remain, perfect strangers to each other. And, again, I give to 'perfect' its double meaning.

"Let us elaborate further upon ourselves. 'Close' is not so far from—is close to—the word 'closed.' The Company itself is not closed, but each of its members is closed off from each other. Perfection implies closedness, isolation, that which is set apart, completed.

"A company is a group, and a 'company' may also be rendered a 'companionship.' Companions in virtue of strangeness to one another. Companions because we are not friends. And we reinforce that rare companionship with a selection of humanity's most tradition-encrusted links: mystery, festival, wine, and the quest for gold.

"As you know, my friends"—his eyes shone with a smile—"for some years it has been our amusement to draw upon the resources of our varied group for adventure and for profit. The lost, the legendary, the rumored—buried in bank vaults and beneath the sea, under landslides and under the roofs of the unaware—we have engaged to recover. We collect pieces of stories and fragments of memories, and we ask each other. What became of these things? And each year we select one such shard of time and track it down. Search, research, common sense, and luck are our tools, integrity the tightrope we select as our path. We find only what we are free to find.

Time is a thief; we set ourselves against it. Nature is a grasping mother; we unclasp her curled fingers. If we triumph, we triumph equally. If we admit defeat, we are sped home to bed on Christmas night with a good tale from the old year and bright expectations for the new.

"We have a new prospect tonight, upon which we shall vote. The Renaissance Man has a suggestion that sounds promising; you will decide. So let us hear from him. Let us hear also from our treasurer about the state of our collective purse. Let us, before the evening is out, remember with affection and gratitude a man we never knew and whom no one now will ever learn to know. Let us celebrate our origin and our originators. But first, let us speed our proceedings with a toast." He lifted his glass. "To our past and to our enduring! God rest you merry, ladies and gentlemen—whoever you are!"

Laughter, a furious clinking of glasses, a confusion of responses, scattered applause that quickly swept the room. Lou Butterton bowed.

The evening hurried on. In the near dark, Will relaxed. It was unlikely that either Mrs. Ruth or Mr. Crowder would dislodge him now. And if they did, it didn't matter.

Leonard Crowder got awkwardly to his feet and reported that the Strangers were possessed of eighty dollars or so, after the dinner had been paid for. Then the Renaissance Man rose. He wished, he said, to put before them the case of some missing tapestries, used as bed curtains by an Englishman whose Rhode Island home was looted and partially burned in 1778. Had the tapestries gone with the Englishman—who had fled to the Islands, where he had wept for his lost silver and china and written of the glories of his former home—or with the thieves? Had they, by chance, stayed in Rhode Island, unrecognized for what they were? For in recent months a panel had turned up there, neatly folded in a trunk in a neighboring house. And the eighteenth-century neighbor had run a shipping firm—until he retired at an early age.

His chair was getting hard. Will eased himself into another position as quietly as he could. It creaked if he leaned too much to the left. He slid his glass toward Mr. Dale for a refill.

He had scarcely heard the Renaissance Man's tale. Mrs. Ruth's head, however, was bent toward the latter slightly, in an attitude of listening, so that he couldn't see her face very well. It would have suited Tom, Will thought, to keep up such a friendship with Poppy Ruth, a one-night-a-year Christmas romance. Of sorts. Until Mrs. Ruth escalated matters, as she'd evidently done.

He could imagine Tom bending over her on these evenings, his face crinkled with laughter, looking elegant in his tuxedo and dark tie.

Will remembered Dora and flinched. The rumpled hair, the uncertain sense of style, the cluttered office and apartment. Tom must often have laughed at her, to himself. But Tom had deliberately latched onto the Crosscreek way of life. He made himself get used to the snow and the old classrooms, to Louise, to Dora, to the emptiness. And he knew he would come back at Christmas, to a pink-lit cellar, a crowd of absurd New Yorkers, and Poppy Ruth to match his own crisp urbanity. A game to play, founded on McCrocken's game.

The difference between Tom and Poppy Ruth was that Tom would have acted his way through all this. New York, these feasts, Crosscreek. Poppy Ruth took it all seriously. No sense of humor. And that, he thought, was one similarity between Mrs. Ruth and Dora.

So Tom had gone to Crosscreek to find the McCrocken treasure. But why hadn't he begun by going to Maisie Moffat? Why, in all these months, had they never met?

Assuming Maisie had told him the truth about that.

The Renaissance Man's proposal was discussed and accepted. A presentation was made to Bess and Brandy, a special twelfth-anniversary gift tied up with a great deal of pink ribbon. Brandy didn't bat an eye, but Bess was flustery with pleasure: It was a superfancy, high-powered orange-juice squeezer and a set of green glass grapefruit bowls—suitable to life in Florida, the Strangers thought.

At last Lou Butterton got around to Tom.

"We are happy tonight," he announced, "but that does not mean we have forgotten there is an empty place, that we are one short. Last summer, with our blessing, Dr. Tom Donahue took leave of his professorship here and submerged himself in a little bare town in the Midwest, to trace an order placed almost fifty years ago with another of our members, the Blind Jeweler, when he was a boy learning his trade. Last week Dr. Donahue died there, caught out in a winter storm. His reports to that point were scanty. We expected tonight to hear the full tale. We never shall.

"I do think he must have found what he went for, for he called me the day before he died. He was very cheerful and excited, but he would say only that he'd have a story for us. He promised to call again in a day or so." Mr. Butterton smiled. "I was so enthusiastic that I passed the good news on to Mrs. Ruth so we could await our good fortune together, but our next intelligence, a day later, was word of his death.

"And so that particular treasure appears to be lost to us once more. We let it go without regret. We can regret two things only: that Mr. Collier has not, at least, the satisfaction of knowing the framework of those odd events that occasioned the search, and that Dr. Donahue is beyond even our finding. Tonight we discover a scrap of truth, my friends: that some treasures *are* beyond our reach."

There was a pause. At her end of the table, Bess blew her nose softly.

"And now," said Lou Butterton, "Christmas night is drawing to a close. God bless you all, and thank you for coming."

And that was all. The Strangers got to their feet, in a rush of talk and commotion. "I'll speak to Mr. Crowder," Jonah Dale volunteered, and made his way to the head table. While they waited, Will saw Poppy Ruth glance at him at last, then stiffen with recognition. Her face went cold with dislike. Mr. Dale and the Etruscan started back.

"Shall we go?" Mr. Dale asked as they came up. "Cabs will be scarce."

"We can walk," said Mr. Collier. "Coming, everyone?"

"Coming," Will said. He grinned, made Mrs. Ruth a half bow, and followed the others to the stairs.

FIFTEEN
Mr. Collier's Story

"**O**ne November night in 1939," said Mr. Collier, "I was at work in the back of Fitton and Sons, a jeweler's here in town. A little place, very old, with a good reputation for doing imaginative work. Only old Mr. Fitton ran it, he being the younger of the original sons, and he'd recently taken me on to assist him.

"The shop closed at five, but I stayed late some nights—I was just learning, you see, though I wasn't quite the boy Lou Butterton said I was, and many nights I stayed late to study and to practice gem cutting. I was anxious to be good at my trade."

The four men were gathered in Mr. Collier's room. It was small and shabby but tidy, with a minuscule kitchen at one end. Mr. Collier sat in the only armchair; Jonah Dale had taken a bentwood rocker. Will sat cross-legged on the floor, and Mr. Crowder had found an ottoman in the shadows under the windows, where he sat quietly, his hat on his lap. They all held little glasses of cognac Mr. Collier had passed around.

The room was full of doors. One to the hall outside, one to the bathroom, and two for closets. Between the doors, strips of green wallpaper ran up to the ceiling, sixteen feet from the floor. The green-striped drapes were open.

"About ten o'clock," the Blind Jeweler went on, "there was a knock on the shop door. I went to see—I supposed it was the police, checking up because of the light in back. When I lifted the shade and saw a man standing there, all wrapped up in a tweed overcoat and a soft hat, I shook my head and motioned him to go away. He looked respectable enough, but I was alone and saw no reason to run the risk that he might be a well-dressed thief.

"He didn't go, however. He took money out of his pockets, handfuls of it, in big bills. Some thief, I thought. He held them out to me so that I could see the denominations. Hundreds, every one." Mr. Collier chuckled. "I've never felt such a surge of curiosity. He had a pleasant face, I remember—an elderly man with a long gray mustache and smiling dark eyes. So I unlocked the door."

Outside the apartment, Will heard footsteps on the stairs. "Here she is," he said. He opened the door almost before Mrs. Ruth could raise her hand to knock. "Come in. We've been waiting for you."

Poppy Ruth stood resolutely on the threshold. She was shivering, damp, displeased, and worried. "You sneak," she said.

"Well, I wouldn't put it quite that way."

"What are you talking about up here?"

"You can guess."

"You have no right."

"Oh yes I do. Come on in."

They had left a chair for her, near Mr. Collier, but she pulled it somewhat out of the circle and sat up in it very straight.

"Shall I go on?" Mr. Collier asked.

"Please do. I think we're complete."

"Well, then. He gave his name as McCrocken. What he wanted, he said, was almost a quarter of a million dollars' worth of stones. Diamonds, emeralds, and rubies were among them, but there were also others. Jade, for instance, and tourmalines and pearls. And he produced a sheet of paper covered with designs. Circles, oblongs, triangular shapes of all sorts. A minimum of cutting and polishing at most, he said. Fourteen cabochon garnets, for instance. Thirty-five teardrop diamonds. The emeralds were the oddest shapes. And then a mixture of the others in squares and rectangles.

'Get the shapes right'—he was strong on that point. Only slightly polished, no faceting at all. That was it. Could I do it?

"I could, I thought. But I was distressed. I told him he was asking for an end product that would look like cheap glass. He didn't seem to care. I pointed out that I was, after all, only an apprentice still and wanted to refer him to Mr. Fitton himself. He said that wouldn't suit him and turned to go, with his money and his paper. I said maybe I could do it myself but that finding and preparing the stones would take months. He said he would come for them in the spring.

"I got almost no sleep that winter. When I wasn't buying stones, I was trembling over what I had undertaken."

"Did he pay you in advance?" Will asked.

"Enough for the uncut jewels."

"That was quite a lot of money, Mr. Collier," Mr. Dale said, in awe.

"At the end of May he came back. He walked in one afternoon, when the shop was empty of customers and the door wide open because it was a warm day. It was an unforgettable day, the first nice one after weeks of cold spring rain. I still think about it. Bright and sunny with the plane tree outside the door in new leaf and sunshine streaming in through the shop door. Mr. Fitton was at home that day—he suffered from arthritis, which kept him in bed increasingly—so no one was there but me. Suffering myself from a bout with spring fever. And then there was a shadow in the doorway and the old man came in.

"He said he hoped his stones were ready, spilled them out of the leather bag I brought, and matched them up against his sheet of paper, one by one. You could hear the traffic and the birds outside, but not a sound in the shop except for the rustling of that paper. It was an old, yellow sheet of ruled paper, the same one he'd had the first time, but dog-eared by then.

"When he was done, he put them all back in the bag and drew the cord, counted out what he owed me for my work, thanked me very kindly, folded up his yellow piece of paper, put it in the inside pocket of his coat, and walked out. I never saw him again."

"You had no idea who he was or how to trace him?"

"None. Just his name—that's all I ever knew about him."

"You didn't guess what he meant to do with the jewels?"

"My dear Mr. Gray, that has puzzled me for four decades."

"And at the end of them, you told the story to Tom?"

"Yes, I did. That winter day in the park."

"And, of course, McCrocken's name meant something to him. His parents must have talked about the story of the will when he was a boy."

"That's what he told me. He didn't recall any details, but he remembered the name and something about some missing money. It made me curious enough to think it should be pursued." Mr. Collier smiled. "You know, I've often told that story. It sounded as if, after all those years, I'd finally told it to someone who actually had a line on the ending."

"But there was no indication—" Will began.

"Exactly," Mr. Collier said. "That occurred to me, too, of course. No indication that those jewels were free for the finding. But Tom thought people in general had somehow been searching for the lost money, so they must have expected to profit from it. He didn't see why we couldn't, too. In any case, he said, it would be fun to look into it."

Mr. Collier reached for his glass. "He was a friend of yours, you said?"

"Yes. More or less."

"Less, I hope."

"Why?"

"What I don't understand is why Tom didn't tell us about Mr. McCrocken's daughter. He certainly found out that she was very much alive—and he probably found that out that spring, before he began making arrangements to go to your college for the year. But he never said a word."

"How did you find out about her, then?"

"I wrote a letter to the president of your college. Mr. Dale had looked up his name for me, in a directory of colleges and college presidents. I asked him if Gabriel McCrocken had any descendants who were still living."

"And he said yes."

"Living right there in Crosscreek." Mr. Collier's fingers toyed with the stuffing coming out of the arms of his old maroon armchair.

"What moved you to write?" asked Will.

"I didn't care for Tom much, I guess. He was too slick. And I did like that old man. It was after Tom had gone out there. His first report was full of jokes about your town. He wasn't being funny; he was making fun. Very much above it all."

"So he was" came from Mrs. Ruth's chair. They all looked at her, but that was apparently all she had to say.

"What, exactly, did Tom tell you?"

"Nothing substantial," Mr. Collier answered. "He said he was having great difficulty in getting information about the missing part of the estate. Someone had evidently rifled all the public records for miles around. The newspaper files and the libraries in Crosscreek were stripped; he had tried most of the neighboring towns with the same result. His greatest concern was to find a copy of a letter Mr. McCrocken had left with his will. He had learned, at least, that this letter contained the clues to the whereabouts of the fortune."

"That part was true," Will said. He had guessed as much, but Mr. Collier's remarks confirmed the reason for the gasoline credit-card slips he had found among Tom's papers. So when had he gotten Bo's copy of the letter, and how?

"That was the first note from him. Still, he was convinced that, with diligence, he could find it, and that when he did, locating the jewels would be a simple matter."

"Mrs. Moffat would have had one, of course."

"I know. And at that point I told him what *I* had discovered, and asked for an accounting of why he had failed to mention to us the existence of a proper heir. I am certain—though in his next letter he was very gay and funny about it—he was unprepared for my knowledge of her.

"He congratulated me on my cleverness and put himself down as a blockheaded idiot for not having thought of doing the same thing. He said that no one had told him about her and that it had never occurred to him to ask. He'd just assumed all the McCrockens were long since dead and gone. I wrote that I found that hard to believe. In the meantime, Mr. Butterton, whom I'd kept apprised of all this, was alarmed and confused. He was away from New York for the year himself, but he wrote me right away. If Tom had been openly looking, as he should have been—for we meant to be honest about it—how could he have failed to hear of Mrs. Moffat in such a small town? Secrecy was useful, sometimes, but there was no need to be surreptitious. Had Tom been so cautious for the Strangers' sake? If so, he was in error. Or had he—and such thoughts upset Mr. Butterton badly—had he really known of Mrs. Moffat's existence after all? If he had, Mr. Butterton dreaded to think why Tom had not told us of her."

"But Tom played innocent," Will guessed.

"Yes, with all his charm and humor. He blamed himself for overlooking the obvious, for too youthful an attitude, for vanity that had tripped him up so thunderingly. He painted an entertaining picture of himself as sleuth in disguise, overtaken by the fun of conducting a secret adventure, the better to surprise his friends there in the end. He was warm, apologetic, earnest, and cheerful.

"He said he would get in touch with her right away and offer her our services. Possibly she would reward him—and therefore all of us—with a portion of the treasure if he found it. He chattered on so, with such evident good nature about it, that eventually Mr. Butterton and I were satisfied that he had meant no harm. We left it at that." The black glasses seemed to stare at Will. "*Did* he speak to Mrs. Moffat about us, and ask for her help?"

"No. He never did. At least she says he didn't."

"Would she have any reason to lie about that?"

"I don't think so."

"She's devious," Poppy Ruth said darkly.

"You should know," said Will, and turned to Mr. Crowder. "Was it this year you took over as treasurer?"

The Etruscan flushed. The whites of his uptilted eyes were startlingly noticeable from the gloom of his alcove. He nodded quickly.

"And the first thing you did was to go over the books?" Again the sharp gesture of assent.

"Why?"

Crowder's face looked suffocated with worry and self-doubt.

"Mr. Gray," said Jonah Dale softly, "Mr. Crowder is very timid."

"But not too timid," Will answered, "to attempt an heroic bit of investigation on the Company's behalf."

Mr. Collier raised an eyebrow, Mr. Dale looked puzzled, and Mr. Crowder reddened deeply.

"Shall I tell them what happened?" Will asked. "I think I know."

"I would . . . I would rather tell it myself." The Etruscan's voice was just above a whisper. "I really didn't do much after all—except watch as best I could, and then let you both know it. I didn't trust you, either, you see. I was frightened of going much further."

"Mr. Crowder was in Crosscreek?" It was quite warm in the room. Mr. Dale mopped around the edges of his gray curls with a handkerchief. "Really, Leonard? What for?"

"The books." In his effort to speak at all, Mr. Crowder almost shouted, and then swallowed and got his voice a little more under control. "The books were incorrect. Accountants cannot be tricked. Even if the arithmetic is right."

"But why Crosscreek, Leonard?" Mr. Dale repeated. "The books were Dr. Donahue's fault?"

"No, no. Mrs. Ruth was in Crosscreek."

"Ah," said Mr. Collier. "I see now."

"I don't," said Mr. Dale. And then, after a short interval of silence, "Oh dear. Yes. I'm afraid I do, too. Oh dear."

"What made you suspicious in the first place?" Will asked.

"Last Christmas the Fat Twins located a famous coin collection," said Mr. Crowder, his tongue loosened at last. "It had been stolen during the war from the home of an army captain while he was overseas. When we came to dinner, our checks were distributed. I opened mine; I saw at once that the amount was much too small. I happened to know what a collection like that would bring, what their expenses would have been, how many were in the Company. It was all wrong. But there are other knowledgeable persons among us, and no one else appeared concerned."

"What did you do?"

"The only thing I could think of. I spoke to Mr. Butterton during dinner. I said we were getting too big and too prosperous for an amateur to have an easy time with our finances, especially if she had to be secretary, too. I offered my services as treasurer. After dinner he brought it up, and I was appointed. I took the books home. That night I started going over them."

"And when did you find out that you were right?"

"In the spring."

"Whom did you talk to about it?"

"No one. I would have gone to Mr. Butterton, but he was in South America. He does missionary work there. I thought it best to wait till he came home."

"And he came back . . . ?"

"A week ago. Last Tuesday morning, for the feast. I called him the day after that to ask if he could see me that night. He said he could, and then he told me the apparent good news about the jewels. He was very excited."

Mr. Crowder stopped to catch his breath.

"My plan," he went on painfully, "my plan, you see, had been to talk to Mrs. Ruth first. I thought that was only fair and that she . . . she might have amends to suggest, or . . . or want to go to Mr. Butterton herself." He glanced at her nervously, as if aware at last just how coldly she would have responded to any such suggestion. "So I called her next and found out she'd gone away."

Will's face was kind. "And so you went to Crosscreek after her, to be sure something strange didn't happen to the McCrocken treasure."

"Yes."

"Did you speak to Mr. Butterton when you got back?"

"No. It didn't seem necessary. But I am meeting with him tomorrow afternoon."

Jonah Dale was clearly shocked. He had mopped around his curls so much that they stood on end about his face. Mr. Collier looked ready to cry. "Oh, my dear lady."

"Tom didn't tell you anything in the end, did he? Did you ever figure it out?" Will asked her.

She was giving Mr. Crowder a hard look. "You have no proof at all," she told him, and then said to Will, "Figure out what?"

"What McCrocken did with his sack of jewels."

"No. How could I?"

"Well, by reading the letter. That, at least, was available to you—as it wasn't to Tom for a long time—from the flyer."

"It made no sense."

"Yes, it did."

She stared at him. "Do you mean you found them?"

"I'm afraid so."

She sprang up, white-faced, in a fury, but Will went on, unperturbed. "What's it like to go broke?" he asked her. "You'll have to go out and work all day, you know."

The room had helped, he thought. Despite its neatness, it had probably terrified her a little. Faded drapes with stained linings. A musty smell. The rug was brown and threadbare, the kitchen fixtures discolored.

The night was black through the windows. In the building

across the street, lights burned behind a few drawn shades; in other windows, people lived their lives visibly.

It was warm and stuffy and quiet. Mr. Collier's hands had stilled and his face was in shadow. Mr. Dale's fingers worked at the cloth of his trousers over his knees. Mr. Crowder gripped the hat in his lap.

"Tom seemed weak about it, didn't he?" Will said. "In the end, he was going to let it go. He knew where it was and he could have had it, but he wouldn't just take it. And he deliberately told Mr Butterton first. But when Mr. Butterton passed the word along to you, you went to Crosscreek anyway, in a final attempt at talking him around. You thought you could, and that Butterton could be dealt with somehow. Tom had known early on that the treasure belonged to Maisie, but you had continually talked him into concealing that. He wanted it, too, maybe, for a while. Or maybe he just had trouble telling you no. It must have been frustrating to you, the way he kept putting you off, changing his mind, making you persuade him again, saying wait till we find it and then we'll decide."

"Tom was like that."

"For how long," Will said, "had you been stretching the Strangers' coffers to supplement your own income? It was easy, wasn't it? —as long as they trusted you and didn't think to examine their own books. You could add a few names to the rolls and make the checks out to 'Bearer.' This screen of anonymity, this use of nicknames, came in handy. There must be many legitimate Strangers whose real names no one knows. You could falsify the amounts of the deposits from the various treasure hunts—as long as you made certain that the handful of financially canny souls in the group got a plausible amount. The others' checks could be for much less. And you found it necessary only to make the totals of the checks equal the total income you noted down; you didn't list each check individually. But you neglected to respect Mr. Crowder's acumen."

The Etruscan was nodding sharply at the end of each sentence.

"And you wanted more," Will continued. "All this, after all, amounted to only a few thousands, irregularly. A little easy pin money. This time around was something else entirely. It could bail you out of your financial troubles and give you a chance to start over. It must have seemed so easy—for one thing, Tom was fond of you. In private I expect you laughed at the Strangers, at the whole idea of the Company, at Butterton and Bess and at the way all of them looked forward so to the Christmas feasts. Tom followed your lead and laughed, too. And when it turned out that Tom himself was involved with the best story of all, one that promised more money than the Strangers had ever before aspired to, you set out to have it for yourself, or half of it, through him.

"He needn't ever tell them that he'd found it, you said. He could report no luck, and the two of you could split it. Why not? It wasn't theft; it didn't really belong to the Company. It belonged to the finder. It would be foolish to find such a fortune and then invite a lot of strangers to share it with you.

"But Tom was hard to manage. Sometimes he agreed; sometimes he wasn't so sure. He wouldn't give you away, but he wasn't especially greedy. He wanted his name in the papers, and his picture. He wanted to be able to tell the world, in later years, how he found the McCrocken treasure. He wanted to distribute largesse among the Strangers, to stand up on Christmas night with his story and his fistful of checks. He could see himself announcing his find to Crosscreek. He would do it with flair and modesty and charm. He liked all that better than socking away money he didn't really need and having to lie about it."

"He was stupid," she announced.

"He was vain," Will corrected her. "That was where you slipped up. You should have played on his vanity, showing him how much handsomer and more entertaining and interesting he could be if he were rich. You had a chance; he never did go to Maisie Moffat. He never let on to anyone in Crosscreek that he had the least interest in the McCrocken money. He always kept himself covered in that way, I think because of his cousin Louise. Once he revealed his interest in the money to Maisie, Louise would come to know about it sooner or later. And any sudden wealth he displayed after that would make her wonder about it. He could disappear from the Strangers' circle, but she would always be there.

"Maybe, of course, I'm being too hard on him. Maybe he just liked the intrigue of it all, of finding the fortune the hard way, all by himself. In any case, you didn't convince him to go along with you, and when he found it, he called up Butterton and said so. In the meantime, he'd done it the way he wanted to, for whatever reason. He had found the other person who'd been looking for it, had laid hands on the letter, and had solved his own little mystery within a mystery. And he'd called up Mrs. Moffat at last."

Mr. Collier cleared his throat. "Can you tell us, please, where the stones have been all these years?"

"The front door of the old McCrocken house. The stained-glass fanlight isn't all stained glass."

"Ah." The jeweler's lips moved in an expression of satisfaction.

"What is it that's important, then, for you to find out from me?" Poppy Ruth looked tired. "Why are you here?"

"I came to find out who you all were, and what you were up to. For what light it might shed, for instance, on why Tom was murdered. And on who did the murdering."

"I don't know who murdered him. It wasn't me." She closed her eyes wearily. "Not that I know how to prove it."

"You don't have to. You could, all things considered, have killed Tom, given a lot of unlikely planning and flying back and forth, but I don't see how you could have known about Lucy. What you might know is some detail from Tom that could help us out. When were you last in touch with him, for instance, and what did he say?"

"About a week before. We just chatted about this and that."
She shook her head slowly. "I really don't know anything that
would help you. I can't imagine who would have wanted to
kill him."

She leaned back in her chair, eyes closed again. "Mr.
Crowder, what do you mean to do?"

"I don't know." The Etruscan looked profoundly agitated. "I
am so sorry for you. This matter"—he twisted his hat—"well,
it came to nothing, it appears. But our books—Mr. Butterton
must know."

Mr. Collier turned to him. "How great is the discrepancy?"

"About twenty thousand dollars, all told."

He bent his head in Mrs. Ruth's direction. "And your own
debt?"

"I don't know. Twice that, maybe."

"But you own your apartment?"

She flinched. "Yes."

"My dear, we so much need a sign of good faith. If you were
to sell—"

"Yes?" she said wearily. "You don't understand. I have very
little capital left to live on."

"Nor do we." He smiled at her. "You see, we do understand
after all."

"And so?"

Jonah Dale was struggling with himself. "I could use a
helper in my shop," he said. "I really could. I'd . . . I'd
welcome you, I think."

She didn't make a sound, but in a moment tears escaped
beneath her eyelashes and ran slowly down her cheeks.

"It beats jail," Mr. Collier said solemnly. "By quite a lot.
And Mr. Dale is really rather nice. You could give it a try, I
think."

"I guess I have no choice." She opened her eyes and stared
at Mr. Dale. "Yes, I do. I don't need to burden you, too.
There'll be other ways I can make a living."

"Well, if not—"

"If not, I'll come back. Thank you." She busied herself collecting her belongings. "Thank you all, I guess I must say."

Will finished his drink. "What did you want from Tom's house, by the way? Anything I should know about?"

"Is that your last question? I do hope it is," she said. "You know what I wanted. Something, anything, that would tell me where he had located the treasure. I didn't even have a chance to look." She got to her feet. "I think I hate Christmas."

"Before you leave—there is just one small thing that continues to puzzle me," Mr. Collier said. "It seems that, in the end, Tom ceased to be ambivalent and proposed to restore Mrs. Moffat's fortune to her. But can we be sure of that? That he wasn't wavering still?"

"I don't think he was," Will answered. "He'd made an appointment with her, for one thing, as soon as he found it. For another, given its location and the fact that he couldn't take possession of it till after Christmas, he would have had to declare himself in order to make his presentation to you. What he never knew," he added, "was that the Strangers would have gotten more than he expected." He explained about Maisie and the flyer, which had come out the next day. "I don't know what Tom thought you would get—the ten percent the family had originally offered, or some suitable reward, or nothing at all but the satisfaction of having solved the puzzle. As it happens, though, the prize would have been substantial."

"Poor Tom," said Mr. Collier.

Mrs. Ruth's face was sour.

The hotel room was pitch-dark. Will turned on the lights and went into the bathroom to wash his face. When he came out, he found a note from Roy Hill beside the phone: *We got baby toys for Christmas, and we're off to play with them. We hope your dinner was all you wanted it to be. Just before we left,*

you got a phone call from Sheriff Winterlin. (We're impressed.)
He wants you to call him back.

It was nearly two o'clock—one in Crosscreek—but Will did
so. Mack Winterlin answered right away.

"Something occurred to me," he said, "when I found out
where you'd gone."

"Who told you?"

"Oh, Maisie's been around, dropping hints."

"I should have guessed."

"And then Mrs. Gray called, all frantic about what had
become of you."

Will sighed. "All right. So what did it suggest to you?"

"Well, if the McCrocken treasure is involved in all this, it
made me wonder something. Something along the lines of"—
he hesitated—"well, symbolism."

"Symbolism?"

"Yeah. There could be something in it. What I mean is, why
would Donahue have been sent out the old McCrocken Road
to his death? It could fit in, somehow."

"The old McCrocken Road? What happened to ten-
sixteen?"

"They're the same. Ten-sixteen used to be called that, a long
time ago. Gabriel owned property out there once. Now, who
thinks in symbols? English professors do, it seems to me. So
I've been wondering about Joey Livingston."

"Oh."

Will leaned back against the headboard of his bed and
thought over what Winterlin had said. "Symbols have nothing to do with it. Forget Joey. He's probably a minor saint
anyway. But," he added, "I think you've just solved the case."

"Excuse me?"

"You remember that envelope, don't you?"

"Yes."

"Hang onto it. I'll explain when I get home."

SIXTEEN
The Last Bid

On the day after Christmas, Parson Road was empty; the few cars parked along the curb still wore two-day-old caps of snow, and their windows were glazed with frost. The houses were mostly dark. No one seemed to have turned the lights on yet.

Will left his car in the driveway and went in through the back. He turned on the kitchen lamp and put a kettle of water on to boil before he took off his coat. Only two of Amigo's food bowls were empty; he always lost his appetite when Will went away.

He found him, asleep, in the armchair in the living room. He mewed when Will touched him, and got up, arching his back and stretching his legs, purring. For a moment he let Will hold him in his arms; then he scrambled down and ran into the kitchen.

Will made supper from a TV dinner he found in the back of the freezer. While he ate, he looked through the paper. The double murders of Lucy Mellon and Tom Donahue occupied most of the front page. There was a two-page spread about Christmas in Crosscreek, a story about the treasure hunt with a big picture of Maisie Moffat, an account of the special Christmas dinners the local restaurants had offered, and an interview by phone with Luke Vondervorste about Paris during the holidays. There was a notice as well, on a back page, to the effect that the auction of the contents of the McCrocken-Mellon house would be held on Friday, starting at one-thirty. Everybody had known that for a week, at least, along with the murder news and the treasure hunt story.

Jed must fret over old news, not that he could help it.

After supper Will sat on the floor of the living room and opened his Christmas presents. There were several packages from his parents, in shiny green paper with silver trees and no bows, since they'd come through the mail. A box from his sister and her husband; a gift each from his brother and sister-in-law. A big box from his grandmother. She had put a large blue bow on. It was squashed flat.

He put the lids back on the boxes and gathered up the crumpled papers. The trash can in the kitchen was full. He mashed the papers down on top and carried it all out to the garbage pails behind the garage. Louise should know, he thought. He could call her, of course. There was no reason why he couldn't tell her about it on the phone.

He started back to the house. It was breathtakingly cold. He didn't have to go out again. And she probably had something to do tonight.

How, he asked himself, as he searched under the sink for the box of plastic garbage-can liners, how do you charge anyone with murder on such evidence? A pretty dream, a stolen letter, a house being dismantled, a laughing newcomer, and a name on an envelope. And there was still a gap in the story he was going to have to try to fill before anyone—Winterlin, for instance—was going to begin to listen to even those tenuous scraps. At the moment he didn't know how. He stuffed a new bag into the trash can and set it back in its corner. He could call Louise now. Make a drink first and sit at the kitchen table and talk to her. Or he could wait, save it a little. It was early yet.

He got a bottle of Scotch out of the cabinet. If he couldn't fill that gap, what business had he so much as mentioning a name to Winterlin at all? And yet it was all they had. No more evidence was likely to turn up now. No more killings. No one had seen a thing; the treasure was found. *Louise*. Will threw ice cubes into a glass and splashed some Scotch in. He thought about water and decided against. They would always have to catch Tom's murderer some other way. But when, and how? Tonight? Tomorrow? Friday? Friday, come to think of it, might be their only chance.

He took his glass over to the table and set it down, gathered up the *News* he'd left there and, absently, thinking about Friday, dropped it into the newspaper basket by the door. Dropped it and picked it up again. Under it was last week's paper, and on the front page, looking up at him, was an article about the new library wing and the plans for the opening ceremonies.

Will got it out and read it. He had seen it before but, he remembered, had scarcely glanced at it. This time, standing in the middle of the kitchen in a bad light, he read it carefully. It began and ended with an interview with Tom along the lines of "Crosscreek Newcomer Takes Pride in Its Past."

Maisie was quoted in it here and there. So was Luke, at length. Jed must have caught him before he left for Paris. And at the end were some comments from Tom about the content of his talk.

Not that Tom had much to say. Just what a great guy Gabriel McCrocken must have been and that the more he found out about him, the more impressed he was. The old stories—the ones everyone had heard—were supported by outside evidence, too, so it wasn't just local pride. He'd been given, for instance, a book called *The Men Who Made the Midwest*, which dealt with him extensively. . . .

That, then, was how Tom had done it. Will peered over his glasses at the wall clock. It would be 2:00 A.M. in Paris. Too bad for Luke, but the university was closed for the holidays. He had no other source. He reached for the phone.

"The guard's name is Spaulding," Luke told him, sounding groggy and confused. "Will, this just isn't kosher. That just slipped out. It's not fair to wake people up and ask them confidential questions about the rare-books room staff. Why do you want to know?"

"First name?"

"Jerry. Damn. What is this, anyway?"

"Are you having fun?"

"Fun? It's *cold* here. I've never been so unhappy."

"In Paris?"

"I hate it."

"Are we ever going to see you again?"

"Soon. We've got a booking . . ."

"That's wonderful. Good night, Luke. Sweet dreams."
Louise.

He poured the drink out and put on his coat.

Amigo was asleep on his rug. He raised his head in apprehension when he heard Will getting his things on, and struggled to his feet. But Will was on his way out the door.

From the corner of Victory and Main he could see the light blue street lamp on the corner in front of the bookshop and the deeper blue neon sign of the Capricorn Theater catty-corner from it. In between, he knew, was the yellow glow of curtains across the four windows on the second floor.

The downstairs door was unlocked, the entrance cold and dark. His footsteps were quick on the wooden stairs.

On Thursday morning the skies cleared and stayed clear for two days. The sidewalks rang with the clank of snow shovels against concrete; the streets roared with a swarm of yellow snowplows, grinding and tossing the snow aside with hard iron hands.

After them droned the sand trucks, and soon the streets, scraped down to their rutted shells of ice, turned brown all over town. In spite of the blue sky and the sun, it went on getting colder all morning. The radio said the temperature at noon was one degree above zero. From then on, the snow-plows and the sand trucks chugged about in subzero weather.

The ice on Pebble River thickened and changed from blue-gray to white. Skaters were out on the pond in their new Christmas clothes.

At the Northside Apartments, Jerry Spaulding gave him the information he wanted. Spaulding was the denimed, bearded student Will had seen in the library the night of the reception at Mellon's. Will sat at his tiny dining table and drank a Coke.

The boy looked as if he had just come out of the shower. His blue work shirt smelled of soap; his cheeks were scrubbed.

"Donahue was there, all right," he said. "Last Monday night. From four when I came on until about nine-thirty."

"Tell me as much as you can remember about it."

"That's not much. He had some books and was sitting at one of the tables for a long time. Later he moved around some. I wasn't paying him any special attention. He just read, did some writing."

"But he could see the room door from where he was sitting?"

"He could see everywhere."

"Many other people around?"

"Quite a few. About like it was the night you were there."

"Do you have the sign-in sheet for that night?"

"Sure. I turn them in at the end of the month. Till then, they just stack up on my clipboard."

"I'd like to see it."

"That's easy." Spaulding went to his bedroom and came back with a book bag, fished around in it, and brought the clipboard out. He flipped pages back till he got to the right one. "Here you go."

Will hunched over it, looking down the list of scrawled names.

"Can I ask why you want to know?"

"Not yet. But"—Will found the name he was looking for—"don't lose this, Spaulding. The sheriff's office will want it."

"You're kidding."

"Nope. Thanks for the Coke."

* * *

On Main Street, Will ran into Dora. She was wearing a new navy coat and a smart red wool hat. He looked at her in surprise.

"Who gave you those?"

She seemed aggravated. "Nobody. I buy my own things." And then, "Where have you been?" she asked.

"When?"

"Christmas. Day before yesterday. I called you."

"Oh, around," he said. "No place special. Why did you call?"

"I'm lonesome. I wanted to go out."

"What about your mother?"

"What mother? I practically never see her anymore. She and Mrs. Moffat have been spending all their time together. Thick as thieves. They've been helping Mr. Mellon pack up."

"That's nice of them."

"I guess so." She looked disconsolate. "How was your Christmas?" she asked. "Fun?"

"Fun," he agreed.

"I don't see how."

"I ate out. With friends."

"Oh. Well, I'm glad. Where are you going now?"

"Dora . . ." he said.

"Oh, never mind. Maybe I'll go to Mellon's, too. See if I can wrap cups or something. Except I think he's gone by now."

"Then you can help unwrap them. Make your mother proud of you."

"Why not."

The *News* office was alive with activity when Will climbed the stairs. The two reporters who constituted Jed's staff were there—Mowkington on the phone, Crenshaw leaning against his desk, talking to Jed.

The paper couldn't afford a full-time photographer. Ed Malone, who got paid by the hour and who worked when he was off duty from the sheriff's office, fiddled in a corner with the paper's ancient camera.

Jed's fingers drummed idly along the edge of his desk. There were doughnuts on a paper plate in front of him, and a half-empty box of Christmas chocolates someone had sent over.

"Pictures of the house," he instructed Crenshaw. "Tagged furniture, bare rooms. Chandelier above uncarpeted stairs. You know." He peered at Ed Malone over his half-glasses. "That work?"

"Does now."

"Mellon by the fireplace, maybe. Or Mrs. Moffat. Outer edge of a rolled-up rug. Dusty sunbeams. Good stuff like that. Listening, Ed?"

"Constantly. Furniture tags and sunbeams."

"Wrap up, then," Jed said. "Chilly out." He selected a doughnut. "Have one?" he offered when his staff had gone.

"Um." Will sat down in a straight-backed chair, without taking his coat off. "Thanks."

"What's up?"

"I want to know where that article came from in last week's issue. The one on the new wing."

"Why should I tell you about that?"

"Because you misled me, for one thing. You told me the other night that there wasn't any new material on McCrocken."

Jed stopped chewing and frowned at him. "Well, there isn't."

"Well, now, I would have—"

Jed waved a hand at him impatiently. "Yeah, he was mentioned there, all right, but we would have put that in Maisie's file." He settled back in his chair. "Anyone interested in Gabriel should have had the sense to check that also. Any more complaints?"

"Guess not."

Jed sharpened a pencil. "Good. That piece was Tom

Donahue's idea. He called me up one day, said he thought there was material for a story. Went on about it till I thought so, too. So I went around and talked to him."

"That Brewster book he mentioned—"

"Which? Oh yes." Jed made a face. "I don't know what was wrong with him on that subject. He carried on and on about it." He shrugged. "I couldn't see that it was all that interesting, so I didn't print much of what he said. But I had to mention it, he kept dragging everything back to it so."

"What the hell," said Winterlin. His brown eyes were furious. "You mean that window is it? And I didn't know about it till now?"

"No one needed to," Will told him. "It was safe until the auction tomorrow. Still is."

"And then?"

"I've got a story to tell you first."

When he had finished, Winterlin stared at him for a long time. "That's the damnedest fairy tale I've ever heard," he said at last.

"Yeah."

"So we leave the window alone."

"It's the only thing to do."

Will found the door of the Mellon house open, in spite of the cold, and the walks covered with strips of old carpet. A good many cars were parked out front. The blue shadows of the iron fence already stretched far across the lawn, though it was only three o'clock.

Inside, Crenshaw and Malone were still at work. Malone was setting up his camera in a corner of the dining room. He had directed the lens across the foyer at the French doors that opened onto the veranda from the living room.

The foyer was empty except for a mahogany costumer with curled arms. Will saw that Malone had placed it so that its carved branches arched in front of the French doors, far in the background. A sunbeam cast a halo around it.

Crenshaw was in the living room, out of camera range, talking to a representative from the university by the fireplace. The mantel was for sale; Crenshaw appeared to be taking notes while its virtues were being explained. Both men wore their overcoats and gloves.

People wandered through the nearly empty rooms, alone or in pairs, bundled up against the cold. The floors were bare, the drapes gone. Almost everything had belonged to Mr. Mellon and Lucy and had been taken away in the moving van before noon.

Most of the remaining pieces of furniture had been Gabriel McCrocken's. Each was tagged and numbered; the tags fluttered in the draft.

A few things, also up for sale, were university property, used in the 1960s when the house had done service as a dormitory. An overstuffed armchair with most of its buttons missing. A glazed maroon lamp. A black iron fire set with brass-and-amber handles.

Joey Livingston floated through the hall with a vague smile and a nod. Will started for the library to look at the glass-fronted bookcases but came up short at the door. Barney Nealsson, still in the throes of a cold, was inside with his mother, who was tapping the gilt frame of a mirror with a fingernail.

"It's only wood," she was saying. "Painted wood."

A corner cupboard in the dining room, with etched glass doors. A pair of wing chairs. A table full of cut glass vases and candy dishes. Four old clocks. More andirons and fire sets. A small table with a black marble top. Cornices and doors and carved moldings. Incongruously, a set of redwood garden furniture. A seashell made into a night light.

In the kitchen, Will found Claire Bordeaux standing before a massive dresser with a counter made of flowered blue tiles. Above and below were shelves and cabinets and drawers trimmed with porcelain pulls. Claire was running her fingers across the tiles.

"You could do something with these," she said.

The door to the back stairs stood open, and he went up. In one bedroom, an enormous black wardrobe. In another, a straight-backed chair and a blanket chest. A third held only an empty trunk and a stack of old paintings. The fourth was empty. The fifth contained half a dozen rolled-up rugs and boxes of folded drapes, some more faded than others.

He stepped over them and looked out the windows. The room faced the university, hulking dormant in the sun and snow for the holidays. The windows were black; many of the shades were drawn, the panes dust-streaked in the light

Directly below Will, people were still drifting in to look at the things for sale. Ellen Powell was among the latest bunch, coming up the sidewalk to the front door. Will stepped back from the window and picked his way again among the rugs and the drapes to the door.

He went down by the front stairs. Over his head the stained glass burned fiercely, with the late-afternoon sun behind it. Its tag swung from an extralong string: *Fanlight, ca. 1900. Item #119.* So it came up relatively soon. Not good for the auction, probably, but better for him. He'd be glad when it was over.

He crossed the porch and headed for his car.

Will spent most of the evening with Maisie Moffat. She made him burned steaks and fruit salad and warmed up some sweet rolls for dessert.

"I do hope," she said, "that there's hot food in Heaven. One can imagine cold things—ambrosia and mead and melons— but not lamb chops. It wouldn't be fair if there aren't any. Just think of all the lonely people who have been eating oranges and frozen fish sticks all these years."

"On the other hand, think of the lambs."

She put him at the dining-room table set with a lace place

mat and a crystal goblet of water. The dining room was dark except for some bare bulbs in brass sconces on the wall. Not till he had started on the sweet rolls did she remember to light the candles on the table.

Afterward they sat in the green chairs in the living room and talked of town news and the past.

"So many changes," Maisie said, putting her feet out toward the fire. "I sometimes get a queer, lost feeling in my own town. But always a strand of continuity keeps emerging. The old house being torn down, but the library wing going up, with Papa's name over the door. You coming to tell me, after all these years, about Papa in New York and I'd almost forgotten how he used to have the *Sun* sent out by mail when we were small. And next week this grand opening coming up. I'm so glad they asked Tippy Roberts to make that speech. I remember him when he was a child, before he and his people moved away. He was always a quiet little boy, but a smart one. And now he has Papa's job and is going to be giving a scholarly talk about him. I think about things like that when I see the river, especially in the summer."

"The passage of time?" Will didn't try to guess what the summer had to do with it.

"No. About how the water goes. Shallow places, with all the water spread out, and then deep parts where some of it is hidden and then shallow stretches again where the hidden water runs along on the surface. In the summers it's quiet . . . everyone is gone . . . you can watch the water lying in the sun."

After a bit, she continued, "I was at the library yesterday. They were hanging Papa's portrait. A whole bunch of administrators came around. They all studied it very thoroughly. And Mr. Bordeaux, who painted it, was there. Such a nice young man—he has done it in the old style, with a bit of the university the way it was behind the figure. And on the other side, the open fields and the roads running into the grass. . . . I wonder how he knew to paint it that way." She laughed. "But afterward I drove to Bo Jenkins's to have the tires checked. I had my own car for the day, you see. I needed some steadiness. Mr. Bordeaux might be nice, but he's awfully edgy."

Then Maisie made him fetch a box of treated wood chips from the kitchen. "I found them at the hardware store," she said. "I haven't thought of them for years."

Will flung a handful into the flames. The fire burned red for a moment, then shot up with tongues of blue and green and purple.

"If Mr. Collier could see," Maisie said, "I would invite him to come out for a visit. I think he would like to see what Papa did with his stones."

"They'll be worth much more, considering inflation," Will said.

"And you will be so much the richer," said Maisie. "The terms of the treasure hunt still apply, you know."

Will, startled, looked at her. That part of the treasure would come to him had not, amid the business of finding it, ever occurred to him. He had had other reasons for looking for it.

"No," he told her. "For one thing, Tom did the original finding. Any reward should go to Louise, and to the Strangers."

"*If* you can get them to take it, you may give them some. But I only claimed a hundred and fifty thousand. Anything over that is yours."

Will began to shake his head. "No, Maisie."

"Why not? I have no one else to inherit. The university gets it all." She reached for the box of wood chips on the glass table and threw a few more on. "I'd rather there were a limit to what the trustees are free to misspend."

By one o'clock on Friday, the house was filling up rapidly. Someone had brought folding chairs from the university; boys were setting them up in the living room with a great clatter. Administrators moved about among the crowd; a thin lady whom no one had ever seen before stood at the front door handing out mimeographed lists of things for sale; a professional auctioneer brought in from Sioux Falls stood at one end of the living room talking to several strange men.

Maisie Moffat arrived early, hatted, gloved, and in her best black dress with a diamond pin. Mr. Mellon had declined to come; without having to be asked, Maisie graciously took over the role of hostess, chatting with people and greeting them warmly. Claire Bordeaux, with bent head, drew heavy lines around the number of the kitchen dresser on her sheet, and Bo Jenkins studiously hefted and examined two iron bookends shaped like sombreros, with a calculating eye.

Louise had closed the bookstore to come. She took a seat at the end of a row, toward the middle of the room. "It's just as well," she told Will, who stood beside her for a while. "Everyone in town is here anyway."

The heat had been turned on, too high this time, so people who had sat down in their coats kept jumping to their feet to take them off. Crenshaw was back, and Malone lounged in a corner with his camera.

"I'm definitely going to get something," Will heard Bo Jenkins announce to Dora as he sat down beside her and her mother. "I don't know what, but I'd like a remembrance from the old house. Something little. Maybe one of those glass dishes."

"I thought you wanted the bookends," Dora told him, and Bo looked annoyed.

"Well, don't say it so loud." And then, anxiously, "You don't want them yourself, do you?"

Dora shook her head.

It was hard to tell who was there and who wasn't. The rows in front were soon full—of farmers and their families, townspeople, and faculty members. A few students had taken seats and sat looking uncomfortable, as if they wondered whether to offer them to someone else. Will recognized Janie Lacey and Jed's blue-eyed assistant standing against the wall opposite the fireplace.

In the back of the room a crowd had gathered. Mack Winterlin craned his head around, sizing everyone up. Truitt Roberts in his ordinary old suit, Jed by the hall door with his notebook ready, Dr. Lollo McIngling in a corner with his wife. Geoff Bordeaux had just ducked in and dropped into a seat beside Claire.

"Lots of these people," Jenkins said complacently, "never saw the inside of this house before. I'll bet that's what they're here for, mainly."

Dora absently nodded agreement. On her right, her mother and one of her new friends had their heads together over the auctioneer's list and were conferring animatedly. Will—who had gone up to have a word with the auctioneer—smiled at the sight of them as he came back down the aisle; they had evidently zeroed in on some finds.

It was past time to begin. The auctioneer took his place behind a rostrum and rapped on it with his gavel. "Ladies and gentlemen! Ladies and gentlemen!"

Will lowered himself into his own chair, on the aisle near the foyer. Beside him was a wiry, dark-haired man in plainclothes whose name he didn't know but whose function he did; behind him, two larger ones were fanning themselves with their lists.

Everyone was shy at first, and the bidding began slowly. But then Maisie broke the ice by making a bid on a Chinese figurine in a blue and yellow robe. There was a momentary pause while the auctioneer bent over his master list, whispered to one of his helpers, who looked too, and then said, "Mrs. Moffat, that was yours to start with."

Maisie wasn't at all flustered.

"I know," she said. "And I've decided I want it back."

Everyone laughed, and of course no one would bid on it after that. The auctioneer looked disapproving, but he went on. And the tautness went out of his face in a few moments, for the pace picked up nicely as everyone relaxed. Maisie just folded her hands in her lap and smiled at him with her bright eyes.

Item 7 was the sombrero bookends. Red-faced, Bo got them, after an initial frozen panic and then a brief but heated struggle with Jed's assistant. Item 45 was a hall runner that Andrea Mateas coveted and won. Item 63 was the kitchen breakfront. Claire Bordeaux's opening bid was so low, and her tone so laconic, that everyone stared—and then fell silent. Will could almost hear the thoughts of the others who'd wanted it: *There must be something wrong with it*. It went to Claire.

He glanced over his shoulder. Mack Winterlin was still standing quietly in the back of the room.

Item 119 was the fanlight.

"If you'd just look behind you," the auctioneer instructed the crowd, "and into the foyer. . . ." Everyone twisted around and stared at it obediently.

A voice from the crowd near the hall door opened the bidding. Will had trouble, at first, seeing who it was, and then recognized Mary Linnet, the rector's wife. Geoff Bordeaux's hand went up; Claire looked at him blankly. That modernized house. . . . There were two or three raises from others.

"A very unusual piece," the auctioneer was saying as the rays of the afternoon sun shot under the porch roof and illuminated it. "Some of the glass has *quite* a good color. . . ."

"I always did think that was pretty," Bo said to Dora in an audible whisper.

But Dora was biting her lips and looking uneasily at her mother, who had turned in her chair and was peering at it through the foyer door with a fixed expression.

"The bidding now stands at four hundred dollars, ladies and gentlemen," the auctioneer said.

"Five hundred."

Will's shoulders slumped with relief. He'd been right. He held himself in check while the bidding went on, with the voice in the rear firmly raising each competing bid, until the sum stood at a thousand. In the silence that fell then, he caught the auctioneer's eye and made the small, doubling sign he had previously conferred with him about.

"One thousand . . . *two* thousand." The whole room gasped.

"Three, then," said the other voice.

Will doubled it again.

"I have six now."

In the stunned silence Truitt's voice came clearly, almost amused: "Who *is* that? I don't mind doubling, too, if this is some kind of game. Twelve."

And on it went. Will, leaning forward, his elbows on his knees, his chin on his hands, looked around the room for the other bidder when everyone else did, and made it twenty-four. Truitt hesitated, standing alone now, his hands in his pockets, in the middle of the small space.

The pause drew out. Will knew he would bid again, knew also what was beginning to occur to him.

"Is that all, sir?"

"No. Make it thirty-five." But there was a small quaver in his voice. This time the auctioneer's glance turned too directly to Will, and Truitt saw it.

"Is that you, Will Gray? You don't *have* thirty-five thousand dollars."

The auctioneer's eye went to Maisie, who smiled at him. Will stood up. "Forty."

"Forty-five."

"Fifty." Will turned as he said it.

Truitt's fists were clenched at his sides; his body—rocked a little forward on the balls of his feet—was rigid; his face was tense. It wasn't a question of ready money; Will knew he would sign over his house if he had to. It was another question altogether, a bitter and desperate one.

"Fifty-five," Truitt said.

"Sixty."

"Sixty-five."

"Seventy."

There was a silence. Into it, at last, Will said, "If you raise it again, I'll double." Double it to a hundred and fifty. The intolerable number. The amount Truitt could have gotten it for last week, by telling Maisie he'd found her father's treasure. The amount that Tom's death, and Lucy Mellon's, had come to represent.

"Mrs. Moffat," Truitt said loudly. "Mrs. Moffat, this man can't make good on such a bid. I know he can't. Don't allow it."

Maisie had been sitting for the past few minutes with her head bowed. Most of the others in the room didn't understand what was going on, but she did. Will was appalled. He had never meant for the burden to be dumped on Maisie's shoulders like this.

He started to speak, to say anything, but she was ahead of him. She lifted her head and looked at Truitt, with a face that suddenly showed her age. "I'll take a postdated check from Dr. Gray, Truitt," she said. It was the first time she hadn't called him Tippy.

"Damn you!" Truitt said. "Damn you!" He lunged forward across the aisle toward Will. "You won't keep me from it!" His hands were curled for Will's throat, his small body heavy with fury. Will caught him, shook off the strangling touch, pushed him aside, and then chairs were going over and the men behind Will were seizing at them, lifting Truitt away, doing things with handcuffs.

"Truitt Roberts," Winterlin was saying, "I arrest you for the murders of Tom Donahue and Lucy Mellon." Will mopped his brow, brushed himself off, looked at the stunned auctioneer—who whispered, "Done"—and left the room.

SEVENTEEN
The Treasure Brought Home

Louise caught up with him just past the sidewalk gate. Will hadn't any particular plans; he had only felt the need to walk a few blocks in the cold air. Neither one of them had much to say.

For fifteen or twenty minutes, Will strode along the snowy streets, his hat pulled down on his head. The last of the sunlight shone on Louise's auburn hair as she scuffed along beside him.

Presently they found themselves nearing Main Street. "Let's go home," she said. "Unless you'd rather keep walking for a while."

"Home is fine," Will answered.

Upstairs, sitting on the living-room floor, they had hot chocolate and raisin toast in teetering buttery stacks. While they ate, Will told her all about it.

"First," Louise said, "what put you onto him?"

"Don't you eat the crusts? Can I have them?" Will took two from her plate. "It was three things," he told her, "that the murderer had to match up to. He had to be a close enough acquaintance of Tom's to have plausibly called him for help. Second, he had to be free twice during that evening, to siphon the gas out of the car and to make that phone call to Tom. And third, the most important one in the end, he had to be an old-timer here."

"But how did you know that?"

"Look." He took a pen from his pocket, bent over the coffee table, and sketched a portion of the envelope on a paper napkin. "You saw this—we all did. Mack showed it all around. I didn't read it right, though, for a long time."

He pointed to the word "McCrocken" crossed out beside Maisie's name and her address alongside the set of directions the murderer had given Tom. "I thought at first that meant either of two things, both unimportant. That 'McCrocken' had been written separately from the directions, as a reference to his upcoming speech, crossed out because he had finished preparing it or finished looking up something. Or, in writing Maisie's name and address, in connection with his appointment with her, he might inadvertently have written 'Maisie McCrocken' at first, then marked out the last name and put 'Moffat' under 'Maisie' in the only space he had left. But neither of those explanations matched up with Tom.

"The first was no good because Tom wasn't a meticulous person. He would never have dug that old envelope out of the mess on his desk in order to cross out that word. The second possibility was really just as unreasonable. Tom never knew her as anything but Maisie Moffat. Mack Winterlin or Dr. McIngling or Bo might forget and refer to her as Maisie McCrocken, but Tom wouldn't have.

"So how had Tom come to jot down that word? I never came up with any better ideas. And then Mack called New York Tuesday night and said something that made everything slide into place. He referred to Highway ten-sixteen as the McCrocken Road. It was the first I'd heard of it, which wasn't surprising. They changed the name in 1944.

"Whoever called Tom told him to take the McCrocken Road, but Tom didn't know where that was, and the caller amended it to ten-sixteen. It was natural for Tom to write down 'McCrocken' as he heard it, then to question it, mark it out, and put 'ten-sixteen' instead.

"So the murderer had to be someone who'd lived here long enough to have known the old name for ten-sixteen. By then, Truitt Roberts was the only one who came anywhere near fitting, and he fit exactly. It was an easy slip for him to make. He grew up calling it the McCrocken Road."

"There were other old-timers, surely," Louise said doubtfully.

"Sure, but no one else who then fit the other criteria. Maisie, for instance, hadn't met Tom at all. And besides, I was with her that night while Tom's gas was being stolen, and afterward she was at Jed's, looking over his shoulder while he put the flyer together. So she couldn't have made the phone call.

"Bo just might have done it—he knew Tom and only he knew whether he'd actually even filled up the gas tank in the first place. But he was here visiting with you while he was waiting for Maisie to get her fill of helping Jed with the flyer. On top of that, he wasn't at the Mellons' party, and he couldn't have heard what Lucy said. So if he'd been involved, it could only have been with Maisie as accomplice, and as I've said, that was out because neither was free to call Tom the night he died."

"I don't see why Maisie would have had a motive anyway," Louise said. "She hadn't yet announced the terms of the treasure hunt, except to you and Jed. At that point the old terms still stood, I guess—what were they? That the finder could keep ten percent?"

"Ten percent was at least twenty-five thousand dollars she wouldn't have had to give up. That's a fair amount in itself, not to mention the possibility that she might have thought Tom meant to abscond with the whole thing."

"Could she have known that?"

"Well, there were wheels within wheels here. Did you know she used to go out with Tom's father when they were young? Maisie was almost your aunt, for all I know. And given that connection, she could have been far more in touch with Tom's activities than anyone had reason to believe. However, all that came to nothing, as it turned out."

Louise got up. "Did you ever really think it was Poppy

Ruth?" She cleared the plates away and went into the kitchen to heat up the rest of the cocoa.

"I didn't know," he said when she came back. "She was never around at the right times, of course, but that was only what she told us, not what we ourselves knew. Except for Mellon's party. After that I was sure enough that she wasn't guilty. On the other hand, I didn't really know what she was up to, or any of that bunch, until I got to New York. I guess her chief importance to me, though, was that her existence, and what she said about herself and Tom, and that telephone message, made Dora someone to consider as well." He traded the floor for a chair and stretched out his long legs. "But, of course, Dora wouldn't have known about the McCrocken Road, either. Nor would Geoff and Claire Bordeaux. They seemed to have been mixed up in it, too, for a while." He told her about Maisie's seeing Claire at Tom's house.

"Why did Tom want that painting?"

"I don't know. Perhaps because it was very good. Perhaps as a kind of memento of the treasure hunt."

"Just because McCrocken had once owned the house?"

"No, there was more to it than that. Last night Maisie told me, when I asked her about it, that Truitt Roberts had grown up in that house, with Gabriel as his parents' landlord. It's possible Tom knew that—if, for instance, he'd talked to Truitt at any time about where he was from, his childhood here, all that."

"Truitt seems to have been bound up with McCrocken in a number of ways."

"I know. I think that goes a long way toward explaining why the whole thing happened the way it did. McCrocken was always sort of *there*, in ways he couldn't escape. His father's landlord when he was a kid, and therefore central to their lives, at least until he moved away with his parents when he was ten or so. And then, when he came back here to college, McCrocken was one of his professors in the history department. When McCrocken died, while Truitt was still in school, there was all the to-do over the first treasure hunt—the biggest news Crosscreek had had in years. Then Truitt went away to teach, and when he came back here, he was eventually appointed to McCrocken's old job, with even his desk for company.

"Doubtless, he had thought about that missing money all those years he was away. And at some point after his return, maybe inspired to it by that desk, he began to think of looking for it. Eventually became obsessed by it. It must have surprised him, when he came back, to hear that the money had never been found. And surprised him, also, that it had been almost forgotten, even. It must have intrigued him at first. And seemed much more than just intriguing when he really thought about what he could do with a quarter million dollars. If it were all his.

"Anyway," Will finished, "Tom saw the painting at Geoff's last Tuesday, just a few hours after he'd found the treasure. He found it when he laid hands at last on a copy of Gabriel's letter. As it turned out, he'd stolen that letter from Truitt's files."

Louise's face darkened. "He shouldn't have done that. And I still think the painting makes an odd memento. It would always remind him of . . . of his own theft."

"I doubt he saw it that way. Truitt had taken the stuff first. He had no more right to it than Tom had. Less, actually, since he'd taken public documents—newspaper clippings and so on."

"Still," Louise said sadly, "he could have gotten the letter in no time if he'd gone to Maisie in the beginning. So even if he viewed his getting the letter from Truitt as just a bit of cleverness and good thinking on his own part, the painting was still a symbol of duplicity."

"I suppose so." Will smiled at her. "Maybe, though, that shows a better side of Tom than we're giving him credit for. Some tangible reminder of sins he came close to committing. A kind of constant mortification of the soul. Or it could have been something more of a lighthearted impulse that inspired him to buy it. He would have been riding high that day—he certainly was at five o'clock, when I ran into him in the history department. He'd found the treasure, he was going to see Maisie the next day to tell her about it, he had called Lou Butterton and shaken himself free—he thought—from Poppy Ruth. It would have been easy to feel, just then, that he'd always meant to do the right thing in the end. And after all, we can't say that he didn't. I think that the complications he found when he got here would have appealed to him. Maybe he liked having it made as hard as possible; it was more fun that way. And he would have liked finding it on his own, without help from Maisie or anyone else.

"And then, too," he added, "you know Maisie. If Tom had gone to her for the letter and said he was trying to find the treasure, it would soon have been all over town. Tom wouldn't have had any peace, other people might have joined in the search, and if he hadn't found it after all, he wouldn't particularly have wanted everyone to know he'd failed."

"Thank you." Louise stood up. "Let's have a real drink." And when Will cocked an eyebrow at her, she smiled. "I've been so *worried* the last few days, thinking Tom had done wrong. But you're making him seem like a much better person than that, and I feel—well, enormously relieved."

"To the kitchen, then."

They had just broken into a couple of Louise's stubborn ice trays and were shaking the ice cubes into a plastic bowl when there was a knock on the front door. Louise went to answer it and came back with Mack Winterlin. He declined a drink, so Louise made him some more cocoa.

"I thought you'd like to know," he told them, "that he confessed."

They both stopped what they were doing and looked at him. Winterlin shrugged. "His lawyer was there and everything, but he couldn't stop it. I practically didn't even say a word to him before he started in on telling us all about it. I don't think anybody could have *kept* him from talking."

Mack and Louise took armchairs, Will leaned against the wide windowsill. Mack sipped his cocoa and frowned when he burned his tongue.

"It's a good thing he did talk," he told them. "I'm afraid we'd never have been able to make a case against him that a jury would buy. Not for murder. All we had, really, was that assault on Dr. Gray here, and some pretty strong suspicions. That was enough to detain him while we looked for more, but I don't know that we would have found it."

"Why did he confess, then?"

"He was just so damned undone by that experience this afternoon, for one thing. When he didn't get that window, and saw that Dr. Gray knew the jewels were in it and that he'd never get it now, it was too much. He'd waited for it for years, is probably even in debt on account of it—they've got that unpleasant kid Angela signed up for an Ivy League school, you know—and had murdered two people for it. He saw right away that his life was pretty well over. Even if we couldn't have convicted him, everyone in town would have known he'd done it, once it came out that Dr. Donahue had found the treasure. Dr. Gray established this afternoon that Dr. Roberts was the only other person in town who knew that window's value, and everybody saw what happened when he realized his next bid was going to carry him up to where the murders became meaningless. So—no money and a burden of guilt and he couldn't have held his head up in town again." Winterlin spread his hands. "It was too much for him."

They sat quietly for a moment. Then Will asked, "Did you have a chance to go through that desk?"

Mack nodded. "It's all there, where you thought it must be." To Louise, he explained, "That's where the letter was, in McCrocken's old desk in his office. Roberts gave out that it just had old department files in it, but no one ever knew for sure because he always kept it locked. What it really was full of was all the stuff about McCrocken he'd stolen over the years. Including Bo Jenkins's shoebox."

"Did you find anything written by McCrocken himself?"

"Yes. Old copies of those three pamphlets you told us might be there, as well as copies of the books he wrote and a bunch of other articles. All that stuff Roberts had written his own name on, and the date, on the flyleafs—1938, 1939, mostly."

"And the Brewster?"

"Just that one page, like you said."

"And the clipping from last week's *News*, the one about Tom?"

"That, too."

Louise was looking confused, and Will smiled at her. "Until yesterday or the day before," he said, "I couldn't figure out exactly how Tom had found out that it was Truitt who'd been ahead of him. We knew from Poppy Ruth that that was how he'd gotten the letter at last, by uncovering the other searcher. But not what put Tom onto him. Or even whether Tom engineered it or found out by chance. It turned out to be the former."

"I don't quite see how."

"A couple of weeks ago he'd been given the Brewster book by Luke Vondervorste for his talk. It had a lot of McCrocken material in it, you know, yet not all that prominently. He was just one of a number of people mentioned. And it was a book that had gone in and out of print very quickly, in the early thirties. Furthermore, there had been a copy of the book all along in the public library, untampered with, undefaced.

"It gave Tom an idea. Here was maybe the only McCrocken information left in town. Quite likely it had survived because the other searcher didn't know it existed. If that person was still around, he might be lured out."

"I see," Louise said. "So Tom got Jed to do an article about the new wing—"

"Right. And to interview him about plans for the opening

talk and so on. And Tom made sure he spent a lot of time talking about the Brewster book."

Will lighted a cigarette and dropped the match in an ashtray. "As it happened, Jed did mention the book, though grudgingly. And before the paper came out last Monday, Tom ripped out the whole McCrocken chapter from that public-library copy. He wanted to incite the other searcher, you see, and also he couldn't be in two places at once. Then he put his own copy back in the rare books room, and on Monday evening he was up there, waiting, pretending to be working.

"Sure enough, someone—Truitt—showed up there that night. His name is even on the student guard's sign-in sheet. He probably looked the book over, found it intact, found also that the place was too public and too well guarded for him to remove everything, at least to do so all at once. And he couldn't check it out, even if he'd been willing to run the risk of having his name associated with it; that stuff all has to be used on the premises. He did, however, see that the only thing really useful to anyone else was that information about McCrocken's past, indicating his original training in medieval history. And he did remove that one page."

"So then Tom knew who had stolen all the other materials," Louise said. "And who, therefore, might still have them, including copies of the letter."

"That's right. And chances were, Truitt would have kept them in his office where he wouldn't have to explain a locked drawer or two, unlike at home. So that's where Tom went after he left the library. Back up to Jaeckel Hall, where the fifth floor was deserted at that hour. It evidently wasn't a problem for him to spring the locks on the history-department doors and to jimmy the drawers of Gabriel's old desk. Where he found what he was looking for. And where Truitt caught him."

"Caught him!" Louise sat up straight. Winterlin nodded.

"Well, not literally," Will said. "He didn't let Tom know he was there, and watching. But he must have been. Otherwise.

you see, how would Truitt have known that Tom was involved in the thing at all?"

"You mean, you think Truitt also went up to Jaeckel Hall that night and found Tom going through his desk."

"Yes. And stood in the shadows and watched. It seems to me Truitt must have gone to the public library after he left the university library. He would have wanted to see if the book was there, too, and it accounts for the necessary time lapse before he turned up at his office. I think he had planned to go up to Jaeckel Hall that night anyway, to remove those files. That was Monday night, don't forget, and on Tuesday the men were coming to take the desk away. Truitt had summoned them himself, maybe, doubtless because Luke was driving him crazy about it—the desk had to be refinished before it got moved into the new wing as part of the McCrocken display. Or possibly Luke had arranged it in Truitt's name before he left and told Truitt what day to expect them. Anyway, those guys were so sure they had been sent for, and they had been. Only Truitt was too shaken by finding Tom there the night before to get the desk cleaned out after all."

"Do you think he knew for sure that Tom had found the jewels?" Louise asked.

Will looked at Mack. "Here I am rattling on about what I'd guessed and what I'd conjectured," he said. "If Truitt confessed the whole thing, you know all about it by now. Why don't I shut up and let you talk."

Mack smiled. "You're doing fine. That's how it happened, all right, according to what Dr. Roberts told us. He did get alarmed about that article; he did go to the two libraries, in that order; he did mean to clean out the desk in privacy that night; and he did find Dr. Donahue there. He says he hid and watched while Donahue took one copy of the letter—it happened to be Bo's—and made a photocopy of it on the office machine. Then he put the original back, restored everything to its former order, and went down the hall to his own office to read it. After a while—maybe an hour or so—he left and went home. Dr. Roberts followed him, but Donahue didn't stop by the Mellon house or anything like that. He just went home. So Dr. Roberts didn't have any way of knowing anything. Of course, he didn't have any indication that Dr. Donahue already knew so much—that the treasure was in the form of jewels and that they were cut in certain shapes—so he felt pretty secure. As far as he knew, Dr. Donahue was starting from scratch. Which didn't seem like much of a threat."

"Then why," Louise asked, "did he murder him the very next night?"

"Because," said Mack, "when he left the campus Tuesday afternoon, all those green signs had been put up. He'd known for some time, of course, that the house was going to be torn down, soon. That's what he was waiting for: the chance, at last, to acquire, without violence, what he had years ago discovered. For several years there had been talk that the house would have to go, but no date had been set. For the past few months, as you know, plans were being laid—but still, no certainty about exact dates of demolition. And then, without Truitt's knowledge, it was suddenly all set. And he walked out of Jaeckel Hall that night into an established time and date for the auction of the contents of the Mellon house.

"It was unsettling. A few days away—all he'd been waiting for. And the night before, he'd come upon another contender. He couldn't afford that risk. Tom was bright and clever and just the kind of person to pull off some coup. But even if he'd been slow and stupid, it would have been almost more than Roberts could bear. It drove him a little nuts, I think. Sent him to Louise's, trying to round up any other copies of the book that might be floating around, with a story about how he'd ruined Maisie's copy—as in fact he had—and caused him to decide to get rid of Tom. The only thing he couldn't do was recover Tom's copy of Bo's letter. He had to maintain his alibi that night, and by morning the police were too much involved."

Mack stood up. "That window is coming down this evening, by the way," he said. "I'm going over there now."

"Can you look after it overnight?" Will asked. "That would probably be the best thing."

Mack nodded. "First it goes to Mrs. Moffat's, though. She says she wants to look at it awhile."

By the time Will and Louise got there, a small crowd had collected in the front yard of the McCrocken-Mellon house. Under the glare of the porch light, some workmen were struggling to free the fanlight from its frame.

"Which is which?" Will heard somebody ask.

"Diamonds," someone else said. "All them daisies is diamonds."

They leaned against the fence and watched. "Hold it!" one of the workmen shouted. "Hold it!" His ladder wobbled on the lumpy old quilt they had spread on the porch floor. "Prise that corner some, Milt. Easy now."

Ed Malone's camera was going off in the dark at regular intervals. Will saw Jed McIngling roaming the front yard, listening to the various groups standing on the packed snow. He stopped beside the construction crew's pickup truck, parked at the curb. A red-eared boy leaned against the cab door.

"Where are you taking it?" Jed asked him.

"For a little while, to that lady's." His pointing finger picked out Maisie Moffat, standing on the other side of the yard. Not much of her showed from beneath her coat, hat, shawl, and the grocery sack she clutched in her arms. Beside her, with more groceries, was a darker figure Will finally identified as Mr. Mellon. "She's a friend of Dr. Gray, who bought it at the auction," the boy said. The weight he gave to Will's name indicated profound admiration. "There's a bunch of them having a get-together tonight, to look at the jewels. After that it goes right to the sheriff's office and gets locked up. That's a pretty valuable item we've got there."

"I heard."

Jed wandered over toward Dora, who was standing alone with her hands in the pockets of her new coat; her red wool hat was somewhat askew. She looked at him anxiously. "Mr. McIngling?"

"You got it."

"I'm Dora Gray."

"I know, sweetheart. I came to see if I could give you and your mother a ride to the party tonight."

Her face was white, her eyes determined. "I'll ask Mother if she'd like to go, but for myself, I don't really feel like it. Thank you for asking, though."

"I was afraid of that." Jed gave her a pat. "You're mistaken, I think. It seems like a nice ending to what Tom came here for. He did find it, you know."

"Well, maybe that's right," Dora said slowly. "It just hurts so much to know—"

"Don't take it out on that beautiful thing. Remember him by it. And that it gave him a good adventure."

She thought that over. "All right, Mr. McIngling. We'll go for a little while, anyway."

"Good."

Mack Winterlin was standing a few feet away with Joey Livingston and Geoff and Claire Bordeaux. "It's been quite a couple of weeks, hasn't it?" he said.

"I was just thinking that." Geoff's arm was draped over Claire's shoulders. "What a funny town this is. Good place for an artist."

"How do you mean?"

Geoff gestured vaguely. "Campus buildings decorated with jewels. Professors finding them to pay for the new library. Murderers growing up where I live. Adds color to one's days."

"It does that."

They watched the progress on the porch. The construction crew was making a big job of it. Through the cold night air came the sounds of nails tearing loose and a board splintering.

"Get a rope around that end," they heard one of them say. "Hold it from inside, Milt."

"Well, I'm sorry it's all over," Joey said. "I wish Truitt hadn't done what he did, but I enjoyed looking for that treasure."

"I didn't know you were," Claire said.

"I think everybody was, one way or another. I was just sure I knew where it was, too. In Gabriel's old desk. I was wrong, of course." He blushed. "I guess I shouldn't admit it in front of the law, but I, um, I *investigated* it one afternoon, when nobody was around. Just found all those old clippings Truitt was saving up."

Mack just stared at him. And behind them, on the other side of the fence, Will closed his eyes.

"Some people," he murmured to Louise, "really do seem to go with God."

Maisie and Mr. Mellon had evidently decided to set out for home. They made their way slowly across the trampled lawn and reached Will and Louise just as Bo Jenkins got out of his car, and crossed the sidewalk toward them.

"Don't leave yet," Will said, "right here at the climax."

Maisie smiled at him. "All right, my dear. A moment more." She held out her bag of groceries, and Will took it.

"I've been adding up," Bo said as they watched. The window was being lowered carefully to the porch floor. "Roberts came back here in 1962. Right after that, my box of souvenirs disappeared. Do you suppose he's been looking all that time?"

"I expect he was. Tippy Roberts always was a little cloth-headed." Maisie leaned forward, grasping the black iron fence with her gloved hands. "Look, Bo, isn't it pretty. Did you ever *dream*—"

"What in the world is going on?" The speaker, coming up

behind them, sounded so aggressive that Mrs. Moffat jumped. And then recovered herself.

"There's our ship coming in, Mr. Vondervorste," she said, "thanks to Dr. Will Gray."

Will turned. Luke, teetering on the curb and wearing a beret, looked at Maisie uncertainly and apparently decided he was safest pretending that she hadn't spoken.

"You know," he said, "I expect you can help Truitt Roberts with his speech—" He stopped. Maisie's smile was fixed; her gleaming dark eyes made Will think of Gabriel's in the photograph. "What did I say wrong?" Luke asked frantically.

Bo opened his mouth to explain, but he didn't have a chance. The men were bringing the fanlight, swathed in blankets and tied up with leather straps, down the walk to the truck. Mrs. Moffat turned to watch. Beside her, Mr. Mellon drew in closer, and she put her hand on his arm.

Mack Winterlin was walking down to his car and getting in.

"It looks like that's about all," said Will. He glanced around at the others. "Shall we go?"

"Go where?" Luke asked. "Am I invited?"

"Yes," Maisie told him. "Yes indeed."

Will opened his car door for Louise Tree and made sure she was safely inside. A car or two away, as he closed the door, he heard Luke saying, "Why would anybody want that old window? I always thought it was rather funny-looking myself. Way too many different kinds of glass."

Will smiled and got in beside Louise.